IMPOSTOR

A NOVEL SET IN THE KINGDOM OF NAPLES

C. DE MELO

ISBN 13 978-0-9997878-7-8 (C. De Melo)
ISBN-10 978-0-999787

DEDICATION

Thank you, D.

PROLOGUE
KINGDOM OF NAPLES
JANUARY 1760

Celeste Carducci crept into the ancient chapel before hastily adjusting her starched white wimple. Sinking to her knees before the altar, she assumed the position of prayer with a racing heart. A Paternoster rushed from her swollen lips, the whispered words flowing like holy water over her tightly clasped hands.

His scent lingered on her fingers, his taste on her tongue...

Rusty iron hinges creaked as the esteemed Sister Assunta pushed open the heavy studded door. The nun genuflected and crossed herself, then rushed toward the altar with light steps.

"There you are, my child. I've been searching everywhere for you."

Crossing herself with a trembling hand, Celeste stood. "I've been here all morning, praying."

Sister Assunta took a step closer to her ward. A beam of early morning sunshine spilled from an open window, illuminating only half of her wrinkled face. Dust motes floated in the air between them. "I checked the chapel earlier and you were nowhere to be found."

"Oh," Celeste said, her mind racing to conjure another lie. "Ah...I did leave once to use the privy."

"Come along. Someone is here to see you."

"Valentina?" Sister Assunta slowly shook her head. The nun's pinched brow and worried eyes alarmed Celeste, who demanded, "Who is it?"

"Your uncle has sent a miniaturist to paint your likeness."

Celeste's face fell. "No..."

The matronly nun placed a comforting arm around the girl's shoulders. "Don't worry, my dear, we'll pray together on this matter. God will provide a way out. He always does."

Chapter 1
Kingdom of Naples
February 1760

Ferrante degli Spini checked his silver pocket watch for the second time. Exhaling an impatient breath, he scanned the lively sunlit square. Hearty vendors cried out to passerby while toothless old women selected their wares with meticulous care. To his left, a pair of servants bargained with a cloth merchant for a better deal on a measure of dyed linen. To his right, a boy peeked from behind the base of a statue. Ferrante watched with wry amusement as the lad darted from his hiding place, swiped an apple from a cart, and then vanished down an alley.

Across the piazza stood an outdoor tabernacle housing a painted statue of the Madonna. The amateur artist had selected garish colors in which to portray the Queen of Heaven. Draped in dried yellow roses and cheap green glass beads, the effigy gazed down at the Neapolitans in the square with a wan smile. Fresh posies tied with faded ribbons and flickering candles littered the base of the icon.

Clad in black from head to foot, an old woman paused to cross herself before the statue. She kissed her meaty palm and placed it over one of the Madonna's chipped feet, her lined lips moving in a silent prayer. The crone possessed only three teeth, and Ferrante couldn't help wondering if she had been a great beauty in her youth.

Someone nearby shouted a greeting, breaking his reverie. He noticed a dazed young man calling out to a pretty girl leaning from an open window. The enamored couple stared at each other as if they were the only two people in the city.

Young love.

Ferrante had never experienced such a frivolous emotion. A practical man, he focused his energy on running his small empire with an iron fist. Love was for peasants with nothing better to do with their time.

Speaking of time...

Checking his pocket watch again, he frowned and tapped his well-shod foot. His late father used to say that 'punctuality veered on sacred' and Ferrante strictly adhered to that concept. To be kept waiting—even if only for a few minutes—catapulted him into a foul mood. Resisting the urge to go home, he reminded himself that the outcome of this meeting could prove beneficial for both him and his daughter. Besides, he had already spent several months searching for a suitable girl and couldn't afford to waste any more time.

A ruddy-cheeked figure rushed across the square, his unadorned hand gripping the edge of a tricorn hat. Ferrante took in the shabbiness of the man's velvet coat and resoled leather shoes. Camillo Custozi had spent most of his sizeable inheritance on whores and gambling. The fool's fortunes were dwindling, which explained his desperation to strike a deal.

Camillo came to a halt with an apologetic smile hovering on his thin lips. "Signore Ferrante, please forgive my tardiness. The carriage wheel got stuck in—"

Ferrante lifted a jeweled finger. "*Don't*. There is a café over there where we can talk."

Camillo prudently refrained from speaking as he followed the nobleman.

Ferrante cursed under his breath. Once again, he failed to control his temper. He possessed a harsh personality, rendering him older than his thirty years. His intimidating persona served him well when dealing with rivals, but in social situations it proved disastrous. No wonder people gossiped about him.

They ducked into the cool shade of a portico and headed toward an elegant establishment brimming with gentlemen engaged in animated conversations. Some discussed politics, others art and finance. The rich aroma of freshly brewed coffee mingled with the sweet smoke of pipes in the crisp morning air. The men placed their order, then settled around a small table where they could privately discuss their business.

Casting aside the customary niceties of polite conversation, Ferrante inquired, “Have you notified your niece?”

Startled by the man’s brusqueness, Camillo replied, “Not yet. I wanted to obtain confirmation from you before making an official announcement.”

The firstborn men of the House of Spini were required to marry women of noble blood. This edict had been clearly stipulated in his late father’s will under threat of forfeit of inheritance to his first cousin, Ruggero, who currently served as a bishop in Rome. Celeste Carducci was the only child of a duke, rendering her perfectly acceptable to the terms of the will.

“Tell me more about Celeste,” Ferrante said.

Camillo spread out his hands. “My lord, I have told you everything about my niece in my letter. Did you not read the copies of the reports from the last five years?”

“Yes, but I want to hear it from your lips.”

“My widowed sister died shortly after Celeste’s fifth birthday. Fortunately, my late brother-in-law had already made provisions for his only child by endowing her with a handsome dowry. As Celeste’s legal guardian and uncle, it is my responsibility to select a suitable husband.”

While shamelessly profiting from the arrangement, Ferrante thought. “Why didn’t you take her into your own household?”

Camillo emitted a deprecating laugh. “An old cantankerous bachelor like me raising a girl? I figured my niece would be better served by the nuns of Santa Patrizia.”

“Do you visit her often?”

“Not exactly,” he replied sheepishly.

“When was the last time you saw her?”

Camillo rubbed his chin in thought. “Five—no, I believe it was six years ago.”

Ferrante regarded the man with skepticism. “Your letter offered a precise list of your niece’s accomplishments and character. If my memory serves me well, you described her as domestic, submissive, and comely.”

“According to the reports I’ve received from her chaperone, Celeste is all of those things and more. The respected nun has been her constant companion for the last twelve years and loves my niece as her own daughter."

"In those reports you forwarded to me, I noticed that Sister Assunta mentioned Celeste's 'delicate constitution' and 'frailty' on several occasions."

"My niece is healthy enough, I assure you."

Ferrante's eyes narrowed. "How can you be so sure when you haven't seen her in six years?"

Flustered, Camillo's face reddened. "Sister Assunta would have alerted me to any *serious* health problems. Remember, my lord, convents are drafty places and the nuns consume a sparse diet. A bit of rest and good nutrition will make Celeste truly robust." In an attempt at humor, he added, "I doubt she'll be accompanying you on the hunt any time soon, however."

Ferrante's face remained stoic. "I don't need her to hunt. I need her to run my household and, in time, give me a son."

"I understand perfectly. My personal physician will conduct a thorough examination to put your mind at ease."

"No. I'll send my own physician."

"As you prefer, my lord. May I ask you a personal question?" Camillo waited for Ferrante's nod to proceed. "Although my niece is of noble blood, she was raised among nuns. She has never attended parties or worn fancy dresses. I doubt she even knows how to dance."

"What is your question?"

"Celeste lacks sophistication and the feminine wiles expected from a lady of noble breeding. I daresay that she is innocent to a fault, and I fear that you may find her rather disappointing. Perhaps even dull. I would imagine that many noble ladies would eagerly avail themselves of your courtship. Are you sure you wish to marry my niece?"

Ferrante pinned the man with a hard stare. "My late wife was coddled and spoiled throughout her childhood. She grew into an exigent, frivolous, and arrogant woman. While I regret that God saw fit to take her in the prime of her life—for I wish ill upon no one—I am grateful for a second chance at a fortuitous marriage. This time, I want an obedient wife with a mild temperament. It's true that I have noblemen offering me huge dowries to marry their daughters, but I am not interested in another foolish woman. In answer to your question, yes, I am certain that I wish to marry your innocent, unspoiled niece."

Camillo begrudgingly admired the unconventional man. "In that case, I am confident that Celeste will not disappoint you."

"Assuming the nun's reports are indeed true, then your confidence is well warranted."

"You can rest assured, my lord. I will notify Celeste at once. When can she expect a visit from you?"

Ferrante cocked an eyebrow at the loathsome man. "I have no intention of paying her a visit."

"You wish to marry my niece without so much as meeting her beforehand?"

"Why bother? I have all the information I need."

Camillo found this odd but who was he to question the man's methods? Reaching into his pocket, he said, "I have taken the liberty of having a miniature painted so that you can appreciate her physical attributes."

Ferrante accepted the tiny oval portrait and brought it up to his face for closer inspection. A pale girl with a straight nose, rosebud mouth, and wide-set eyes stared back at him. "Pretty," he murmured before handing the trinket back to his companion.

Camillo shook his head. "Keep it. It's my gift to you."

Ferrante pocketed the tiny portrait. "Thank you."

"So, do we have a deal?"

"Marriage to Celeste will be contingent on her good health. The moment my physician sends me a full report, I will contact you. Only then will I transfer the land in your name."

"Fair enough," Camillo said, satisfied.

The men shook hands to seal their agreement.

***

Ferrante remained in the city to run some errands after his meeting with Camillo. Animals and people competed for space on the crowded streets, which were littered with dung and refuse. The endless noise and vile smells irritated him. To make matters worse, he ran into his aunt's acquaintances after exiting his solicitor's office. The tedious couple tried to ingratiate themselves through social invitations and banal conversation.

Ferrante sagged with relief in the saddle when he finally returned to his stately villa on the Vomero hillside. Late afternoon sunshine covered his home in a burnished gold veil. Two long rows of cypress trees created elongated shadows along the pebbled drive leading to the villa's entrance. Fortunately, he owned enough acres to enjoy the peace and tranquility of isolation, far from the vile smells and constant noise of the city below.

The stallion's hooves crunched along the pebbled path, lulling Ferrante into a thoughtful reverie. The mighty horse suddenly reared as it neared the imposing iron gates.

"Achille," he warned, pulling on the reins. Spotting the source of the animal's hesitation, he cried, "Berta! How many times have I told you to keep my daughter away from the gate? You know I don't like it when you take her outdoors."

The nursemaid scurried to fetch the adorable toddler, who stared at her father in terror. "Forgive me, Signore Ferrante. We were playing by the front door and she ran out here when she heard your horse."

"I should have you whipped for disobeying me."

"Nadia is getting too fast for me."

"If I catch my daughter playing by the gates again, I'll find a competent replacement for you. Am I clear?"

"Yes, my lord. Come, Nadia."

Nadia wailed as she was swept off her tiny feet and carried into the villa. Ferrante cursed under this breath while studying the retreating face of his daughter. The girl eyed him in the same level of contempt as one would an enemy. Given that his late wife's blood ran in her veins, it was no wonder.

"My lord!"

Ferrante turned toward the voice of his trusted valet, Sandro. He also noticed his aunt's carriage further up the drive. "If you have bad news, I don't want to hear it."

Sandro winced. "Your aunt is waiting for you in the library."

"So?"

"I'm afraid she already knows."

Ferrante dismounted as a stable boy ran over to take the horse's reins. "Did you tell her?

"Of course not, my lord."

Ferrante pinched the bridge of his nose. "Women are the source of men's woes. Remember that, Sandro."

"Yes, my lord."

Taking a deep breath, Ferrante entered the villa and veered toward the library.

Clad in one of her signature black gowns, Livia smiled a bit too sweetly when he entered the room. "Ferrino."

"You know I hate that nickname."

"Yet it suits you perfectly, my beloved nephew, for you are an unbending bit of iron. Even as a boy you were stubborn."

Ferrante kissed the severe woman's rouged cheek. "Hello Aunt Livia."

"What is this I hear about you seeking a nun for a bride?"

"She's not a nun. How do you know about her, anyway?"

"Donna Elvira heard it from Signora Teresa who personally knows Camillo Custozi. You're to wed his niece, Celeste."

Ferrante spread his hands in supplication. "Cristo Santo! It's only been a few hours since my meeting with Camillo and already people are gossiping about it? You women with your wagging tongues never cease to amaze me."

Livia quirked a black penciled eyebrow at him. "You're the topic of conversation in every salon and drawing room from Naples to Rome. Even now there are noblemen hoping to parade their daughters before your eyes."

"I'm not interested."

"Really, Ferrino. You shouldn't disregard—"

"I'll not have another spoiled creature defying me under my roof. Endless balls and dinner parties, vapid fops and frivolous women roaming about my home. Enough is enough."

"Calm down, my dear."

"Caterina cost me a fortune and provided me with nothing more than a useless mute daughter and countless headaches. What's more, she was a negligent mother who never cared a fig for Nadia. The only things that mattered to that selfish woman were her gowns and her stupid friends."

Livia puckered her vermillion lips as she watched her angry nephew pace the room like a caged animal. Several strands of shoulder-length black hair escaped the leather strap tied at his nape, affording him a wild appearance.

She ventured, "I'm here to convince you to reconsider."

"Too late."

"Ferrino—"

He stopped in his tracks. "Stop calling me that!"

"*Ferrante*, be reasonable."

"You're the one who is constantly pressuring me to remarry. Every week you remind me that my respectable period of mourning is over. I swear you've mentioned Ruggero's name at least one hundred times since Caterina's death. Now you're telling me not to wed?"

"You should marry but—"

"Nadia needs a mother *and* a brother."

Livia clicked open her fan. Eyeing her nephew above the curve of painted fabric, she inquired, "Have you met the girl?"

"No, but I know enough about her."

"Aside from the fact that she was Count Emilio Carducci's only child and raised in a convent, what can you possibly know about Celeste?"

"What's there to know about a seventeen year old girl who has spent the last twelve years of her life surrounded by nuns? She's *seen* nothing, *done* nothing. Her mind is a clean slate and I happen to find that quite appealing in a woman."

"What if she's hideous?"

Ferrante crossed the room while extracting the tiny oval portrait from his pocket. "She's not. See for yourself."

Livia examined the piece. "Hmm, attractive."

"More importantly, she is docile, obedient, and accustomed to the frugality of convent life. In other words, Celeste is the exact opposite of Caterina."

"Caterina was challenging, I admit..."

"Try insufferable, demanding, rude, and unfaithful."

"We can't prove the latter…" Ignoring her nephew's harsh glare, she continued, "Anyway, I agree that you were ill-matched the first time. You'll offend quite a lot of nobles if you marry this girl, however."

"I realize that selecting my bride from a convent will perhaps shock my peers, but I don't care. I refuse to be saddled with another Jezebel."

"May I accompany you to the convent?"

Confused, he said, "I'm not going to any convent."

She stared blankly at him. "Aren't you going to meet the girl before making a decision?"

"No need. I've already read all the reports."

"Reports?"

"One of the most highly respected nuns in the city sends Camillo an account of Celeste's health and accomplishments every six months. From what I've ascertained, the girl is perfectly suited to be my bride. There is only the matter of her frailty."

"Let me see if I've understood you correctly. You wish to marry a girl you've never met *and* she has health problems?"

"She doesn't have health problems. Camillo described his niece as fragile, which sums up most women."

Livia clucked her tongue in annoyance. "Don't listen to that old fool. What does Camillo know? He's a bachelor."

Going to the sideboard, Ferrante poured himself a drink. "You can put your fears to rest, Aunt Livia. I'm going to have my physician examine Celeste. My deal with Camillo is contingent on the health of his niece."

Livia went over to where he stood. "Don't trouble yourself, darling. I'll send my own physician, whom you know is very good. I'll even accompany Dr. Bernardo so that I can judge the girl for myself."

"I'm not sure I like that idea."

"Why not? You have so many things to worry about. Allow me to do this small task for you." She waved her hand to make a point. "One of us should meet Celeste Carducci before she becomes a part of this family."

"Very well, but don't try to scare her away."

"I daresay she'll want to bolt the moment she discovers the name of her betrothed."

Unamused, Ferrante said wryly, "Your faith in my abilities is always a source of encouragement."

"You know that I love you." Livia closed the fan and tapped the ivory spine against her palm while thoughtfully regarding her nephew. "Well, I've done my duty to my beloved late brother—your father. I've tried to talk sense into you but I see now that my attempts are futile."

"Don't be like that, Aunt Livia. All I want is an easy wife who will care for Nadia and bear me a son. I believe Celeste will fulfill those roles without any fuss."

Livia hesitated before asking the next question. "What about that other matter?"

"What other matter?"

She pinned him with a pointed look. "I'm referring to *her*."

"Nothing will change where she is concerned."

"Celeste may object."

"She'll learn to live with it." Livia was about to say something then stopped. Seeing this, Ferrante added, "Nothing you say will change my mind. We've already argued enough on the matter."

"I don't wish to argue with you."

"Good," he snapped.

"You know how I feel about it."

"I do, but can't you be happy for me?"

She sighed. "I'm tickled by the prospect of Celeste Carducci being your bride. *Better*?"

"Actually, yes."

"Good. Now, what's for dinner? I'm famished."

CHAPTER 2
MARCH 1760

The Countess of Saponara, Ippolita de Monti, lost three sons at the same time. The culprit? *Poison.* This alone must have been quite a tragic blow to the poor woman, but to discover that the murderer was none other than their uncle for reasons of inheritance…

I would have killed the man. Murdered him in cold blood. I would have severed his head from his neck in the same manner the biblical Judith decapitated Holofernes. Perhaps poisoning would have proven a better punishment.

A taste of his own medicine.

Rather than seek revenge, the noble Ippolita commissioned the great sculptor, Giovanni da Nola, to create a funerary monument unlike any other in Naples. She had insisted that her sons, each slain before the age of twenty, be depicted as they were in life—full of vitality and movement. Giovanni did not disappoint. The *Sepulchers of the brothers Filomarino* immortalized Ippolita's sons in the prime of life. Splendid work, indeed. Despite being created from marble, the handsome young noblemen seemed capable of jumping from their perches at any given moment. Their tomb served as a constant reminder of the fragility of life.

People milled about in the church after the conclusion of Holy Mass several minutes ago. To my left, a broad-shouldered man ushered his wife and small children toward a neighboring chapel. I discreetly lowered my gaze to admire his hard ankles and chiseled calves beneath the white stockings. As I studied his impressive form, I wondered what he looked like devoid of clothing. Curiosity of the male anatomy prompted the wicked thought, not lust. More than seeing men naked, I wanted to know what existed *inside* of them.

Last year, this burning desire had prompted me to sneak into the university and spy on the medical students. A professor spotted me while the young men were performing autopsies, forcing me to flee the scene. Two months ago, I popped into the morgue and saw two bloated men who had drowned in the bay.

Only one subject piqued my interest more than anatomy, and that was alchemy. Great debates were currently underway on the topic. Some argued that alchemy was a legitimate science while others branded it as quackery. The well-known chemist and physicist, Robert Boyle, insisted that alchemy and chemistry were two distinct subjects, defining the latter as a legitimate science. Some still believed in the process of alchemy for diagnostic tests while others disagreed. Having contemplated both sides, I still hadn't made up my mind on the issue. Not that my opinion mattered since these discussions were held among men, not insignificant girls like me.

My interest in science could be traced directly to my late father, who had worked as a chemist in an apothecary. He had fostered a deep respect for the mechanisms of our natural world and had often pointed out the chemical properties of things whenever we were together. Sometimes, he would prove his points in banal ways, like baking a perfect loaf of bread. The passion he had displayed for his work inspired me to read and reread his books.

I turned away from the exquisite chapel and headed down the nave toward the exit. The heels of my suede shoes clicked lightly against the impressive intarsia marble floor. I paused, as I always did, at the tomb of Belisario Corenzio. The Greek artist fell to his tragic death in 1646 while frescoing the marvelous ceiling of the church. To have died in such a terrible manner while creating something so splendid…

"Valentina!"

The gentle voice of my dearest friend, Celeste, prompted me to look up and smile in greeting. Every Sunday, after attending Holy Mass at the chapel of Santa Patrizia, she and her chaperone left the convent to stroll to the Church of San Severino in my parish. I waited for them each week with eager anticipation.

Alarmed by her pale face, I inquired, "What ails you?"

Placing a gentle hand on my arm, she whispered, "Valentina, I have much to tell you. You must come visit me soon."

"Perhaps this week—"

"You must come today, I beg you."

"Very well. First, I need to run an errand for my aunt. I'm sure she won't object if I slip out afterward."

"Thank you."

Sister Assunta greeted me with a nod before turning to her ward. "Have you told your friend?"

"Not yet," Celeste replied.

I looked from one to the other. "Told me what?"

Celeste urged me outside and Sister Assunta followed us. Once we had descended the steps to the street level, she said, "My uncle commissioned someone to paint my portrait."

"He's finally paying attention to you. How delightful."

She shook her head vehemently. "No!"

"Hush," the old nun admonished, her beady eyes darting toward a gaggle of old women exiting the church. "Keep your voices down. Lord protect us from gossipmongers."

I whispered, "I don't understand. Why are you so upset over a portrait?"

Sister Assunta sighed in irritation and took it upon herself to reply. "Don't you see, Valentina? This means that Camillo Custozi has found a potential husband for our dear Celeste."

"Oh. Who is it?"

The nun frowned. "Does it matter?"

I didn't particularly care for the shrewish old matron who coddled my friend, but I treated her respectfully nonetheless. "I am merely curious, Sister Assunta. I hope that Signore Camillo has chosen someone worthy of my honorable friend."

Celeste's eyes glistened with unshed tears. "My uncle did not reveal the man's name in his letter. He only stated that it would be a 'fortuitous marriage' for all parties involved. I haven't slept in days. I can't eat or think. It even hurts to breathe. I'm in desperate need of consolation."

"I'll come and see you as soon as I can," I promised, giving my friend's hand a reassuring squeeze.

"We'll be expecting you," Sister Assunta said with a nod.

The nun urged her ward forward and I watched their retreat with a mixture of concern and sorrow. Pulling my white lace head covering low over my brow, I headed home with heavy steps. People passed me on the street but I barely noticed them. I couldn't get Celeste's sad face out of my head.

"Mamma!"

A rosy-cheeked boy pointed at a sweet bun in a baker's window. His mother grinned indulgently before extracting a coin from her crocheted purse. The little boy's face lit up with the simple joy of anticipating a delicious treat.

For the majority of the city's inhabitants, Sundays were for thanksgiving and rest. *Church and food*. The sacred day involved attending Holy Mass, then roasting meats or fish, playing with children, and consuming wine. *Lots of wine*. Music and singing filled the air as people digested their meals.

My parents and younger brother had loved Sundays too. The three of them had perished within a week due to plague. I was only ten years old when it happened—too young to be on my own, too old to be adopted by a couple. The only place for an orphaned girl from a respectable family was a convent. I had been sent to the same one where Celeste Carducci resided, the Convent of Santa Patrizia. Being the same age, she and I instantly became the best of friends. I wept when my mother's sister had shown up a month later to claim me. Through a blur of tears, Celeste and I vowed to always be true to each other no matter what life doled out to us.

"Valentina!"

Craning my neck, I waved at the plump adolescent who watched me from the window high above. Guido and his parents lived in the building across from where I lived with my Aunt Gloria.

"You're looking quite comely today, Valentina."

At age twelve, Guido fancied himself in love with me.

I smiled at him. "Thank you, Guido."

"Will you marry me?"

Laughing, I shook my head and the boy appeared stricken.

Guido's mother ushered her ambitious son away from the window before I ducked into the butcher shop to make a quick purchase. A moment later, I walked into the apartment that I shared with Aunt Gloria. Cluttered with threadbare rugs, a pair of decent paintings, and a chaise longue in desperate need of reupholstering, the space felt both cozy and comfortable.

I set the parcel on the table. "Hello Aunt Gloria. Are you feeling better?"

"I am," she replied from her resting place on the chaise longue. "Did you go by the *macellaio*?"

"Yes," I replied while removing my lace head covering. "Natalino gave me the meatiest bone."

The best butcher in our quarter had a soft spot for my aunt, whom he fondly referred to as *Glorissima*.

Draping the lace over the back of a chair, I continued, "He asked after you, as always."

"That was kind of him," she said primly before taking a sip from the glass in her hand.

I unwrapped the bone and dropped it into a pot of water, which my aunt had already set to boil. "He's a good man."

Adjusting her linen mobcap, she said, "I know. Once upon a time, I was a beauty like you with flowing locks and a nice figure. You may not realize this, but I had more than my fair share of admirers."

Appealing to her vanity, I said, "I'm sure you did. You're still lovely, Aunt Gloria."

"You're a good girl, Valentina."

"When are you going to marry Natalino?" I teased while quickly chopping some carrots and celery to add to the broth.

She waved her hand dismissively. "What does he want with a sickly old woman like me?"

I smirked. "Shouldn't you be in bed?"

"I felt better after you left." Lifting the glass in her hand, she added, "This tonic that the apothecary prescribed is beneficial for my health."

Taking in Aunt Gloria's plump cheeks and florid

complexion, I wondered if she sometimes faked her bouts of illness to garner attention. To be fair, she often suffered headaches so severe that she was forced to take to her bed. She claimed that impurities blocked her nose to the point that she couldn't breathe. These symptoms usually became worse with the changing of the seasons, particularly in the spring and autumn. During these months, our home emitted the odors of camphor and peppermint oil.

I ventured, "Since you're feeling better, do you mind if I pay Celeste a visit?"

She pouted. "I hoped that you would read to me."

"I'll read to you once I return."

Tilting her head to the side, she sighed. "I suppose that will have to do. Perhaps you can brew me a bit of peppermint tea before you go?"

My spinster aunt thrived on being pampered. I had learned long ago how to navigate through the contrived petulance and melodrama in order to get my way. I set a small pot to boil before walking across the room to a sunlit window. A cluster of potted herbs sat on the maroon tile floor in a pool of sunshine. I tore a few leaves from a thriving peppermint plant.

I sighed loudly while tossing the fragrant leaves in the water. "Such a shame..."

"What is?"

"That a virile man like Natalino must live a lonely life. How long ago did his wife die?"

"Two years, I believe."

"A good woman is what he needs." I deliberately paused. "Donna Francesca recently lost her husband too. Do you recall how long ago?"

"Six months."

My eyes slid to where my aunt sat. "Did I mention that she was also there purchasing bones for broth?"

Alarmed, Aunt Gloria sat up straight and placed the glass of tonic on a nearby table. "You most certainly did not."

"Forgive me. My mind is on poor Celeste who looked so pale this morning."

"How did Donna Francesca seem to you?" When I feigned confusion, she clarified, "Did she look…attractive?"

"As a matter of fact, yes. I don't recall ever having seen her wearing that yellow silk—"

"Yellow silk?" She snorted in disdain. "The woman is barely out of mourning. What did she say?"

"Let's see," I said, tapping the side of my face as I pretended to recall something. "Oh yes. She sends warm greetings and wishes you a speedy recovery from your convalescence."

"Convalescence?"

I carried on nonchalantly despite her horrified expression. "I think Donna Francesca made a comment about illness being the bane of old age."

"The nerve! Francesca is older than me."

"Is she, really?"

"Yes! Besides, I'm not *that* sick. Knowing her, she'll tell the entire neighborhood that I'm on my deathbed." Gloria's expression went from anger to worry. "Did Natalino overhear this conversation?"

"I'm sure he did since he was right there and, as you know, the butcher shop is quite small."

"What did he say?"

I shrugged and made a face. "I think he said something about it being a pity that you're not doing well."

"Were those his exact words?"

"I believe so," I replied while pouring the tea into a tea cup. "Here you go, Aunt Gloria. I saved a bit in the pot. Shall I add camphor and make you a compress?"

She nodded distractedly before indulging in a careful sip of tea. I resisted the urge to smile as I dipped a soft cloth into the aromatic brew. She liked to apply the damp cloth to her face since she claimed that it helped her condition.

Stirring the simmering broth, I suggested, "Tomorrow I can get us a bit of beef liver to make a nice pie."

"No need, dear. I'll go and get it myself."

I did my best to maintain a straight face. "Are you sure? I mean, you've been sick. I don't mind..."

"As I said, I feel better. After applying the compress I'll be good as new. Besides, it's been a while since I've seen Natalino." Something occurred to her and she removed the mobcap. Patting her unruly hair, she inquired, *"Is it that time?"*

'That time' referred to her gray hair beginning to show. Peering at her head, I offered the same reply as always. "It wouldn't hurt."

At my solemn confirmation, she stood and rummaged through a cabinet. A moment later she began boiling walnut tree bark, which had been ground into a powder, along with the inner shell of the nut. Once it boiled, she added red beet seeds. My aunt would often apply this concoction to her hair before going to bed, then rinse it out in the morning. The result was a brownish pink color that nature never intended, but at least it hid the unsightly gray hair.

"Off you go to see Celeste," she said, for she didn't like me witnessing her beauty ablutions.

I scurried out the door before she changed her mind. Walking slowly, I admired the people on the street as I made my way toward the Convent of Santa Patrizia. A fancy lady on the arm of an elderly gentleman strolled past me. Cream brocade was a daring color to wear since it was so difficult to keep clean in a city crammed with people and animals.

Sidestepping a steaming heap of horse manure, I turned my attention back to the elegant woman. An ostrich feather adorned her powdered coiffure, and shiny topaz stones hung from her earlobes. An exquisite lace shawl served to cover her décolletage. I offered her a smile but she only regarded me with bland disdain.

Glancing down at my shabby linen dress, I wondered if I would ever own such a fine gown. It seemed unlikely, especially since my parents had left me a meager inheritance. We weren't poor but our limited finances forced us to live modestly. Last year, Aunt Gloria sold the last silver candlestick holder that had belonged to my grandmother.

I rounded a corner and the looming volcanic stone walls diverted my attention. The convents of Naples served as safe havens for orphaned girls of a certain social status. The Convent of Santa Patrizia was no exception. The seventh century saint, a chaste virgin and descendant of Constantine, was revered as a role model for nuns and novices alike.

Immense dark walls were rampant within the center of Naples because of the staggering number of women who chose religious vocations. Neapolitan streets were made according to Greek design, so they were quite narrow. The locally quarried black stone gave them a mysterious aura, especially at night under the burning flames of street lanterns. I used the heavy iron knocker at the gate to announce my presence. One of the nuns opened the viewing door and recognized me. After being granted access, I went straight to the tiny cell where my friend resided.

Celeste opened the door. "Thank you for coming."

I stepped into the modest space. A simple wooden crucifix adorned one of the cream plaster walls. "I hate seeing you upset like this."

"My heart is heavy, Valentina." She picked up a letter from the nightstand beside a narrow cot and waved it in the air. "To make matters worse, *this* arrived for me only a moment ago."

"What is it?"

"A letter informing me that a physician will be coming here tomorrow to perform an examination on me at the request of my betrothed."

I leaned forward to peek at the sheet of parchment. "Does it mention his name?"

"No."

"How odd. Why the secrecy, I wonder?"

"Isn't it obvious? He wants to make sure that I'm healthy enough to breed before sealing the deal and revealing his identity to the public." Crumbling the note in her hand, she added, "I've always known this day would come. At least I've had twelve years with Sister Assunta and the other nuns. My uncle could have married me off sooner, so I suppose I should be grateful."

"That's a positive outlook."

No sooner had I said this than her brave mask shattered. Tears welled up in her eyes and her lip quivered.

Desperately searching my brain for something to cheer my friend, I said, "You'll always have me, no matter what comes your way."

"I know that I can always count on you."

I touched her cheek. "Don't forget that."

She forced a smile. "Do you remember Chiara and Donatella?"

"The twins? Yes, of course I do."

"Their eldest brother found good husbands for both of them." Celeste rolled her eyes. "All they talk of now are gowns and parties. I can't bear to be around them anymore."

"I think it would be fun to own fine garments and host grand parties. Don't you?"

"I prefer the peacefulness of the convent. I enjoy working alongside Sister Assunta in the apothecary. Which reminds me…" She went to a shelf and grasped a small ceramic vessel. "I made some arnica unguent for your aunt."

Aunt Gloria often complained of aching hands and feet so I accepted the gift with a grateful smile. "I know she will appreciate this, thank you."

"Healing people is what I was meant to do. It's what *God* wants me to do, Valentina. Who am I to question Him?"

"God sanctioned marriage—it's a Holy Sacrament. Being a good wife is another way of serving Him. There's no reason why you can't continue brewing tonics and mixing curatives once you're married. I'm sure your future husband will find your skills most valuable."

A shadow settled upon Celeste's features. "While that may be true, it's not the same as being surrounded by my fellow sisters in the faith and living a cloistered life."

"I'm only trying to make you feel better. What does Sister Assunta say about this situation?"

"She puts on a brave face but I know she's as devastated as I am. Sister Assunta is the only mother I have ever known and it pains me to think that I'll soon be leaving her here alone."

Celeste had been orphaned at a much younger age than me. I remembered my parents with clarity whereas she did not.

Throwing up her hands, she continued, "I wish I could simply convince my uncle to desist in this matter."

I ventured, "You could send him a letter stating your feelings on the matter."

"I haven't seen him in several years. I barely know the man. I doubt he would take pity on me."

"Maybe Sister Assunta will be allowed to accompany you to your new home."

She shook her head. "My uncle will aim high. I'm a Carducci, remember? I can't imagine a nobleman tolerating an elderly nun glued to his wife's side."

"Your husband won't object to visits, I'm sure. In the meantime, you'll be living a comfortable life in accordance to your social status."

"What use will I have for comfort if I am unhappy?" Celeste shot back, indignant. "There is nothing that a rich man can provide me with that would compensate for the loss of Sister Assunta."

I imagined a jewelry box overflowing with sparkling gems, an armoire filled with lovely gowns, a table laden with succulent roasted fowl and tender beef. Sweetmeats galore. Finally, I imagined a library filled with books. *Dozens of books.*

"Having your own home, servants to command, a bountiful table—these are privileges that few people will ever enjoy in their lifetimes. Celeste, you must see the positive in this situation. Otherwise, you'll always be sad."

"I concede to your point, but what if he is unkind? Worse still, what if he's cruel?"

"Have you so little faith in your uncle?"

"It's not that…"

"I know he hasn't been a part of your life, but I doubt he would saddle his niece with a monster. You are the sweetest, kindest, most sincere person that I know. God will grant you a good Christian husband who will cherish you."

Celeste stared at me. "What if he's hideous?"

I made a face as I searched my mind for a suitable answer. "I don't know much about carnal matters, but I hear that men seek the beds of their wives in the dark so you'll be spared the sight of him."

At this, Celeste laughed. "Oh Valentina…"

"I'm trying to help you make the best of this terrible situation."

"I know, and I thank you for that. I've been asking the Madonna and Santa Patrizia for strength. I'm sure they'll help me when the time comes."

"There's something else you should consider."

"What's that?"

I shrugged. "You may fall in love with your husband."

Looking me straight in the eye, she said, "Never."

The vehement manner in which she said this puzzled me.

She continued, "Let's talk of pleasant things, shall we?"

"Yes."

Celeste extracted a deck of playing cards from a drawer and glanced at me. This was my devout friend's only vice. I nodded to her unspoken suggestion. We laid the subject of husbands to rest and enjoyed the remainder of our time together by playing a few rounds of card games.

I left the convent an hour later and returned home to find Aunt Gloria propped on the chaise longue eating sweetmeats. A cloth was wrapped around her hair like a Moorish turban.

"Celeste sends her warmest regards along with a gift," I said, handing her the ceramic vessel.

She opened the lid and took a whiff. "Bless her heart. I used up the last bit of arnica unguent a few weeks ago."

"The next time I go the convent, I'll ask her to teach me how to make it for you."

"How is Celeste? You mentioned that she wasn't well."

I sat in a chair and sighed. "She is extremely upset."

Aunt Gloria slathered the unguent on her hands. "Let me guess. Camillo Custozi has found a man for his niece to wed."

"How did you know?"

"A mere guess. Who is he?"

"We don't know but he's most likely rich. Celeste's uncle commissioned a miniature, and she received notification that a physician will examine her tomorrow."

Aunt Gloria's eyes narrowed pensively. "Camillo Custozi is known for striking good bargains so I'm certain that it will be someone of importance. I realize this isn't what your friend wants but she should consider herself a lucky girl."

I toyed with a strand of my long dark hair as I pondered my own future. There would be no such advantageous arrangement made on my behalf since I had no male relatives—or an attractive dowry. As for my husband, he definitely wouldn't be noble, wealthy, or powerful. I would be lucky to marry a chemist like my late father.

Aunt Gloria popped a piece of dried fruit into her mouth and held out the small plate. "Would you like one?"

I accepted a dried fig, relishing its flavor.

Seeing the serious look on my face, she said, "Don't feel too bad for your friend, Valentina. Most girls in the city would trade their left eye for the chance at being a rich man's wife."

"Celeste isn't like most girls."

"Neither are you, but I'm sure you wouldn't scoff in the face of such a good opportunity."

She was right but I said, "Remember, Celeste is pious."

Aunt Gloria's eyebrow shot upward. "A bit *too* pious if you ask me."

"What do you mean by that?"

She shrugged and selected another piece of fruit instead of answering my question.

CHAPTER 3

Furtive kisses tasted sweeter in the moonlight. Languid embraces and whispered words spoken beneath a blanket of twinkling stars held more value. At least this was what she believed to be true. Caressing his bearded cheek, she offered him a heartfelt smile. He smiled in return, then kissed her forehead before hastily rearranging his robe. The mere thought of these precious moments coming to an end filled her with tremendous grief. The exquisite pain in her chest caused her to heave a sad sigh.

He paused in his task. "Do not despair, my love."

"How can I not?"

"I will find a way, I promise."

She hugged him tightly. He meant more to her than anything on Earth or in Heaven. Surely, God couldn't find fault with an emotion as pure as true love? God created male and female, did He not? God instilled people with hearts and the capacity to fill that special organ to the point of bursting.

"I must go," he whispered.

She glanced over her shoulder at the quivering shadows of leaves disturbed by the wind. Every sound, every movement seemed amplified whenever they were together. Every fiber of her being felt wonderfully alive when he held her in his arms.

He continued, "Meet me tomorrow. Same time. I love you."

"I love you."

He scaled the wall as silently as a cat as she tiptoed back to her cell. Once inside, she fell upon the bed and wept in fear of their love coming to an end because of her damned uncle.

***

Livia's carriage came to a halt outside the walls of the convent. The footman aided her in alighting the vehicle, then turned his attention to the weathered man still within.

Shaking out the creases in her black satin gown, she said,

"Here we are, Dr. Bernardo."

The physician emerged from the carriage in a somber coat and knickers, gray stockings, and brown leather shoes. A black tricorn hat sat upon his balding head. "Lead the way, madam," he said, lugging a worn leather satchel full of implements and ointments—the tools of his trade.

Pulling a sheer dark veil over her face, Livia strutted to the main gate and made use of the iron knocker.

The viewing door slid open. "Yes?"

Livia said haughtily, "I am here to see Signorina Celeste Carducci. My personal physician will examine her today."

The plain featured nun opened the gate and stepped aside, granting access to the tall, gaunt woman. "Ah yes, we received your message. This way, my lady."

Livia's eyes darted right and left, taking in the manicured garden with its citrus trees and the cloister's frescoed walls. The convent seemed clean and well-maintained, which she took as a good omen. A few nuns sat on benches reading prayer books.

The nun led Livia down a hallway to a door. Three sharp raps later and a nondescript girl in a plain gray nun's habit appeared in the doorway. Livia studied the creature with an appraising eye and deduced that the miniaturist had obviously exaggerated Celeste's beauty.

"You have visitors, Signorina Celeste," the nun said before retracing her steps.

Celeste took in the stranger's fine gown and painted face but said nothing.

Livia frowned slightly at the girl's lack of good manners. "Celeste Carducci?"

"Yes?"

"I am Signora Livia, aunt of Ferrante degli Spini. Dr. Bernardo will be examining you today. You received my note, did you not?"

"Ferrante degli Spini?"

Livia hesitated. "Yes, the man you are destined to marry."

Celeste's face blanched in horror.

Afraid that the girl would swoon, Livia stepped into the cell and led Celeste to a stool. "Calm yourself, child."

Dr. Bernardo went directly to the pitcher on the table and poured some water into a ceramic cup. "Here, drink this."

Livia waited for the girl to take a sip. "I'm well aware of Ferrante's reputation, but I assure you that his bark is worse than his bite. The fact that you fear him tells me that you have some good sense in that head of yours."

Sister Assunta poked her head in her ward's room. Seeing the girl in such a panicked state, the old woman grew alarmed. "Celeste, are you all right?"

"I am to marry Ferrante degli Spini," Celeste replied in a trembling voice before tears ran down her cheeks.

Livia's brow knitted together in irritation. "Take a moment to calm yourself."

Placing a comforting hand on the girl's back, the nun whispered, "Don't be afraid, child. God never gives us more than we can bear." To Livia, she added, "I am Sister Assunta, her nurse and chaperone."

Livia inclined her head in greeting. "I am assuming that you have prepared Celeste for this day."

The nun gave a curt nod. "I was well aware of Signore Camillo's intentions when he dropped off his niece at the convent twelve years ago."

Livia glanced disdainfully at Celeste. "Good. I expect there will be no more of these theatrics in the future."

Celeste hastily wiped her face with her sleeve. "Forgive me, my lady. I meant no offense."

Sister Assunta added, "You must understand that Celeste is an innocent girl with a tender soul—a spiritual creature who has dedicated her life to God."

Livia's icy stare silenced the nun. "I'm glad to hear it. Now she will dedicate her life to my nephew and be a mother to his children. Each of us have our duties to fulfill in God's plans, wouldn't you agree?"

"Yes," Sister Assunta replied, albeit reluctantly.

Livia turned to the physician. "Shall we get on with the examination, Dr. Bernardo?"

The older women retreated to the opposite side of the room. They positioned themselves in a manner that allowed for Celeste's privacy, yet their sharp eyes missed nothing.

Dr. Bernardo opened his satchel and removed various devices, setting them in a neat row atop a nearby table. He checked Celeste's pulse, eyes, and ears, then proceeded to ask a list of questions before prodding the girl's firm flesh in various places.

Gently patting the sides of Celeste's throat, he said, "Stick out your tongue."

Celeste did as she was told, her eyes darting nervously to where the older women stood like a pair of sentinels.

The physician turned to Livia and said, "She seems to be in excellent health."

Livia's brow creased. "Are you sure?"

The physician nodded. "Hearty and hale, madam."

This information struck Livia as odd given that the reports Ferrante mentioned described Celeste as frail. Her eyes slid to Sister Assunta, the nun who had penned those fictitious reports. Livia suspected something foul afoot and, rather than confront the old woman, she thought it prudent to wait. Sooner or later, the puzzle pieces would fall into place.

Dr. Bernardo turned his attention back to Celeste. "Signorina, I need you to lay back on the cot."

Celeste's eyes were wide with fear as the physician lifted the hem of her habit. "Please don't." When the doctor persisted, she cried, "Stop, no!"

Sister Assunta's face melted into an expression of concern. "This is a common practice, my child. Men want to *know*." To Livia, she added, "Perhaps I should hold her hand…the poor thing must be terrified. She's never been touched by a man."

Livia gripped the nun's arm. "Leave her be. She'll need to get over her fear of men if she's to become Ferrante's wife."

Averting his gaze, the physician performed the examination as quickly and as gently as possible. He stood and wiped his hand afterward, his expression puzzled. Next, he collected his things.

Livia escorted him to the door and they shared a pointed look before the physician whispered something into her ear.

Livia's face blanched. She took a moment to compose herself, then said, "Please wait for me in the carriage, Dr. Bernardo. I'll be along in a moment." To the nun, she added, "I would like to have a word with Celeste in private."

Sister Assunta tossed an apologetic look at her ward before vacating the room.

Livia closed the door then wandered to the cell's tiny window. Gazing up at the sky, she said, "My nephew has been scouring the nunneries these last few months in the hope of finding a good wife. I was skeptical when he told me about you. For this reason, I insisted on accompanying Dr. Bernardo today. I wanted to see for myself what kind of woman my nephew has chosen for a bride. He believes you to be submissive, devout, obedient—"

"I *am* all of those things," Celeste interjected.

Garnets and sapphires flashed in a ray of sunlight as Livia's hand shot up in protest. "Ah, but not *chaste*."

Mortified, Celeste hung her head in shame.

Livia turned away from the window and pinned the girl with a cold stare. "Despite being cloistered and ignorant of the outside world, you have managed to find a way to play the harlot."

"It's not like that."

"Camillo Custozi would have you whipped and stripped of your good reputation if he were to discover the truth. More precisely, that old whoremonger would gamble away every penny of your dowry."

Celeste nervously wrung her hands. "My uncle can never know the truth. Please, I beg you."

"Who is he?"

"I'm sorry but I cannot tell you. I'm sworn to secrecy."

"May I remind you that you are in no position to bargain?"

"Please don't make me break my promise to him."

"I asked you a question and I expect an answer." When Celeste refused, Livia shrugged. "Very well. I shall notify your uncle at once that you've been playing the whore at his expense for years."

Celeste hesitated, then placed her head in her hands. "There is a monastery across the way…"

Livia gaped at the girl. "Your lover is a *monk*?"

"Luigi was forced into monastic life due to lack of inheritance. He's the only man I've ever known and I love him. I don't believe that constitutes being a whore."

"How far along are you?" At the girl's blank look, she demanded, "When did you last have your monthly?"

Confused, she performed the calculations in her head and whispered, "Six weeks ago."

Livia tapped her jeweled fingers on the table and mused aloud, "You are at the onset of your pregnancy. That's good."

A mixture of fear and bewilderment settled upon Celeste's features. *"I'm pregnant?"*

Livia froze, her fingers hovering above the wooden surface. "You didn't know? Santa Madonna. You are naïve, aren't you?"

Still in shock from learning about her condition, Celeste placed her hands on her belly. A hint of a smile touched her lips, then realization lit up her features. "Does this mean you will call off the wedding?"

Livia went back to the window, her mind racing with thoughts. She mused aloud, "A virgin who gave her maidenhead to a monk. Was he a virgin too?"

"Yes."

"I'll be surprised if the baby isn't born with a halo around its head," Livia murmured to herself.

"What did you say, madam?"

"Never mind. Who else knows about your illicit affair with Luigi?"

"No one."

"Not even the nun?"

Celeste shook her head.

Livia recalled Ferrante's pale face and hollowed eyes. Her nephew had spent three days in bed due to fever last winter. The fear of him dying without an heir had consumed her throughout the duration of his illness. Enough time had been wasted in finding Celeste. To tell Ferrante of the girl's folly meant searching for another suitable young woman. One who could be barren…Livia's gaze rested on Celeste. The girl was young, strong, and somewhat innocent despite the circumstances. Better that her late brother's legacy fall to a bastard raised as a Spini than to her sister's son, Ruggero. Her corrupt nephew was the embodiment of debauchery and decadence.

"You will tell no one of your pregnancy," Livia said at last.

Celeste gaped in disbelief. "You would have me marry your nephew while carrying another man's child? Forgive me, but I thought the whole purpose of Dr. Bernardo examining me *down there* was to determine if I was still a virgin."

"Ferrante has no doubt that you're a virgin. Dr. Bernardo examined you at my request. My nephew requires a healthy wife who will conceive and carry a child to full term. He desperately needs an heir. You should be grateful, Celeste. This means that you will have fulfilled your duty as a wife before the year is out—assuming the child is male, of course."

Celeste's brows knitted together in supplication. "Luigi and I wish to marry."

"Can he provide for you and the baby?"

Averting her gaze, Celeste replied, "Not yet, but we love each other and that's what matters."

Livia laughed derisively. "Do you think love will feed your hungry baby?"

"God will provide."

"As if God doesn't have better things to do than help a pair of fornicators. Wipe the foolish thought from your head this instant! You will bid Luigi farewell and that will be the end of it." The words propelled the distraught girl into a weeping fit, so Livia added in a gentler tone, "Think of your future and that of your child. Ferrante is determined to claim you as his bride, and when he sets his mind to something there is no stopping the man. He's tired of searching and wants to marry as soon as possible. This wedding will take place whether you like it or not, so I suggest that you start accepting your fate."

"I-I d-don't want t-to m-marry him. Please…"

Resisting the urge to strike the girl, Livia said, "Take comfort, child. Ferrante isn't a bad man. I won't vouch for my nephew's charming personality or easygoing nature, but at least he isn't stingy. Brash, moody, yes…but never cruel."

Celeste did her best to staunch her tears while nodding to the woman's words.

Livia continued, "I know you'll fall in love with Nadia."

"Who?"

"Ferrante's three year old daughter. She's a sweet little thing. Unfortunately, my grandniece is mute. God willing, she'll soon have a brother."

Celeste sniffed. "What will I tell Luigi?"

"You will explain to him that you have a duty to fulfill, then bid him farewell. Obviously, he knows nothing about the child growing inside of you and it should remain that way for everyone's sake. Afterward, you will get down on your knees and thank the Lord that you have been gifted a dignified way out of your current state of disgrace."

Celeste nodded distractedly at the woman's sobering words. "When is the wedding scheduled to take place?"

"On the first of April, so I suggest you pray for courage and tranquility of heart and mind. Ferrante won't take kindly to you moping about the house. You will be expected to perform your wifely duties with cheerfulness and efficiency. Do you understand what I'm telling you?"

"Yes, Signora Livia."

Livia regarded the girl with narrowed eyes. "Tell me, was it your idea or the nun's to send false health reports to Camillo?"

Celeste's shoulders sagged in defeat. "I begged Sister Assunta to pretend that my health wasn't good in order for my uncle to postpone his search for potential husbands."

Livia crossed her arms and studied the little schemer. At least she had the good sense to lower her head in shame. "Marriage has its benefits. In time, you'll learn to accept your fate and derive joy from motherhood."

"Is that what you did?"

"Unfortunately, no. I'm barren." *And everyone in Naples knows it too.*

"I'm sorry."

Livia's eyes turned hard. "At least that won't be the case for you, Celeste. We'll meet again on your wedding day and I hope to see an improvement in your spirits."

"When will I meet your nephew?"

Livia hesitated. "Ferrante is not coming here."

"Doesn't he want to meet me before making me his wife?"

Livia sympathized with the girl's bewilderment. "He's a *very* busy man, my dear, and he has placed his trust completely in your uncle."

"And you."

"And me, yes. You'll meet Ferrante on the first of April at the wedding. Until then, I suggest you pray for fortitude and begin reconciling yourself with what's to come."

"I'll do exactly as you say, Signora Livia."

"That's better. You'll see, everything will work out for the best. I promise."

***

Celeste forced a smile as the overbearing woman exited the cell. The moment the door closed, she fell into a fit of tears.

Sister Assunta hurried into the room a bit later. Seeing her ward in such a wretched state, she grew anxious. "What happened?"

"I'm getting married on the first of April…God has abandoned me, Sister Assunta."

"We'll find a way out of this mess."

"How?" Celeste snapped.

"I don't know yet…"

Fresh tears formed in Celeste's eyes. "*Please*, I beg you! Find a way for me to escape my fate or I will die of sadness. If you truly love me, then you will help me out of this mess."

The old nun wrung her papery hands. "I will, I swear."

Celeste took to her bed and made a great show of suffering from her sadness.

CHAPTER 4

Aunt Gloria made several deliberate attempts throughout the week to prove her robust health to Natalino. In addition to finding excuses to run to the butcher shop for "forgotten" ingredient items, she made it a point to pass in front of the establishment once or twice a day. This inevitably resulted in shy waves and nods between the two of them.

What I found particularly humorous was the carefully contrived manner in which Aunt Gloria crossed in front of the window. Sometimes, she pretended to be laughing or chatting animatedly with me. Other times, she pretended to sniff a flower or admire a child in the street. She always made sure to pat her hair into place and smooth any creases in her garments beforehand.

Natalino eventually interpreted Aunt Gloria's rouged cheeks, dyed hair, and coquettish smiles as an invitation for courtship. Old women in the marketplace exchanged whispered rumors of the widower courting the spinster.

"Can you imagine behaving like that at their age?"

"A butcher? She'll never go hungry, that's for sure!"

"Isn't she well past childbearing age?"

"Shameful, I tell you. Both of them."

"Donna Francesca is heartbroken, the poor thing."

"Ah, love..."

By the time Sunday rolled around, the entire neighborhood knew that Natalino and *Glorissima* were officially courting. Aunt Gloria awoke early that day in order to prepare herself for Holy Mass. I watched in amusement as she sat at the vanity applying rouge with expert precision.

"Aunt Gloria, would you like me to set out your Sunday dress?" I asked, throwing open the armoire.

"Good idea. Everyone will be looking at me today."

I shook the garment to remove wrinkles, then carefully set it upon the bed. Dainty white embroidered flowers graced the neckline of the pale violet gown.

"I'm so nervous," Aunt Gloria confessed.

"We're only going to church."

"No. I haven't told you yet…"

I went to the vanity and took up the comb to style my aunt's pinkish brown hair.

She continued, "Natalino wants me to dine with him and his mother today. We'll be sharing the midday meal together."

I met her eyes in the mirror's reflection and grinned. "Donna Pasqualina is fond of you. What's there to be nervous about? Make sure you save me some sfogliatelle. She makes the best in the neighborhood."

"I will, my dear." She heaved a giddy sigh. "Believe it or not, I feel like a young maiden."

"That's because you're in love," I said with a wink.

"Someday, you'll feel this way about a young man."

"I already do," I said with a straight face.

"Male protagonists in novels do not count."

I snickered. "What about male authors?"

"I'm serious, Valentina. I sincerely hope you find love."

I embraced my aunt. "I already have. I love you."

Church bells rang throughout the city as we made our way to the church of San Severino e Sossio for Holy Mass. Aunt Gloria strutted by my side with nervous steps. A beaded amethyst necklace adorned her plump, perfumed neck—a recent gift from her beloved Natalino.

No sooner had we entered the church's dim interior than Aunt Gloria nudged me. "Look at Donna Francesca's face."

Sure enough, the woman stood near the entrance as if she had been waiting for us. I resisted a giggle, for the crafty widow appeared stricken at the sight of her rival's radiant demeanor.

Pulling herself up to her full height, Aunt Gloria smiled in greeting to various acquaintances, including Donna Francesca. She practically preened when Natalino came over to say hello to us. He even complimented my aunt's gown, causing several people to whisper among themselves.

“Has he proposed marriage yet?” I asked the moment we settled into our pew for the service.

“Not yet but he will soon,” she replied while looking at him from across the aisle.

Aunt Gloria and Natalino exchanged furtive glances and shy smiles throughout the entire service. Afterward, I lingered outside the church doors in anticipation of Celeste’s weekly visit. When she never showed, I went out into the street and scanned the area. I waited a few more minutes, then turned to go back inside. That’s when I spotted Sister Assunta jogging toward me.

“Valentina, you must come to the convent today,” the nun said breathlessly. “Celeste is ill. She has taken to her bed.”

Alarmed, I demanded, “What ails her?”

“Fear, sadness, anxiety…Lord help us!” Gripping my hands, Sister Assunta’s eyes reflected great sorrow. “I fear for her life.”

A sickening feeling settled in the pit of my stomach. “Santo Cristo. Why didn’t you send word?”

The nun looked away. “She told me not to bother you with her problems.”

“I don’t understand—”

“She is to marry Ferrante degli Spini.”

My heart sank. “No.”

Aunt Gloria approached us and said, “Sister Assunta, hello. Where is Celeste?”

The nun inclined her head. “Hello Donna Gloria. I regret to inform you that Celeste is unwell.”

“Bedridden,” I interjected.

Aunt Gloria’s hand flew to her chest. “Poor girl.”

Sister Assunta said, “She has asked for Valentina. I hope that you will allow your niece to come to the convent today. I’m afraid my ward is extremely sick.”

Aunt Gloria said. “What’s wrong with her?”

“She’s to marry Ferrante degli Spini,” I replied.

Aunt Gloria’s eyes widened. “Really?”

“I’m afraid so,” Sister Assunta said sadly.

“I’ll accompany you to the convent, Sister Assunta.” Kissing my aunt's cheek, I added, "Enjoy yourself, Aunt Gloria. Say hello to Natalino and Donna Pasqualina."

Aunt Gloria nodded. "Tell Celeste I will pray for her and light a candle too."

Sister Assunta and I covered the short distance to the convent in silence. There were simply too many eyes and ears on the street to discuss such personal matters out in the open. The moment we entered the gate, the nun led me to a bench in the center of the cloister where we could sit and talk. An orange tree laden with fruit cast its shade above our heads.

Sister Assunta said, "I've been asking around to discern if what they say about Ferrante is true. Rumors of the widowed lord's fierce temper and dark moods are rampant, as I'm sure you know."

"I've heard a few things, yes."

Assunta's eyes glistened. "He will break my sweet girl's spirit and ruin her purity. He will utterly destroy Celeste."

"Maybe he's not as bad as people say he is," I offered in what I hoped was a convincing tone. "Gossip can oftentimes be exaggerated."

"Celeste is too spiritual for the likes of a man—especially a beastly one like him. Her place is *here*, serving God with me." The nun heaved a painful sigh. "For years I've been sending reports to Camillo Custozi describing the delicate condition of his niece's precarious health."

Confused, I said, "Celeste isn't sickly."

"I know it was dishonest, but my hope was to dissuade him from pursuing a spouse for my ward. Now that the physician has examined Celeste and declared her healthy, there is no way of preventing this marriage." Sister Assunta wiped away a tear. "I cannot tell you how many times Celeste has wept this week. Her tears could easily fill a cistern."

"She must be terrified," I concluded.

"I'm afraid she will send herself into an early grave if she continues like this."

I shuddered. "I wish there was something I could do, Sister Assunta."

The nun's glassy eyes turned hard. "Actually, you can."

Startled, I inquired, "How?"

"I've been thinking on the matter for days, carefully mulling it over in my head. I know it sounds unfeasible but…"

"But what?"

"You can marry Ferrante instead of Celeste."

I stared at the woman, stupefied. "What did you say?"

"You can marry him instead of Celeste," she repeated, her eyes wild. "Think of it. You would have a rich husband and a fine home. Gowns, jewels, stability…"

She had obviously lost her wits. "How can I possibly—"

"You and Celeste have the same coloring, similar height and build, you could easily pass for sisters. Camillo Custozi hasn't seen his niece in *six years*."

I stood. "What you're suggesting is insane."

Her hand darted out like a viper to grasp my wrist. "Sit down and hear me out, will you?"

The nun's determined expression and harsh glare compelled me to obey.

She continued, "Is it really so insane to propose a better candidate for the task? Celeste has no interest in boys. You, on the other hand, possess a roving eye."

My face grew hot, for it was true. "How do you know?"

"I've seen how your gaze is drawn to handsome men."

"Are you questioning my chastity, Sister Assunta?"

"No Valentina. I am only stating the obvious. It's perfectly normal for a girl your age to feel certain *stirrings*...Celeste doesn't have them. Christ takes precedence over carnal desire in her life. You, on the other hand, are better equipped to be a wife and mother."

"I don't know—"

"Celeste is scheduled to leave here on the first of April and be taken straight to the church for her matrimony. It will be the first time she will meet her bridegroom."

"It's apparent that you have given this serious thought," I concluded.

"I've been awake for nights devising this plan. I love Celeste and there is nothing I wouldn't do for the sake of her happiness. If you love your friend as much as you claim, then you will at least think on the matter."

I bit my lip pensively. "If I agree to your plan, where will you take Celeste? Obviously, she cannot remain here."

"There is a small convent in the countryside maintained by wealthy noble benefactress. The sister who mixed their curatives has passed away and I have been asked to be her replacement. I leave within a fortnight, which by miracle falls on the first of April. I plan to smuggle Celeste out of here and she will remain with me."

"Under a different name?"

"Naturally."

"I see."

Sister Assunta stood. "I sincerely hope that you do. This could be a wonderful opportunity for you and a viable solution to Celeste's problem. Come along. She is waiting for you."

I followed the nun in silence, my thoughts crashing within my head like roiling waves of the sea. She opened the door of Celeste's cell and I froze. A dreadfully pale face and sunken eyes greeted me. The unmade cot in the corner signaled that my friend had been abed all morning.

Celeste forced a smile. "Valentina, you came."

I embraced her. "Of course I did. Dearest, what are you doing? You'll make yourself sick if you continue like this. When was the last time you ate?"

Sister Assunta took it upon herself to reply. "She refuses to eat and cries herself to sleep at night. She barely sleeps."

Celeste's eyes met mine. "Did she tell you the news?"

I nodded as I urged her to sit down on a stool. "My aunt is praying for you. I will too, I promise."

"I'm being forced to marry a monster."

Casting a furtive glance at the nun, I said, "I heard he has a daughter. You're fond of children, aren't you?"

"The girl is mute. Three years old."

I touched Celeste's cheek and said, "Perhaps God put you in this child's path. She needs a kind, loving mother and I know you possess both of those qualities."

Celeste pushed my hand away. I stepped back as my friend unraveled before my eyes.

"No, no, no! I can't…Oh God, please help me. I don't want to marry Ferrante degli Spini." Reaching for the nun's hand, she cried, "I don't want to leave you, Sister Assunta. Tell him that I'm dead. He can find another girl. You must help me."

Celeste broke down in tears. Sister Assunta embraced her ward and did her best to comfort the girl. She also gave me a pointed look, waving me away with her hand. My friend's weeping quickly evolved to heart-wrenching sobs so I quietly took my leave and waited in the cloister garden.

I sat in quiet contemplation beneath the shade of the orange tree. In all the years I've known Celeste, I had never seen her break down like that. Sister Assunta came out to meet me a little while later.

Taking a seat beside me, the nun said, "She's asleep. I brewed a draught for her last night and she drank the remainder of it. Do you see what I'm dealing with here? If she continues like this for another fortnight, she'll waste away and die."

Tears stung my eyes. "Santa Madonna."

"I've spoken with the abbess to intervene on Celeste's behalf. I begged her to speak with the priest in order for him to dissuade Camillo or Ferrante, but there's nothing that can be done. Ferrante wants a convent bride and he's powerful enough to be obeyed by everyone. We're only puppets in a world controlled by men."

"Sister Assunta, please don't make yourself sick too."

"Consider my suggestion, Valentina. You're much stronger than Celeste, and I daresay more cunning. You know about the world whereas she does not."

I bristled at the nun's innuendo, unsure whether to be flattered or insulted. "I'm not *that* worldly, Sister Assunta. Most of my knowledge comes from books rather than experience. I'm an avid reader and spend most of my time at home caring for my aunt."

"Speaking of which, she is currently courting the butcher

and will marry soon."

"How did you find out?"

"*Everyone* knows. Donna Gloria can instruct you about life and what to expect from a husband. I can't offer that kind of advice to my sweet, innocent Celeste. I became a nun when I was fifteen and have never known the touch of a man. What's more, where will you go once your aunt is wed?"

It was a valid question and I didn't know the answer.

"Well?" Sister Assunta prompted.

"I don't know."

Fixing me with thoughtful look, she said, "This could be God's way of solving two problems at once."

I left the convent with a heavy feeling in the center of my chest. Sister Assunta's words rang in my ears as I headed toward home. I had never considered the resemblance between my friend and me. Both of us had long brown hair and slim frames. Although my features were sharper, we both possessed oval faces, small chins, golden brown eyes, and straight noses. Celeste's mouth verged on pouty whereas my generous mouth boasted a set of full lips. Finally, we were both blessed with healthy teeth.

Could you really pass for Celeste Carducci?

Outside the convent in the light of day on the busy street, Sister Assunta's plan seemed absurd. Overly dramatic, too, like a bad play. In two weeks, Celeste would no doubt face her fate with dignity and courage.

Do you really believe that, Valentina?

Shaking my head to clear it, I rounded the corner and turned toward the crumbling palazzo housing my aunt's apartment. My thoughts went from my friend to Ferrante degli Spini. Maybe, *hopefully*, the man was a victim of malicious gossip. After all, people loved to exaggerate stories. Besides, who could ever be cruel to Celeste? Divine light practically oozed from every pore of her body. The girl loved God and dedicated her life to serving Him. What husband wouldn't cherish such a wife?

***

Aunt Gloria entered the apartment later that day with a

dreamy smile playing upon her lips. The coppery light of the late afternoon sun lit up her pleasant features as she took a seat across from me at the kitchen table. The burnished sunlight also deepened the pink strands of her hair, making it difficult for me not to return her smile.

"Did you have a pleasant luncheon?" I inquired, setting down the book that I had been reading to get my mind off of Celeste's plight.

"I did. Donna Pasqualina is a most gracious hostess. She served asparagus and beef stew, along with sfogliatelle."

I was extremely fond of the crispy pastries stuffed with almond paste, honey, and pieces of candied fruit. "Did you happen to save one for me?"

"Donna Pasqualina wrapped this one up especially for you and sends it along with warm greetings."

I accepted the treat with gratitude. My teeth bit into the delightfully crunchy layers of the flaky pastry before coming into contact with the silky sweet filling. "Mmm..."

"She's a good baker," Gloria concluded.

"Hmm-hmm," I agreed, chewing.

Squinting at the cover of my book, she asked, "What were you reading?"

"Quotes by Voltaire. Tell me about Natalino's plans."

"He wants to get married as soon as possible. At our age and current situation, nothing prevents us from doing so."

I set down the pastry and clapped my hands in glee. "This is wonderful news!"

Her rosy cheeks mimicked two apples as she grinned widely. "Natalino will finally marry his Glorissima!"

"He's a good man who will make you happy."

"*And* keep us fed. That's the rumor, anyway."

One never went hungry with a butcher or baker for a husband. "I'm happy for you, Aunt Gloria."

"Thank you. Tell me, is Celeste feeling any better?"

My face fell. "It's worse than I thought."

Her expression sobered. "Oh no."

I explained Celeste's predicament to my aunt, who listened

with concern and empathy.

At length, she uttered, "Of all the men in Naples, it had to be that one. Celeste is such a tender and sensitive soul."

I ventured, "Sister Assunta proposed a plan to save Celeste from the clutches of the villainous Ferrante."

"Oh?"

I hesitated. "She suggested that I marry him, instead."

Aunt Gloria stared blankly at me, then laughed aloud. "What a preposterous idea!" My stoic expression prompted her to stop and study my face. "You can't be serious. How can you marry him and get away with it?"

"According to Sister Assunta, Celeste and I can pass for sisters."

My aunt nodded. "She's right about that but…"

"Camillo Custozi hasn't seen Celeste in six years. He wouldn't know the difference. The more I ponder Sister Assunta's plan, the more appealing it becomes. What have I got to lose? There's no money for my dowry and I certainly don't want to end up a spinster."

"Like me?"

"I didn't mean it like that."

Reaching across the table, she patted my hand. "I know you didn't, dearest."

"I love Celeste enough to marry a stranger so that she can live out her life in peace at the convent."

Aunt Gloria made a face. "Wait…if Celeste remains at the convent, then you're treachery will be discovered."

"Sister Assunta plans to sneak her out of Naples under a false identity. Together, they will flee to another convent. No one need know the truth except us. Besides, what's to become of me once you marry Natalino?"

"You make a valid point. Forgive me, Valentina. I'm afraid I've been so focused on my own happiness that I didn't take you into account. I suppose you could live with us."

"You've dedicated your life to me for years and I love you more than anything, Aunt Gloria. Now it's time for you to focus on yourself and your future."

"I love you too, my sweet girl."

"Do I have your blessing to carry out this farce in order to help my friend?"

"This is more than a playful farce, Valentina. I know you love your friend, but what Sister Assunta proposed could have dire consequences in the face of the law. You're not volunteering to marry some pauper, but rather a powerful nobleman."

"I know."

"If he ever discovered the truth, it would ruin your good reputation. Worse than that, you could go to prison for committing a serious fraud."

"I realize that but I can't allow my friend to die."

Aunt Gloria rolled her eyes. "Celeste won't die."

"Her spirit would. You should have seen her today. Sunken eyes, ashy pallor, she can't eat or sleep."

"Think hard on this, niece…Honestly, I'm rather surprised that Celeste would allow you to take such a dangerous risk. Sister Assunta, too, for that matter. Have they given any thought to the repercussions that you could face if things go wrong?"

"Sister Assunta is the one who came up with the idea, not Celeste."

She narrowed her eyes at me. "Are you sure about that?"

"Aunt Gloria, I know Celeste better than she knows herself."

Although she seemed to want to express more on the topic of Celeste, my aunt admitted, "I certainly don't wish to argue with you."

I regarded her thoughtfully. "You never really cared for Celeste. May I ask why?"

"It's not that I don't care for the girl. I find Celeste to be…Well, she's a coddled little creature, isn't she? I blame Sister Assunta for that."

"I see your point, but I feel pity for Celeste."

"Because she lost her parents? So did you."

"Not only that. I had a loving aunt who took me in. She did not. Her uncle let her rot in a convent."

"It still doesn't justify risking your reputation and your

future. That said, you are nearly eighteen—old enough to make adult decisions. Your secret will be safe with me if you decide to marry this man. Know that I will be in a state of constant anxiety over your happiness and well-being."

I bit my lip in thought. "Signore Ferrante has a mute daughter. The girl needs a mother, which would offer me a purpose. I'll have a companion, along with a fine home and every material comfort."

"You speak as though you've already made up your mind."

"What are my other options? Marry a poor boy from our neighborhood? Join a convent?"

Aunt Gloria made a face. "You could work."

"As a scullery maid or a laundress, yes."

"You can read and write. It's not like you must infiltrate the dregs of society. What about being a governess to children? There are plenty of wealthy merchants in the city who would hire a clever young woman like you."

I shook my head. "If I'm going to take care of children, I may as well do it with a wedding ring on my finger and enjoy the security that comes with it."

"You've always been such a practical girl."

I thoughtfully traced the letters on the cover of my book with my fingertip. "Lately, I've been giving quite a bit of thought to my future. I've even considered disguising myself as a man in order to attend university."

Aunt Gloria's hand flew to her chest. "Valentina Gaetani!"

"Don't worry, Aunt Gloria. I talked myself out of that folly."

"Thank the Madonna!"

"I'm aware that life is full of uncertainty. I remember my parents making plans and now they're both dead."

"Your great loss forced you to mature quickly and robbed you of a happy youth."

I smiled. "I'm happy here with you."

She stood and poured wine into two cups, then handed one to me. "When is the wedding scheduled to take place?"

"The first of April, which affords me only a fortnight to learn how to behave like a girl who was raised in a convent."

"That's going to be difficult with your sharp wit and even sharper tongue."

"I admit, I am fond of a clever retort."

"Girls who are raised by nuns in convents tend to be less impulsive. Less mischievous too."

Folding my hands on the table top, I regarded my aunt with an amused look on my face. "Any other faults you'd like to bring to my attention?"

"I'm only being honest. You know how much I admire your intelligence and determined spirit."

"I know. I'll need to put on a convincing performance for this plan to work." I rubbed my temples to ease my gradually increasing headache.

"Are you all right?"

"It's only a headache. I'll be fine." I paused, then asked, "Do you honestly believe that I can get away with it?"

"Marrying Ferrante?"

"Yes."

Her brow creased in thought. "If you're cautious, yes. You'll need to learn how to handle Ferrante degli Spini, which I daresay won't be an easy task. Men like that can't be controlled, but I would venture to say that they can be brought to heel—by the right woman, of course. Physical beauty isn't enough because powerful men can have whomever they please. There are plenty of beauties in Naples. You must get into Ferrante's head and find out how his mind works. Beguile him, and you just might be able to tame the beast."

I nodded, committing her sage advice to memory.

Is Ferrante a beast?

Something suddenly occurred to Aunt Gloria. "If you take on Celeste's identity, you can no longer claim me as your aunt."

"Only in secret can we be our true selves."

Chapter 5

"I will marry him."

Celeste eyed me in disbelief. *"What?"*

I took both of her hands into my own. "You will go to the countryside with Sister Assunta and dedicate your life to God. I will marry Ferrante degli Spini in your place."

My eyes darted to where Sister Assunta stood. The cell's small window cast part of the nun's face in light while the other part remained in shadow, affording her a sinister look.

"The Virgin has answered our prayers, Celeste. The Holy Mother has intervened on your behalf and God has shown you a way out of your dilemma."

Despite the relief etched in Celeste's eyes as the nun uttered these words, she asked, "How will Valentina fool Signora Livia?"

Surprised, I asked, "Who is Signora Livia?"

Sister Assunta appeared sheepish. "She is the aunt of Ferrante degli Spini."

Celeste added, "She accompanied Dr. Bernardo, the physician who examined me."

Irritated that Sister Assunta had conveniently left out that pertinent bit of information, I demanded, "How can I possibly fool Ferrante's aunt?"

The crafty nun met my gaze without a hint of remorse. "Don't worry about that."

Celeste interjected, "As much as I appreciate your willingness to help me, I cannot let you do this, Valentina."

"Yes you can," Sister Assunta countered, rushing forward to place an arm around her precious ward. "Think of your health, *your future*." To me, she added, "Don't worry about Signora Livia. I've figured out a solution to that problem."

Celeste shook her head. "It's too risky."

I said, "I'm willing to listen to Sister Assunta's plan. My

aunt will marry soon, leaving me without many options. My finances are extremely modest—too modest for a decent dowry. That leaves marrying in poverty or working as a servant."

"Valentina—"

"Hear me out, Celeste. Marriage will provide me with a home, food, security. I'll have a child to raise to keep me busy and give my life some purpose."

Celeste made a face. "What of your happiness?"

"Do you think I'd be any happier scrubbing floors or removing stains from bedsheets? Would I be better off in a tiny home eating the meager scraps provided by my aunt's husband? Let's be practical, shall we?"

Sister Assunta added, "Valentina is correct. You would be doing her a great service by trading places. Camillo will provide a bridal gown since you cannot wed in a nun's habit. Valentina will wear the gown and arrive at the church with a veil over her face, as is the tradition. She will only be forced to reveal herself *after* the ceremony. By then it will be too late."

Valentina said, "My only concern is Signora Livia. What if she makes a scene and insists on having the marriage annulled?"

The nun shook her head confidently. "A woman of her status and breeding would *never* create such a scene inside of a church filled with her peers. Imagine the scandal. Signore Ferrante is a good friend of Prince Raimondo di Sangro, who will most likely be present at the wedding."

Celeste added, "Sister Assunta is correct. Signora Livia didn't strike me as the type who would expose herself to scandal."

"Valentina, listen to me carefully," Sister Assunta said, coming to stand before me. "When Signora Livia confronts you, which she will do in private at the first chance she gets, you must tell her that Celeste ran away in the middle of the night. Explain to her how your best friend begged you to take her place. You must also pretend to have no knowledge of her whereabouts."

Celeste added, "If Ferrante degli Spini couldn't be bothered to come here and meet his future bride, what difference will it make who is in his bed? The man wants a healthy young woman to breed, and that's exactly what he'll get with you."

"Well, are you up for the task?" Sister Assunta demanded.

I glanced at my friend. "I'll do it."

A radiant smile stretched across Celeste's face. "Thank you, Valentina. I owe you my life."

***

To say that Celeste's health improved after my decision to marry Ferrante would be a gross understatement. I visited her daily to learn as much as I could about Camillo Custozi and her deceased parents. With each passing day, my friend's eyes reflected newfound hope and the familiar soft smile returned to her face. She put on weight rather quickly, and literally glowed with good health. Her mood significantly improved too. Sometimes, I caught her softly humming. The faraway look in her eyes as she stared out the window made me wonder what kind of thoughts she entertained.

One day, I commented, "If I didn't know better, I would say that you're in love."

Celeste smiled as her hand caressed her belly thoughtfully. "I *am* in love…I'm in love with life, with the freedom you've afforded me, with God and His creations." She shrugged and added, "I'm so happy and grateful to have a friend like you."

Touched by the sincerity and sweetness of her words, I offered her a hug. She embraced me tightly, then looked at me as if she wanted to tell me something.

"What is it?" I prompted.

She smiled and shook her head. "Nothing."

CHAPTER 6

Aunt Gloria sent me on an errand across town. I took the opportunity to visit the waterfront. She didn't like it when I went there alone, but the benefits were worth the risk. Being near the water cleansed my mind and spirit. It also helped me to think clearly.

I strolled along the street with eyes glued to the watery horizon. The brilliant sunshine hit the aquamarine waves, causing them to glimmer like diamonds. The entire bay appeared to be covered in mirror shards. I inhaled the salty air while tuning in to the cries of sea gulls circling overhead.

The coast was littered with fishing vessels, both large and small. I watched as shirtless brown men cast their nets into the sea. Wouldn't it be funny if one of them caught a mermaid?

Castel Nuovo, often called Maschio Angioino, rivaled for my attention against the natural wonder of Vesuvius. The imposing medieval castle dated back to the late thirteenth century. My eyes traced the dizzying height of the enormous towers. I imagined long-haired maidens atop the turrets gazing out to sea, the wind ripping through their wavy golden locks. I also pictured brave knights atop those towers, their crossbows aimed at encroaching enemies.

Aunt Gloria sometimes chastised me for my overactive imagination, blaming the tawdry novels I liked to read. She was right, of course. As much as I enjoyed reading science books, intriguing romances proved hard to resist. What woman didn't dream of valiant knights, handsome and strong, with mouths full of sweet words? Those medieval maidens had troubadours to sing their praises—who would sing mine?

"Watch out, girl!"

I flinched at the barked command as an old man passed me with a basket of full of fish. Dead, glassy eyes stared at me from a round wicker tomb.

The man paused. “Buy some fresh fish?”

“No thank you,” I replied.

The images of medieval knights dissolved as the tip of my shoe rubbed against fish guts on the ground. I side-stepped the smelly pile and continued my stroll, only this time paying closer attention to my surroundings.

My gaze returned to the water and fishing boats. One fisherman caught sight of me and waved. I glanced around before returning the gesture. I reminded myself that Aunt Gloria would not approve of my scandalous behavior.

A carriage passed me on the street and I glimpsed an elegant couple through the window. A red tricorn hat sat upon the man’s head as he leaned toward a woman in white brocade. Smiling at each other, they seemed oblivious to the plight of the poor peasants who gaped at them. I doubted that their shoes ever came into contact with fish guts or horse dung. They probably had servants to run their errands, cook their food, and clean their homes. As these thoughts flitted through my mind, I paused mid-step.

That will be you in less than two weeks, Valentina.

Would I, too, own pretty gowns and ride through the streets in a fine carriage? Overcome by giddiness, I pictured the scenario with great detail. Although terrifying, part of me found the prospect of marrying Ferrante degli Spini—a powerful worldly man—somewhat thrilling. I possessed virtually no experience with boys my own age, let alone a fully grown man who was both a widower and a father. What could I possibly say to him that he hadn’t already heard? Another thought struck me: what if he found me dull-witted?

The ramifications of my decision to help Celeste suddenly hit me full force and I began to panic. Perhaps I had been too precipitous in my actions. My desire to help my desperate friend had clouded my own sense of practicality. This whole thing was pure folly.

My chest tightened and I could barely breathe. Forcing myself to inhale deeply, I gazed out at the water. Two young fishermen leered at me from the shore so I hastened my pace.

There would be no more sneaking off to the waterfront after my marriage to Ferrante—of that I was certain.

An old woman sat shucking clams by her husband's boat and I paused to watch her gnarled hands do their swift work. Catching my eye, she offered me a toothless smile and motioned toward the pile of mollusks in the hope that I would purchase some. I shook my head and she frowned at me before returning to her task.

I didn't want to provoke my aunt's ire by staying out too long, so I began retracing my steps toward home. Sighing, I cast a final look at the stunning landscape.

***

One week later, Aunt Gloria married Natalino in a small local chapel with a spattering of friends from our neighborhood. Donna Pasqualina hosted the celebratory dinner at her home afterward. Roasted suckling pig along with skewers of pigeons occupied half of the table. Freshly baked breads and pastries, along with seasonal vegetables, fruits, and cheese accompanied the meats.

I gorged on delicious sfogliatelle and shared in my aunt's joy at finally having landed a good husband. Natalino's eyes reflected love whenever his gaze rested upon his new wife. This made me feel both relieved and happy.

My aunt whispered in my ear, "How I wish I could attend your wedding next week."

"I wish that too." I glanced at Natalino and inquired, "Have you decided what you will tell him once I disappear?"

She nodded in a solemn manner. "Your late father's first cousin in Calabria has offered you a position in his home as a lady's maid to his wife."

I stared at her, impressed. "Aunt Gloria, I must say, your improvisational skills are superb."

She chuckled slightly. "You aren't the only one who enjoys reading novels."

I couldn't argue with that.

She continued, "I look forward to moving in with Natalino. Caring for his aging mother will give me something to do."

"Donna Pasqualina is a good woman."

"Do you know what she said to me this morning before the ceremony? She told me that she loves me like the daughter she never had but always wanted."

Her words warmed my heart.

She continued, "I only hope that Ferrante proves a good husband to you."

"I'm sure he will," I said with far more confidence than I felt. "What about the apartment?"

"We will either sell or rent it out once you've gone."

An overwhelming sadness swept over me. I had committed to helping my friend at great cost to myself. Nodding in response to my aunt's words, I said, "A profitable solution."

Some of the guests began to sing, making Aunt Gloria laugh. "Come, let's join the others."

I allowed myself to be swept up in the moment in order to temporarily forget my mounting anxiety.

***

The first of April dawned clear and cool. Aunt Gloria snored softly from her bed across the room. Natalino had insisted that she spend the night in order to see me off in the morning, which she had planned to do all along. A heavy sigh escaped my lips as I turned my head toward the window. After today, my life would change. *Irrevocably.*

The mere thought produced a strange heaviness in the center of my chest.

"It's not too late to change your mind."

To my surprise, Aunt Gloria lay staring at me from her bed.

"I'm nervous," I admitted.

Propping herself on the pillows, she said, "You don't owe anyone anything, Valentina. Say the word, and I will go to the convent right now to inform Celeste that you can't go through with it. She will marry Ferrante, as is her duty."

"Thank you, Aunt Gloria, but I am going to carry out our plan. God willing, everything will fall into place."

"I'll be praying for you." She got out of bed, threw open the shutters, and added, "It's a nice day. I'll fix us some tea before

I help you with your toilette."

After breaking our fast with tea and buttered bread, we wandered to the vanity. I sat facing the sunlit window as Aunt Gloria brushed and dressed my hair into something resembling a fashionable style. The simple braided coil at my nape showcased my features.

She stepped away from me and studied her handiwork. "There, your hair is done. Now for your face."

Aunt Gloria applied a lavender and lemon scented cream to my face and hands before adding a hint of rouge to my cheeks.

"That's perfect," I said, admiring my reflection.

"Now, the gown."

The House of Spini had dispatched the garment to the Convent of Santa Patrizia yesterday, surprising everyone. Sister Assunta had met us at the gate later that night to smuggle the bridal gown into our hands. Seed pearls graced the neckline and layers of sheer lace fell from the elbow-length sleeves.

I held my breath as Aunt Gloria tied the laces of my bodice tightly in order to cinch my slim waist. Neither of us had ever handled nor worn anything so fine.

Fully dressed, I stared at the mirror. "Oh my…"

"It's exquisite," Aunt Gloria whispered, circling me. "One thing is certain, Ferrante is a generous man."

"Celeste and Sister Assunta had assumed that Camillo would be providing the gown."

"Why would he? The man hasn't bothered to see his niece in six years." Her brow creased and she added, "You need some jewelry."

I watched as she fished through her jewelry box. "I can't possibly take something yours."

Holding out a pair of simple silver earrings, she said, "A wedding gift."

"Aunt Gloria, those are your favorite."

"All the more reason I want you to have them. You'll think of me whenever you wear them."

I put them on and smiled. "Thank you. I will cherish them."

Lifting a bottle of inexpensive perfume from her vanity, she said, “The final touch. Only a couple of drops.”

She administered the liquid to the exposed hollow of my throat, my earlobes, and the insides of each wrist. I inhaled and smiled, for I loved the clean aroma of vetiver.

“It’s time. Are you ready?”

I nodded. We had gone over the plan several times but now we would finally carry it out. There could be no errors.

Aunt Gloria threw a dark cloak over my shoulders to hide my dress, then carefully brought the hood over my head to cover most of my face. I glanced wistfully at my small collection of books, which I was forced to leave behind. They were the only things of value that I possessed, but since Celeste owned nothing, I was forced to enter my new home empty-handed.

I watched as my aunt donned a similar dark cloak. Pulling the hood over her head, she said, “Let’s go.”

I did my best not to cry as I exited my aunt’s apartment for the last time as Valentina Gaetani. Tears blurred my vision as we walked briskly to the convent. We waited by the gate, side by side, in silence. Sister Assunta appeared at the appointed time and granted us access.

“Hurry,” she whispered before gently closing the gate behind us.

She urged us toward Celeste’s cell. My heart raced as we crossed the cloister garden and passed the orange grove. The sun-kissed fruit at the top glowed in the bright early morning sunshine. Bees buzzed around flowers and birds sang in tree branches.

The nun scratched at Celeste’s door. I pushed back the hood of my cloak once we were safely inside the cell.

“You look so pretty,” Celeste whispered, her eyes roaming over me.

“Were you followed?” Sister Assunta demanded.

“No,” Aunt Gloria replied.

The nun pointed to me. “Take her cloak, Celeste.”

I removed my cloak and handed it to Celeste, who threw it over her shoulders and fastened the clasp at her throat.

Sister Assunta gave us a curt nod. “Good. Now, hand me

that lace veil, will you?"

Celeste came over with a stretch of ivory lace. Aunt Gloria and Sister Assunta carefully placed it over my hair, allowing a generous measure to fall in front of my face.

Sister Assunta inquired, "Can you tell that it's Valentina?"

Celeste squinted. "No."

My aunt added, "The lace design is dense enough to provide anonymity."

"Good. Celeste, it's time for you and Donna Gloria to go," the nun announced with a nervous glance out the window. "Some are already up and about at this hour."

Celeste threw her arms around my neck. "I cannot thank you enough, my dearest and best friend. You have saved my life."

Sister Assunta pried us apart. "Camillo Custozi will be here at any moment. Celeste, I will meet you at Donna Gloria's apartment in an hour. From there, we will embark on our new life. Take courage, my child."

Covering her head with the hood, Celeste went to stand by the door. Aunt Gloria took my hand and offered me a sad smile before kissing both of my cheeks.

I watched in emotional silence as my aunt and my best friend vacated the cell. When would I see them again?

Sister Assunta stood by the window. "If anyone sees them, it will appear as if you and your aunt came here to say goodbye." The nun looked at me. "You're nervous."

"I am."

She came over to me and took my hands into her own. Closing her eyes, she uttered, "Santa Madonna, I beseech thee to look after Valentina. We pray for guidance and protection, and ask that Ferrante treat her with kindness. In the name of Our Lord Jesus, Amen."

"Amen," I whispered.

A loud knock startled us both. Sister Assunta offered me a look of encouragement before opening the door. Camillo Custozi stood in the doorway accompanied by the abbess, Mother Clotilda. Celeste had spoken of her uncle many times yet I had never met him until now.

"Celeste," he said.

I took in his balding head, scuffed shoes, and threadbare velvet coat. He tried to dress it up with starched lace at his throat and a big onyx stone brooch.

Lowering my head, I said, "Greetings, Uncle Camillo."

Camillo entered the room to greet me. Sister Assunta immediately took the abbess aside to distract the woman so that she wouldn't see me.

Lifting the edges of my veil, he said, "Let me look at you."

I raised my eyes to his in a modest manner. Camillo frowned slightly, causing my heartbeat to accelerate. To my relief, he offered me an indulgent smile. "Such a pretty bride. Today, you must make me a *bella figura*. I promised your betrothed that you would be a good and obedient wife."

"I will do my best to honor you, sir."

"Have you already bade everyone farewell?"

Rearranging the veil over my face, I replied, "I have."

Sister Assunta turned away from Mother Clotilda and made a grand show of bestowing blessings upon me. Finally, she hugged me and said, "Be with God my sweet Celeste."

Mother Clotilda also hugged me and offered me a blessing. I murmured something kind in return before being led away by Camillo.

"There's no need to be anxious," he said as we exited the convent gate. "Know that your father would have approved of my choice of husband for you."

"Thank you, Uncle Camillo."

My words prompted the man to appear smug as he helped me into the hired carriage. I kept my face turned toward the window in order to avoid conversation. Better for him to think I'm shy or embarrassed.

People stared at me from the street as the carriage cut a path through the center of Naples. I returned their curious stares through the floral design of the lace hiding my face.

"The Church of Gesù Nuovo is not far from here," Camillo said after a while. "Do you know it?"

"Yes."

"Quite an honor for you to be married there, eh?" I nodded but said nothing. Staring at me, he continued, "Tell me, did that nun of yours teach you anything about the real world?"

"Sir?"

"Did she tell you what your husband will expect tonight?"

I gazed down at my lap and shook my head.

Camillo leered, causing me to instantly dislike him. "No need to be ashamed of something God has created. I imagine you're frightened too. Don't cry or make a fuss, girl. Just smile and lay still. Your husband will know what to do."

Mortified, I barely nodded in response to his crass words.

He continued, "You don't have a mother to tell you these things, and what would a nun know?"

"Thank you, Uncle."

"Don't mention it. Do as you're told and everything will work out fine."

The carriage slowed as we reached our destination. To my astonishment, the Piazza del Gesù teemed with people.

"Apparently, the marriage of Ferrante degli Spini has drawn half the city," Camillo said, his tone one of shock and mild amusement. "Look at that, Celeste. Everyone is here to get a peek at you."

I studied the church. Originally built in the late fifteenth century as a palazzo, the spiked stone façade rendered it the most unique church in the city. I found the edifice's aesthetic quite fitting since "Spini" literally meant *thorns*. I wondered if Ferrante would be as prickly and unpleasant as his surname suggested.

"Come along, Celeste." My hesitation to leave the sanctuary of the carriage made Camillo frown. "Today you will become the wife of an important man. You should be filled with joy and gratitude."

"I am," I lied.

I accepted his hand and allowed him to help me alight from the carriage. He patted my back like a proud father instead of a scheming uncle, then ushered me into the church.

CHAPTER 7

Squinting through the haze of incense smoke and powdered wigs, I stepped into the cool church with a racing heart. Milky sunshine poured from mullioned windows, creating patches of light along the nave. The damp air hung heavy with the cloying scents of burning wax, sweet perfumes, and perspiration. Somewhere toward the front, a child began to cry.

"Well, let's get on with it," Camillo murmured beside me as he pushed me forward.

Many sets of curious eyes studied me as I shuffled down the nave toward the man whom I assumed to be Ferrante. The bridegroom faced the altar, keeping his back to the assembled nobles and onlookers. Broad shouldered and tall, his confident stance struck me as somewhat arrogant. His black hair was neatly combed and secured at the nape by a plain black ribbon. No powder, no frills. As I drew closer, I saw that he wore polished riding boots instead of stockings and fancy shoes. His perfectly cut coat was fashioned from plush dark gray velvet yet hosted no decorative elements except for brushed silver buttons. Everything about the man was deceptively plain while being quite expensive.

A mature woman in a black brocade gown with formal powdered wig stood in the front row watching me with a dubious expression on her painted face. Intelligent eyes competed with a hawkish nose and garish red lips. Although she wasn't attractive, her height and thin frame made her appear elegant. The strand of flawless pearls around her scrawny neck looked valuable enough to feed an entire family for years. According to the description I had received from Celeste, I deduced the woman to be Livia, Ferrante's aunt.

Camillo abandoned me rather abruptly at the altar. I stole a sidelong glance at Ferrante, who couldn't be bothered to return the gesture. Chiseled features, a prominent nose, high cheekbones, strong chin, and black eyebrows knitted together to form what appeared to be a permanent scowl. Thank God it was me who stood beside the intimidating man and not Celeste. My friend would have unraveled into a state of despair.

Ferrante maintained his aloof demeanor throughout the entire ceremony and never once glanced in my direction. I noted that his deep voice carried authority as we exchanged vows. Maintaining a stoic expression, he never raised his eyes to mine as he gently took my hand and slipped a gold ring onto my finger. I couldn't help comparing his big hands to my own smaller ones as I carefully slid a gold ring onto his finger.

The priest concluded the ceremony by urging Ferrante to kiss his bride. My new husband lifted the veil and flinched in surprise at the sight of me. I noted something akin to disappointment reflected in his piercing green eyes.

Averting his gaze, he dutifully pressed his lips to my forehead for the benefit of those present, then allowed the veil to fall from his hands. Men normally paraded their brides with pride after the ceremony. For some reason, Ferrante kept me hidden from the world.

Taking my hand, he placed it in the crook of his elbow before turning around and facing the congregation. My fingers pressed against the hard muscle beneath the luxuriant fabric as he led me down the nave. Well-wishers tried to approach us but he stopped for no one, offering little more than curt nods to their kind words.

His brisk steps forced me to keep pace as we exited the church and stepped out into the street. I discreetly studied the man in the daylight through the lace pattern covering my eyes. We were two strangers who had been bound by God until death separated us, so I expected him to return my curiosity or at least say something. *Anything*. Oddly, he didn't. Someone ran after us and I saw that it was Livia.

Keeping pace beside us, she said, "Ferrino, really? You could linger for a moment."

Ferrino?

Ferrante only shrugged without comment.

She frowned. "You're being rude, not to mention the bad impression you are giving your new bride."

"You're the one who wanted a big church wedding, Aunt Livia. Not me. I would have been happy to wed Celeste in the villa's private chapel." Sparing a glance at me, he added, "I'm willing to bet she would have preferred that too."

I lowered my head as Livia tossed a look my way. "That may be true but we're here now, and many important people wish to speak with you."

"If they were important they would have been invited to celebrate with us at the villa."

Livia bit back an angry retort.

Ferrante led me to a fine carriage painted bluish black. Affixed to the door was the Spini coat of arms—a black thorny branch juxtaposed against a gold shield. He opened the door and helped me take my seat. Settling against plush red velvet cushions and light blue satin pillows, I marveled at the sheer decadence of the extraordinary vehicle.

Ferrante entered the carriage and sat across from me. He was so tall that his knees almost touched mine. To my horror, Livia entered the carriage and settled beside her nephew. A sharp rap to the vehicle's ceiling prompted the driver to merge onto the street with the other carts and carriages.

Livia murmured, "I don't know why I bother."

"That makes two of us," Ferrante snapped.

"You are incorrigible."

He pinched the bridge of his nose and closed his eyes in response to her comment. I watched this exchange with interest, for it afforded me a glimpse of what was to come.

Livia continued, "Everything should be ready by the time we arrive. The servants were instructed to set the buffet table outdoors, as you requested. I had them prepare your favorite cake as well as marzipan in the shape of hearts." To me, she added, "Are you fond of sweets, Celeste?"

"Yes," I replied softly.

Ferrante opened his eyes and his gaze roamed over me in a detached manner.

Noticing this, Livia said, "You can remove your veil now, my dear. Let your husband see your face."

I pushed the veil back, allowing some of the lace to cover my brow. Keeping my eyes and head lowered in feigned modesty, I folded my hands in my lap and stared down at my new shiny gold ring.

"You have such lovely hands," Livia said, leaning over to take my ringed hand into her own. "Soft too."

"Thank you," I whispered.

Her skin felt cold and dry against my own. I had once held a lizard as a child and couldn't help making the comparison.

"Ah, to be young again," she uttered nostalgically.

While Livia busily admired my hands, I risked a glance at Ferrante to find his eyes glued to my face. Although his scrutiny caused my cheeks to burn, I didn't look away.

Livia tore her gaze from my hands to look at her nephew. Her face registered surprise at his expression, then melted into a smile of relief and satisfaction. Turning her head in my direction, the smile instantly vanished. Her eyes widened with shock and begged the question: *who are you?*

My heart raced out of control as I braced myself for the harsh words that would surely pour from her lips. To my astonishment, Livia rearranged her features into a neutral mask and remained silent. Her calculating stare made me squirm in my seat, however. After a long tense moment, she broke eye contact with me and I literally sagged with relief. Convinced that she would not expose my lie, I began to breathe a bit easier. There would be a reckoning later for sure.

The carriage began its ascent of the Vomero hillside, which faced the Naples Bay and the magnificent Vesuvius. I leaned forward in my seat to get a better view of the sparkling blue water and cerulean sky.

"My villa is located at the top of this hill," Ferrante said, breaking the silence. "This makes it rather inconvenient at times, but the peacefulness and stunning views make up for it...I hope that you find your new home agreeable, Celeste."

Once again, Livia gaped at her nephew in surprise.

His green eyes resembled translucent sea glass in the sunlight and I couldn't keep myself from staring into them. "I'm sure I will, Signore Ferrante."

"There's no need to be formal when addressing me. You may call me Ferrante."

"Ferrante," I repeated, causing his expression to soften ever so slightly. "My uncle informed me that you have a daughter."

A dark cloud settled upon his features, making me instantly regret my words. "Her name is Nadia and she is only three. Berta, her nursemaid, will prevent her from bothering you."

"I'm certain that she won't be a bother, sir. I look forward to meeting her."

Relieved, he explained, "Nadia is mute. The physicians say there is nothing to be done, but I hold on to the hope that one day…Only God knows the future."

Silence filled the carriage.

Finally, I offered, "I'll include your daughter in my prayers."

"God listens to people like you," he mumbled, turning his face away to peer out the window and abruptly ending our conversation.

The carriage came to a stop before an imposing villa. The immense size of my new home shocked me. I glimpsed servants scurrying about with plates and trays for the wedding celebration. The footman opened the carriage door, flooding the vehicle's interior with warm sunshine. Ferrante held my hand longer than necessary when he helped me down from the carriage, then turned to help his aunt. I was urged toward the villa's grand entrance. Servants paused and curtsied to me while murmuring words of welcome and congratulations.

Ferrante motioned to one of the maids, then said to me, "The guests will be arriving soon. I suggest you retire to your room for a brief rest."

Livia took firm hold of my arm and waved away the servant. "I shall personally accompany Celeste to her room."

Ferrante turned his back on us to supervise his servants. Livia led me upstairs and marched me down a long hallway. I soon found myself inside a frescoed chamber dominated by a canopied bed.

She locked the door and then regarded me expectantly. When I remained silent, she raised a neatly drawn black eyebrow. "Who are you?"

"As of today, I am Celeste Carducci, wife of Ferrante degli Spini," I replied in a firm voice.

"Celeste Carducci is a mealy-mouthed ninny with a dubious character. I know this because I recently met the girl." She paused, giving me a pointed look. *"Who are you?"*

My first instinct was to defend my friend. Instead, I mustered my courage. "Does it really matter who I am, Signora Livia? To your nephew, one girl is as good as the next. He received the dowry from *my uncle*, did he not?"

"Does Camillo actually believe you to be his niece?"

I removed my lace veil and draped it over the back of a nearby chair. "You saw him walk me down the aisle today, did you not?"

"How dare you take such an impertinent tone with me?"

"Forgive me, madam, for that's not my intention. I'm only trying to make the point that Celeste Carducci was only a bargaining chip and a burden to him. The man went years without seeing his niece. To Camillo Custozi, *one girl is as good as the next.*"

She regarded me thoughtfully and slowly nodded. "You're clever and courageous, I'll give you that."

"I sacrificed my life for Celeste's happiness, nothing more."

"You must love your friend and think very highly of her to commit such an altruistic act."

"I do."

"If you don't want to tell me your name, that's fine. I'll find out soon enough." Wandering to the window, she pointed at her nephew. "All that matters to me is that man. His happiness is my happiness because he is all that I have left in this miserable world. My nephew obviously likes you, which is a rare thing since he tolerates so few people and loathes women." Closing the gap between us, she put her face close to mine and added, "I swear to God and the saints that if you so much as cause him one measure of grief, I will expose you to the world as a fraud and report you to the authorities."

My hands trembled upon hearing her threat. "Signora Livia, I'm not here to hurt you or your nephew. I've never committed a crime in my life, I swear."

The woman softened in the face of my vulnerability. "Save me the trouble and tell me your name."

"Valentina Gaetani," I replied as tears filled my eyes.

"Calm yourself, girl. For God's sake don't cry."

"Forgive me."

Extracting a silk handkerchief from her sleeve, she urged, "Tell me everything."

After dabbing at my eyes, I took a deep breath. "Celeste and I have been best friends for many years. We met at the Convent of Santa Patrizia. We are both orphans, you see. I eventually went to live with my aunt while she remained there, but we still saw each other on a regular basis. Celeste is delicate and pious, a tender soul. She is completely devoted to God. After your visit to the convent, she neither ate nor slept. To see her in such a desperate state frightened me—and Sister Assunta too."

Livia's expression turned sardonic. "Let me guess, Celeste wasted away from sadness and grief, so you volunteered to take her place."

"Sister Assunta suggested the switch in order to save her ward and I agreed. Marriage to your nephew would have eventually killed her—no offense to your nephew, of course. Celeste was meant for a higher calling."

"I see," Livia said, crossing her arms. "Where is Celeste right now?"

"Sister Assunta took her to a remote convent this morning, but didn't disclose its location. She said Celeste will soon take the vows and become a nun."

At this, Livia's eyes widened in disbelief. *"Is that what your friend told you?"*

The way she said this made me wary. "Yes…"

"Tell me something, my pretty impostor, have you ever actually heard Celeste express her desire to become a nun?"

I thought for a moment. "Not in those exact words."

Livia began pacing the room, the fabric of her gown rustling with each step in the ensuing silence.

At length, I demanded, "Why else would Celeste go through these lengths if not to continue living a holy life elsewhere?"

Heaving a tired sigh, she stopped and eyed me with pity. "You poor, gullible, foolish girl."

I stiffened. "I beg your pardon?"

"Your friend is a liar."

"No."

"Celeste has a lover."

I shook my head in denial. "Impossible."

She continued as if I hadn't spoken. "A monk, who not only stole her chastity, but left a souvenir in its place."

I staggered to the bed and sat on the edge. "I don't…No, it can't be…Celeste tells me everything. We're like sisters."

Livia tilted her head and offered me a sad smile. "Celeste has cleverly managed to fool everyone, including you."

The world around me spun out of control. "Are you saying that Celeste is…that she's pregnant?"

"According to my physician, yes." At my stunned expression, she added, "I was forced to purchase Dr. Bernardo's silence, and it was not cheap."

Consumed by a sudden wave of nausea, I dry heaved. Livia quickly grabbed the clean chamber pot and set it under my chin in time to catch the vomit that poured from my mouth.

Wiping my lips with her handkerchief, she whispered, "The world is a harsh and unforgiving place, especially for those who are naïve."

"Dear God," I whispered.

"Ferrante despises dishonesty above all human traits. Your friend did my nephew a favor because, despite marrying under a false pretense, you strike me as an honest girl."

"I *am* honest, Signora Livia. I married Ferrante to save my friend, but I have every intention of fulfilling my role. I will do my utmost to be a good wife to your nephew and a good mother to his daughter."

Livia touched my cheek. "I can see that you are sincere."

Overcome by emotion, a sob escaped my lips.

"There, there, calm yourself. You're as much of a victim as I am in this mess. It won't do for Ferrante or his guests to see you in such a state."

"Will you help me?"

"I have no choice, do I? The opportunity for me to have exposed you has already passed," she reminded me, referring to the carriage ride. Changing the subject, she demanded, "How is your health?"

"Fine. I seldom get sick."

"Good...Are you a virgin?"

"Yes."

"A baby would ease the tension in this household and instantly elevate your position." Her eyes roamed over my face. "Assuming you aren't barren, I'm sure you'll have many babies."

"How can you tell?"

"You do realize the power you possess, don't you?"

I shrugged. "I'm inexperienced when it comes to men."

"I saw how Ferrante looked at you. He likes you."

This struck me as odd since I glimpsed disappointment in his eyes at the altar. "If you say so."

Livia continued, "Caterina was extremely vain and conceited, so your humility is quite refreshing."

"Caterina was Ferrante's first wife?"

"Yes. Their marriage wasn't a happy one so don't bring up her name." She walked over to the vanity and pointed. "There's some rose water and some anisette tonic set out for you. Take a moment to compose yourself. I'll leave you alone now."

"Thank you, Signora Livia."

"You're welcome, *Celeste*."

Livia exited the room and I sat on the bed pondering Celeste's treachery. Why did she hide the truth from me? I suspected that Sister Assunta had been fooled and manipulated by my friend as well.

The voices of guests arriving downstairs yanked me from

my reverie and forced me back to the present. I walked over to the vanity and applied rose water to my neck and wrists. I noticed a porcelain *necessaire* with tiny scissors, file, sealing wax, silk patches, rouge, and other grooming requirements. Next, I swished a generous measure of anisette tonic inside of my mouth to cleanse it, then spat the contents into the chamber pot. I set the porcelain vessel on the bedside table for a servant to dispose of its contents.

I studied the artwork and furnishings of what was now my bedroom. The rose damask on the vanity stool matched the upholstered chair of the mahogany writing desk. The latter was equipped with quills, ink, parchment, and a vase of fresh lilacs. An Oriental rug in pastel shades served as a base for a big canopied bed hung with sheer cream silk. A Bible and a small prayer book sat on the bedside table, along with a tiny silver statue of the Madonna. Three paintings graced the walls, each one depicting a female saint: Lucia, Anastasia, and Agnes.

The sound of footsteps outside of my door made me pause. Floorboards creaked and I waited for whomever it was to announce their presence with a knock, but none came. Tiptoeing to the door, I carefully pressed my ear against the painted wooden surface. A sickeningly sweet perfume wafted through the door crack, making me wince in disgust. Footsteps hastily retreated and I caught the sound of fabric rustling.

How odd.

The sound of music drew me to the window. A group of musicians performed on the terrace while carriages pulled up along the pebbled drive. Elegant ladies with rouged cheeks and painted lips cooled themselves with vibrantly painted fans. Jewels sparkled on their throats, earlobes, and fingers, making me feel rather plain.

Catching my reflection in the mirror, I compared my simple hair style to the complicated powdered coiffures worn by the noblewomen. Some of them teetered precariously, threatening to tumble down their backs and shoulders. The door opened abruptly and my hand flew to my chest as I jumped away from the window.

Ferrante stood in the doorway. "I didn't mean to startle you."

"I was about to go downstairs."

He scanned the room. "Is everything to your liking?"

"The room is perfect," I replied with a small smile.

Walking over to where I stood, he extracted a string of pearls from his coat pocket. "My aunt mentioned to me that you lacked adornment."

I gasped at the sight of the precious jewels. "Oh."

"Do you not like your wedding gift?"

"I like it very much."

"Turn around."

I did as he asked, then felt his breath against my nape as he fastened the necklace with nimble fingers. Grasping my arm, he urged me toward the mirror.

Tearing my gaze from the reflection, I looked up at him. "I've never owned anything so lovely. Thank you, Ferrante."

He let go of my arm. "Come."

I followed him downstairs to where people were gathered in clusters. The guests stopped talking and began whispering the moment they saw me.

"She's so young."

"Exquisite."

"Let's hope this one doesn't—"

"Shhh!"

"I need to visit a convent soon."

I hid my amusement upon hearing the last comment since it escaped the lips of an elderly gentleman. Livia materialized beside me and began introducing me to a few older women. I did my best to commit their names to memory as they each doled out tidbits of marital advice. Most of the guests were mature, significantly older than Ferrante, and I wondered if they were Livia's friends.

At one point, a distinguished gentleman in a patterned velvet coat adorned with gold buttons appeared beside me. Of course I knew him. *Everyone did.* Despite being in his fiftieth year, he possessed a boyish face with wide-set, intelligent blue eyes.

Regarding me with childlike curiosity, he said, "Allow me

introduce myself, Signora Celeste. I am Prince Raimondo di Sangro."

Stunned, I managed to offer him my best curtsy. "Your Highness, I am honored by your presence."

I watched in awe as he brought my knuckles to his lips. My humble hand—*kissed by a prince*!

The seventh Prince of Sansevero was an inventor, alchemist, architect, writer, soldier, and Freemason. He spoke most of the European languages, as well as Hebrew and Arabic. He had been head of the Neapolitan masonic lodge until his excommunication, which was eventually lifted by Pope Benedict XIV. What I found most fascinating about the prince were the legends surrounding him. For example, he supposedly knew the secret of creating blood from nothing. Also, his family chapel was said to have been constructed on an old temple of the Egyptian goddess, Isis. He was currently renovating it according to his own designs, and had commissioned exquisite works of art. Finally, a printing press was rumored to exist in his basement, allowing him to produce self-translated books that were censored by the Catholic Church.

Raimondo searched my face. "Judging by your expression, I'm willing to wager that you've heard all the controversial stories about me."

I hesitated. "I have indeed, my lord."

"Yet you are honored to meet me, despite them?"

"I'm honored to meet you *because* of them."

His eyes lit up with amusement. "How refreshingly honest. A bit brazen too."

"Forgive me if I've caused you offense."

"On the contrary. I'm seldom wrong in my perceptions and I sense that you are an unusual young lady. I wonder what you've seen of this world."

"In the physical sense, nothing."

The prince narrowed his eyes. "What other sense is there?"

"The cerebral sense, my lord. I have been to ancient Greece and Egypt, Medieval France and England, Germany, Portugal, and several other faraway places. What's more, I've learned about the men and women who shaped those societies."

"Ah, you like books," he correctly deduced.

"Very much."

"I imagine they had a limited collection at the convent."

My mind raced to conjure a convincing lie. "Sister Assunta, my chaperone, sometimes procured secular books that she felt were appropriate. She knew my interest in history and often indulged me."

"You weren't allowed to select your own books? How dreadful." Leaning in close, he whispered conspiratorially, "Wait until you see your husband's library. Not nearly as big as mine, of course, but impressive nonetheless."

"Compared to the convent, it will be Alexandria."

Raimondo burst into laughter then offered me a smile, the kind that reflected warmth in the eyes. I returned the gesture.

Raimondo looked to Ferrante, who stood on the far side of the room watching us. "I daresay you don't know much about your husband, do you?"

"That's correct."

The prince held my gaze and I saw genuine concern reflected in his eyes. "May I ask a favor of you?"

"Of course, Your Highness."

"I love Ferrante as I do my own son. His father and I were the best of friends, you see. I ask that you exercise patience."

I nodded in consent to the request.

Ferrante crossed the room and stood at my side.

Raimondo turned to him and said, "There you are, my friend. We've been having a lovely conversation."

Ferrante placed a possessive hand on my back. "Already corrupting her, Raimondo?"

The prince smiled good-naturedly in the face of my husband's teasing. "I will take my leave so that you may enjoy your wife's company." To me, he added, "My lady, it was a pleasure."

"Likewise, my lord."

Ferrante stared at me once we were alone. "What did you say to the prince?"

"He kindly introduced himself and we talked about books."

"Books?"

"I love to read. He mentioned your impressive library."

"What topics interest you?"

"Biology, chemistry, history…I like many topics."

This surprised him. "You're interested in science?"

"Anatomy and alchemy, to be precise."

Livia rushed over and interjected, "Celeste, a few guests have requested an introduction. Come along."

Steering me away from Ferrante, she led me to a group of noble ladies. I was introduced to several women, including Carlotta Caetani dell'Aquila d'Aragona, the wife of Prince Raimondo. I said little and listened much.

Afterward, I took my seat in the center of the long table that had been set up outside. Festooned with spring blossoms, every inch of its surface was covered with trays of delicious food. Ferrante sat next to me, quietly presided over the meal like a medieval king at a banquet. Raimondo sat to his right. The prince stood and offered a public toast to our marital happiness, which prompted Ferrante to bring his glass to mine. Aside from that, he practically ignored me throughout the meal.

The wedding festivities continued with lively music and dancing. I remained on the fringes of the event so as not to draw attention to myself. Dancers moved gracefully upon the terrace, their shoes tapping against the herringbone brick floor. To my immense relief, Ferrante didn't ask me to dance and neither did any of the other gentlemen present. There was no way I could have kept up with their quick and clever steps.

Guests began filing out shortly after sunset. I studied my husband in the fading light as he said goodnight to Raimondo. No sooner had the last guest left than the servants began clearing the table. Chairs were moved inside, as well as platters of leftover food. Ferrante stood speaking with Livia and it appeared as if they were arguing about something.

The courage I had felt this morning turned to dust in the face of reality. I was Ferrante degli Spini's wife, which meant that he could avail himself of my body. The mere thought of that mysterious carnal experience made me afraid and excited at the same time. Another thought occurred to me. Celeste didn't even bother to tell me what to expect tonight. It would have been a kindness on her part to fill me in on the details of sexual intercourse, especially since she was pregnant and obviously experienced in that area. She must have suspected my anxiety and fear, yet she had said nothing.

I tensed when I saw Ferrante heading toward me. Bracing myself, I said, "Such a fine party, my lord."

"Yes it was. You must be tired."

"A bit."

"Your uncle informed me of your delicate constitution. I hope today's excitement hasn't been too much for you."

"Not at all."

He glanced around and hesitated before regarding me levelly. "I'm sure you've heard the rumors about me."

I lowered my head and said nothing.

He continued, "It's no secret that I'm a difficult man, but I'm not a monster. I would never stoop so low as to force myself upon a young lady to whom I am a complete stranger. Rest assured that I won't be *inconveniencing* you until we become mutually better acquainted."

With that, he turned and walked away, dismissing me.

Unsure of what to do, I headed toward the door.

Livia intercepted me. "What did my nephew say to you?"

"He assured me that he's not a monster and won't force himself on me. It seems he's also concerned for my health thanks to Sister Assunta's false reports."

Livia sighed. "Ferrante is not a man to mince words. At times he can be callous. I beg you to be patient."

That's the second time tonight that someone close to Ferrante advised me to be patient. What did I get myself into?

She continued, "Get some rest. I'll see you tomorrow."

I grabbed her hand before she turned to go. "Thank you for everything, Signora Livia."

She offered me a slight smile. "You're welcome."

I slipped into the villa and crept up to my bedroom. A

servant girl came in a moment later to help me undress. She had a pleasant round face and inquisitive eyes.

"What's your name?" I inquired.

"My name is Lisa. Signora Livia informed me that you didn't have a lady's maid and instructed me to take on that role—assuming you find me acceptable."

Lisa unlatched my necklace. Taking the string of precious orbs into my hands, I admired their color and sheen in the candlelight. When I was done, she put them away along with my silver earrings.

Lisa let down my long chestnut hair and brushed it until it shone. Next, she set out a cotton slip for me to wear to bed before neatly storing my wedding gown in an armoire. I donned the slip, relishing the softness of the finely woven cotton. Tiny light blue flowers adorned the neckline and sleeves.

Lisa held out a pot of rosemary-scented hand cream. I helped myself to a dollop and massaged it into my hands. The emollient concoction made my skin feel like silk.

"Did Signora Livia provide these lovely things?" I asked.

Lisa tilted her head to the side. "She gave the servants money to purchase them, if that's what you're asking."

"How thoughtful and generous," I commented, both touched and impressed.

Female laughter drew me to the window. Pushing aside the drapes, I peeked through the glass panes. Candles and torches still burned, casting pools of coppery light on the darkened terrace. More laughter floated up to my window. I traced the sound to two lone figures standing beneath the flickering light of a torch. One of them was Ferrante. The voluptuous woman with him wore a striped satin gown. Blonde curls topped her head and a single love-lock cascaded down her back.

"Who is that woman?" I asked of Lisa while she turned down the coverlet on the bed.

Lisa glanced over my shoulder and returned to her task. "That's Signora Paola Colombo."

"I don't remember seeing her at the wedding celebration."

Lisa pressed her lips tightly together and said nothing.

I continued, "Where does she live?"

She hesitated. "Here, Signora."

I looked at her blankly. "Here? In this villa?"

Her cheeks reddened and she avoided my eyes. "Yes."

I turned my head to the window and studied the woman with renewed interest. Lisa bade me goodnight and hastily exited the room before I could ask any more questions. Not wishing to get caught spying, I extinguished the candles in my room.

I moved about the darkened space carefully and took up my former post at the window. I watched as Ferrante nodded his head to something Paola said, making her giggle. The high-pitched sound penetrated the glass panes, grating on my nerves. He eventually joined in her laughter and the sound of his deep chuckle evoked a strange feeling in me. I suddenly envied the pair and wished that I, too, had someone with whom to laugh and share secrets.

Celeste had someone.

She had kept him a secret from me too. My own best friend had betrayed me. In that instant, I felt utterly alone.

Another bout of laughter broke my reverie. To my astonishment, Paola threw her arms around Ferrante's neck and kissed his lips. Rather than push the immoral woman away, I saw my husband's arms wrap around her waist as he deepened the kiss. I recoiled from the window, deeply disturbed.

Livia had said that Ferrante loathed women.

Against my better judgement, I peeked out the window again. They were gone and I wondered which room in the villa belonged to Paola. The fact that she resided beneath the same roof as I did soured my opinion of Ferrante. While I didn't expect a complete stranger to love me, I did expect a modicum of respect for the sanctity of marriage. At the very least, Ferrante could be a bit more discreet about his adulterous affairs.

I went to bed feeling confused, tired, and emotionally spent. The voices of Raimondo and Livia echoed through my head as sleep overtook me...*Be patient.*

CHAPTER 8

I struggle to pull air into my empty burning lungs. The more I attempt to free myself from the pile of lace suffocating me, the deeper I sink into the fabric. There are thousands of lace veils, their intricate designs scratching into my skin and making me bleed as I try to move my limbs. The immense weight crushes my chest and presses against my face. Someone in the background laughs in an annoyingly high-pitched manner, causing me to panic. I scream but the sound is muffled. Lace fills my mouth and forces its way down my throat. I hear Livia's voice above the hyena-like laughter. Over and over she repeats one word. Impostor...

Clutching my throat, I sat up in bed and screamed but no sound escaped my lips. I still couldn't breathe. Closing my eyes, I forced myself to calm down as I inhaled through my nose. Air flowed into my lungs and I sagged against the pillows.

I froze at the sound of someone gently knocking. A soft glow from a single candle illuminated a crack in the door.

"Signora Celeste, are you all right?"

"Lisa…I had a nightmare."

"Shall I fix you some soothing tea? A draught, perhaps?"

"I'm fine, thank you."

"I'm in the antechamber if you need me."

The servant retreated to the small annex attached to my bedroom. Further down the hall, another door opened. Heavy footsteps sauntered down the hall and paused outside of my door. I held my breath for the knock but none came. I relaxed when the footsteps retreated.

Ferrante.

Mortified that I had disturbed his slumber, I tried to think of pleasant thoughts in order to avoid nightmares. I woke up disoriented the next day due to little sleep. Lisa pulled aside the heavy drapes, forcing me to squint against the morning light.

For a brief instant, I forgot where I was and imagined myself in Aunt Gloria's apartment.

This isn't your bed, Valentina. This isn't even your life.

The memory of Ferrante kissing Paola loomed in my mind.

Lisa came over to the bed carrying a basin with scented water. "Good morning, Signora Celeste."

She dipped a piece of clean linen into the water, wrung it out then handed it to me.

"Good morning," I said before running the soft cloth along my face, chest, and armpits.

"Are you feeling better this morning?"

"I am."

Lisa brought me a tray containing hot chocolate, bread, and fruit. Having consumed little yesterday due to my nerves, I ate ravenously. After breaking my fast, I got out of bed and realized that I didn't have any clothes other than my formal bridal gown.

"I'm afraid I have nothing to wear," I admitted sheepishly.

Lisa threw open the doors of the armoire and pulled out a floral printed linen gown. "Signora Livia took the liberty of procuring a few garments for you. The seamstress has already been summoned to take your measurements for new dresses."

The Spini family generosity continued to impress me. "I'll be sure to thank her later."

Lisa helped me into the dress. "I can procure pomade and powder for your hair, if you wish."

I sat down at the vanity. "I would prefer a simpler style."

She began brushing my hair, then met my eyes in the mirror's reflection. "You have lovely shiny locks, Signora Celeste. I've seen hair ruined by the overuse of powder."

"My hair has been kept covered by a wimple for years," I lied. "I'm happy to finally show it off."

At that, she smiled and proceeded to style my hair.

When she was done, I toyed with the pair of lovelocks that fell over my right shoulder. "Well done, thank you."

I stood, then hesitated.

Lisa inquired, "Is something wrong, my lady?"

"I don't know what I'm supposed to do next and I'm hoping

you'll offer some guidance. What is my husband's routine?"

Lisa set down the hairbrush. "Signore Ferrante wakes up early and begins his day with a ride. After the midday meal, he either leaves the villa or remains in his quarters until dinner."

"What about Signora Livia?"

"She lives nearly a mile away from here and dines with her nephew several days a week."

"I didn't notice his lordship's daughter yesterday."

"Berta and Nadia reside upstairs so that they can remain unheard and unseen."

This saddened me. "I would like to meet her."

"Today?"

"Right now." The enormous villa had several rooms and three stories, so I added, "Would you please take me there?"

"Certainly."

I tracked Lisa out into the hallway and up a flight of steps to the highest floor. The patter of little feet accompanied by giggles made me smile.

"I think I can find her," I said, motioning for Lisa to go.

The servant inclined her head and retreated her steps. I followed the childish sounds to a big room painted in pastel shades. An array of birds graced the frescoed ceiling and various species of animals covered the walls. The docile beasts were depicted in a garden complete with trees and flowers. A toddler with light brown hair stood in the center of the room. Sporting an unbleached linen shift with a pink sash, she stared at me with curious green eyes. Ferrante's eyes.

A middle-aged servant stood off to the side in a neat black uniform complete with starched white apron. Catching sight of me, she curtsied. A white lace mobcap hid most of her grayish-blonde hair.

"You must be Berta," I said to the woman.

"Yes," she replied, her curious brown eyes taking in every detail of my face and attire.

I approached the plump-cheeked little girl and squatted to be at eye-level with the child. "And you must be Nadia."

Intrigued, Nadia only stared at me.

Taking her small hand into my own, I said, "My name is Celeste. I hope that we can be friends. Would you like that?"

Nadia's bottom lip began quivering.

Berta came over at once. "She's frightened of strangers."

"I would be too," I said, rising to my feet and giving the child a bit of space.

Berta lifted Nadia into her strong arms. "There, there. Celeste only wants to be your friend. See? She's a nice lady. This is Papa's new wife."

I smiled at Nadia. "Will you be taking her outside to play?"

"Signore Ferrante prefers that I keep her indoors."

"Why?"

"He doesn't like it when Nadia plays near the gates."

"So keep her away from them. The back terrace is large, as is the lawn behind it." I walked over to the window. "I see there is a formal garden with a fountain too. It's a lovely day. Why don't we take her outside?"

"We?"

"You and I."

Berta hesitated. "I don't want to go against your wishes, madam, but I do have my orders."

"I will take full responsibility."

"As you wish, Signora Celeste," Berta said with reluctance.

I waited for the servant to dress the child in a heavier frock. Together, we descended the many stairs and went out onto the sun-warmed bricks of the terrace. The servants had already cleaned all the traces of last night's festivities, allowing me to study the uncluttered space. A wrought iron table and chairs stood off to the side, and large ceramic pots boasting olive and citrus trees lined the edges of the terrace.

The moment Berta set the toddler on her feet, she took off like an arrow. Nadia grinned from ear to ear when a butterfly fluttered past her face. She began chasing after the colorful insect and I joined in the game. When the butterfly flew away, I began chasing Nadia. She squealed as she ran in a circle, then suddenly froze. Her eyes widened with fear.

Alarmed, I asked, "What is it?"

I turned around and saw Ferrante seated atop a great white stallion. The way he stared at us made me uneasy. He didn't flinch when I waved at him, which made me nervous. A thin wail escaped the toddler's lips, prompting him to urge the horse toward the stables.

"Nadia, it's only Papa," I said, trying to soothe the child.

To my astonishment, she clung to the skirt of my gown.

"It's time for her nap," Berta announced, taking Nadia's hand. "I bid you good day, Signora."

I watched them go with dismay, then took a stroll around the grounds. A wide variety of flowers and trees surrounded the villa and I derived pleasure in attempting to identify each species. I also noticed several birds, a pair of foxes, and a ferret. I wandered through the formal garden, admiring the neatly clipped hedges. Birds bathed and frolicked in a fountain depicting stone mermaids and dolphins. Gazing up at the villa, I caught Ferrante watching me from one of the windows. This time, I didn't bother waving at him.

Feeling uncomfortable beneath his scrutiny, I moved to the front of the villa to enjoy the breathtaking view of the Naples Bay and Vesuvius. A sprinkling of boats and barges floated upon the serene blue surface of the shimmering water. Being so high above the city center meant cleaner air, which tasted sweet to me. Turning away from the view, I focused on the villa. The massive stone structure had been plastered and painted in a creamy apricot shade. Teal blue shutters graced the tall windows. A stone coat of arms with a thorn branch was displayed above the studded oak front door.

I heard Ferrante shouting orders, then a dog began barking. Wandering in the direction of the sounds, I spied my husband atop his horse with a large black mastiff bounding after them. He held a musket over his shoulder and a quiver of arrows was strapped to his back. Would he bring back a deer or a wild hare?

The sound of wheels crunching on gravel captured my attention. Squinting against the brilliant sunshine, I saw a carriage passing through the villa's iron gates. Livia's distinct profile was framed in the window. She waved at her nephew before he slipped beneath the leafy canopy of the forest.

"You're up early," Livia said after her footman had helped her alight from the vehicle. "Most noble ladies don't rise until noon."

I refrained from pointing out the obvious fact that she was also awake. "I've never indulged in such a luxury."

"Neither have I. My nephew has gone hunting, which will give us some time alone to chat."

We entered the villa and a servant soon materialized. She looked from Livia to me, wondering who would give the command.

Livia said to me, "Well? Aren't you going to offer me some refreshment?"

Blushing, I said to the servant, "Please bring some tea and cake into the…"

"Salon," Livia provided. The servant left to get the refreshments and she continued, "What were you doing outside?"

"Exploring the grounds. It's lovely here."

"Yes. Quiet too."

"I met Nadia earlier. We played outside and now she is taking a nap."

Surprised, she inquired, "Ferrante has already introduced you to his daughter?"

"Ah, not exactly."

"You took it upon *yourself* to see my grandniece?"

"Should I not have?"

"I'm only surprised that you would take the initiative, that's all. Nadia doesn't like strangers. What's your impression of the child, if I may ask?"

"I found her delightful. Ferrante is fortunate to have such a lovely, healthy child."

"Do you always speak your mind so plainly?"

"If I've caused offense—"

She held up her hand to silence me. "It's pleasant to deal with someone transparent for a change."

I thought her comment ironic given the circumstances

leading to my presence in the villa.

Livia continued, "Personally, I think Nadia is a special child. It's a shame that her mother didn't think so. Neither does Ferrante, for that matter."

"Because of her inability to speak?"

She shrugged sadly. "Aside from the fact that my nephew needs a male heir, who will want to wed a mute?"

I said nothing as my heart welled with pity for the poor child.

Livia said, "Why don't I show you around the villa?"

"I would enjoy that very much."

She led me to the main room on the ground floor. Oriental rugs in soft muted tones and finely crafted mahogany furniture graced the enormous space. Watching us from above was Athena and a gaggle of pagan gods. The ceiling fresco was punctuated by decorative moldings from which hung three chandeliers fashioned from Venetian glass. Their immense size held the capacity for dozens of candles, and I tried to imagine what the room would look like lit up at night.

"This is the grand ballroom where we hold our annual Christmas fête and other parties. Ferrante hates to entertain so you can't count on him to fulfill social obligations. The man refuses to plan anything. Naturally, the task falls to me. I hope you won't mind helping me in the future."

"It would be my pleasure."

"The salon is this way. We entertain guests here."

The lovely room was done in pastel pink with gold and green damask furniture. A telescope stood by a window and a harp begged to be played in the opposite corner. A servant arrived with a tea tray.

"Set it there," Livia said to the girl. She then positioned herself on a settee and accepted a cup of steaming tea. After taking a sip from the dainty cup, she inquired, "Do you play?"

I glanced at the harp. "I'm afraid not."

"Pity."

I nibbled on a sliver of cake and listened as Livia gossiped about some of the nobles who had attended the wedding yesterday. I was relieved when she finally stood and suggested that we continue our tour of the villa.

My new home boasted several pieces of fine artwork, drapes and cushions fashioned from sumptuous fabrics, and every gadget imaginable. There were clocks, armillary spheres, compasses, telescopes, and a costly orrey. I studied the small-scale replica of our wondrous solar system with keen interest.

"My nephew is fascinated with science," Livia commented.

Pleased by this news, I confessed, "So am I."

"Ah, you two have something in common. Hopefully, we'll discover more commonalities as time passes. Our next stop is the kitchen. You'll be required to devise meal plans for the week." Seeing the clueless look on my face, she added, "Don't worry, you'll learn."

I kept pace with Livia's brisk steps as she moved toward the rear of the villa. Kitchens were usually located where they would cause the least damage to the main house in the event of a fire. The vast space bustled with servants. Copper pots and pans, rolling pins, ceramic bowls, and foodstuffs were scattered on a long wooden table. Two chickens roasted on a spit within the hearth while a cauldron bubbled with thick, foamy broth.

Livia led me to a spritely plump woman in a starched mobcap. "This is Donna Florinda. Head Cook."

I smiled. "Hello."

"Welcome, Signora Celeste," she said, offering me a maternal smile.

Livia said, "Her ladyship may require some assistance in preparing a meal plan. I know I can count on you to help her."

"I'm happy to do it," Donna Florinda said.

"When would be a convenient time to sit down with you to discuss the matter?" I inquired.

Donna Florinda replied, "There is usually a lull in the kitchen at three o'clock."

"Very well. Do you mind if I come today?"

"Not at all, Signora Celeste. I am at your service."

Everyone in the kitchen stared at me as I tracked Livia's steps toward the door. A hint of a smile played upon her painted lips as she led me to the second floor. She pointed out the many guestrooms and sitting rooms, and I admired them in turn. Pausing mid-step, I sniffed the air and scrunched up my face. "What's that horrid smell?"

"Nothing. Let's go this way."

Rather than obey, I tracked the stench to a set of doors carved with symbols. Recognizing them at once, I placed my hand on the latch.

Livia came over to me and gripped my shoulders. Urging me away from the door, she uttered, "Those are Ferrante's private rooms. No one is allowed inside of them."

"Not even the servants?"

"Only Sandro, his valet. Two scullery maids are allowed once a week for cleaning purposes."

I glanced over my shoulder at the door and smiled inwardly. The symbols carved into the wood represented the seven planetary metals: silver, copper, lead, tin, iron, mercury, and gold. Ferrante practiced alchemy, and I eagerly looked forward to learning more about the man whom I had married.

I said, "The prince commented on Ferrante's fine library."

"That's another room best left alone. Ferrante doesn't like people in there." Seeing my crestfallen face, she added, "It would be better if you asked him yourself. I'm sure he'll show it to you."

Somewhat appeased by this, I inquired, "I was told that you live nearby, Signora Livia."

"My villa is about a mile north of here."

"Is it grand like this one?"

"Not exactly. My father had it built for my middle brother but he died, so he gifted it to me after my wedding. He assumed there would be grandchildren…"

"I'm sorry."

Livia shrugged, then spread out her arms. "Anyway, *this* villa belonged to my father, then my older brother, and now it's in the hands of Ferrante. Someday, it will go to your son."

"Lisa mentioned that you dine with us several evenings per week. I admit, I was most relieved to hear this."

"Oh?"

"I enjoy your company."

Livia smirked. "Some people find me cantankerous and rather sharp-tongued."

"I find you interesting and kind." Seeing her grateful smile, I ventured, "May I ask you something?"

"Go on," she replied cautiously.

"Last night after all the guests had gone, I saw someone with Ferrante on the terrace—a woman with blonde hair." Livia's lips puckered in disapproval, but I continued undeterred, "I saw them kissing."

"There's no use hiding the truth, is there? That woman is your husband's mistress, Paola Colombo. She's been friends with Ferrante since childhood, but the nature of their relationship changed after his marriage to Caterina."

"I was told that she lives *here*, inside the villa."

"Who told you that?"

"Lisa, the girl you sent to be my lady's maid."

Livia rolled her eyes. "Servant gossip."

"So, it's not true?"

She sighed. "It's true. Paola's husband died a few months after Ferrante's marriage. The debt collectors and solicitors took everything to pay off his debts, leaving her penniless and homeless. By coincidence, Caterina's lady's maid had run off with the villa's gardener. Imagine! Scandalous peasants. Paola found out and begged Ferrante to take her in as the new maid."

"Which he did out of kindness, I assume."

"At first, yes. As time passed and it became clear that Caterina and Ferrante were an ill-matched pair, Paola seized the opportunity. She took it upon herself to provide him with what he lacked in his marriage—both emotionally and physically."

"I see."

"I can't blame Ferrante, really. You wouldn't either had you known Caterina. She—" Livia stopped herself. "That's a conversation for another day. Suffice it to say that Ferrante suffered in his first marriage. There's something else to consider. My brother was a serious, practical man and he raised his son to be the same way. Ferrante never adhered to silly fashions or devoted time to frivolity. This made him somewhat unpopular in social circles. Given his temper and intimidating demeanor, well, you can understand why women avoided him. I'm afraid my nephew is a bit resentful and distrusting of the opposite sex. Paola, of course, is the exception to the rule due to their shared childhood."

"It seems that Paola has established herself firmly in his life and inside of his home."

"Hopefully, you can change that. In fact, I am counting on you to do so."

"I'm an inexperienced girl—a stranger to your nephew."

Despite the concern on her face, she patted my shoulder. "Don't worry. If my instincts are correct, Ferrante will be eating from the palm of your hand soon enough."

"Do you really believe that?"

"Have you looked in the mirror lately? You're also agreeable, well-mannered, and clever."

"You said Ferrante only trusts Paola."

"You now have an opportunity to gain his trust too. Use it."

"How?"

"Befriend him and be patient." Glancing at the clock on the table, she said, "I'm going to leave you now."

"Won't you stay and have luncheon with me?"

"Thank you, no. I'm expecting a friend this afternoon. I'm sure Ferrante will be here soon."

"Are you dining with us this evening?"

"I'm afraid not."

I accompanied her to the carriage and remained in the formal garden until midday. I retreated to the dining room and took a seat at the elegant dining table. A servant emerged with a covered dish.

"Has Signore Ferrante returned from hunting?" I asked as she set the plate before me.

The girl poured me a glass of wine then replied, "No, madam. Would you prefer to dine in your room?"

"No, I'm fine."

Given that this was my first day in the villa, I found it odd that Ferrante chose not to dine in my company. I picked at my grilled chicken in silence. After finishing my meal, I retired to my room. With nothing to do and nothing to read, I began to pace. I stopped when my eye fell on the desk. Taking a seat, I took up a quill and began writing. At first, I practiced my penmanship, writing the word "Celeste" over and over again. Then I wrote the word "Ferrante" a few times before attempting simple verses of poetry.

At three o' clock I met with Donna Florinda who patiently helped me design a meal plan for the week. I discovered that my husband's favorite dishes consisted of wild boar stewed in red wine with olives, roasted venison, and a variety of fowl, stuffed artichokes, asparagus with fried eggs and truffles, raw and steamed oysters, shrimp cooked in olive oil, and every type of fish in the sea prepared in every manner imaginable. Despite his expansive palate when it came to meat and vegetables, Ferrante remained indifferent toward sweets.

"Maybe that's a good thing," I commented thoughtfully. "A lack of cake and puddings will serve to keep me slim."

The older woman chuckled. "I can bake them just for you, if you'd like."

"I don't expect you to trouble yourself. I will eat whatever my husband eats."

"I could also plan the meals myself to save you the trouble, Signora Celeste. I've been here for so many years…"

"Would you mind?"

"Not at all."

In a rush a gratitude, I hugged the woman. "Thank you. I'm inexperienced and don't wish to make mistakes or displease his lordship."

"I understand perfectly. I've known Signore Ferrante since he was a little boy. At times, he can be…" She blushed and paused. "Ferrino is what everyone called him back then. Now, only his aunt can get away with that nickname."

I giggled, which evoked her laughter.

She continued, "I suggest you ready yourself for dinner. How about a nice hot bath? I'll have the girls bring up the copper tub and boil some water. You must be tired after yesterday and a nice soak will do you some good."

"Thank you, Donna Florinda."

***

Lisa helped me don a gown of rose silk with floral motifs after my languid bath. I made my way downstairs to the dining room with soft steps. Ferrante stood by a window with a glass of amber liquid in his hand. I lacked knowledge of spirits since I never consumed them.

His eyes roamed over me as I entered the room. "Good evening, Celeste."

"Good evening."

"I had my aunt procure a few gowns for you. I hope they aren't too ill-fitting."

I glanced down at my dress. "They fit well enough. Thank you, Ferrante, for your generosity."

"The seamstress will be here next week to take your measurements." He paused to take a sip of his drink. "You met Nadia today."

My face lit up. "I did. I look forward to spending—"

"I don't want her to play outside."

I was taken aback by his brusqueness. "Oh. May I ask why? She's a healthy child."

"She could get hurt."

"Berta and I were supervising her. There's no way—"

"She's *my* daughter and I prefer to keep her indoors," he said in a tone that left no room for further argument.

I stared at him aghast. "As you wish, my lord."

Retreating from him, I moved toward the sideboard and pretended to admire a silver tureen.

Sensing that he had offended me, he said in a softer tone, "Nadia is not like other normal children."

She seems perfectly normal to me. Biting my tongue, I regarded him placidly.

He continued, "My daughter's safety and well-being is of my utmost concern. I hope that you respect my rules."

"This is *your* house."

"It's your house too," he corrected as he pulled out one of the dining room chairs for me. "I want you to feel at home here."

I sat down at the table and watched as the servants filled our plates. Ferrante glanced at me before taking up his spoon and eating his soup. I ate quietly, resolving to allow him to lead the conversation.

At length, he inquired, "Did you get enough rest last night?"

"Yes."

"Are you certain?"

I knew he referred to my nightmare. "If I disturbed you, I apologize."

"I suffered nightmares as a child. I learned how to control them through sheer will. If you want something bad enough, you'll succeed in your goal."

Lowering my head, I said, "I'll be sure to try your method."

"My aunt gave you a tour of the house."

The abrupt change of topic prompted me to meet his insistent gaze. "Yes, but she didn't show me the library. To be honest, it's the one room that I most wanted to see."

"Because you love books."

"Yes."

"Most girls your age care for little else besides pretty ribbons and fancy gowns."

"I'm not most girls."

At this, he searched my face with an intensity that made me uncomfortable. "I will take you to the library after we've supped. Would that please you?"

"Very much, my lord."

The servants cleared our soup bowls and brought out a roasted pheasant and fresh asparagus. White wine flowed into our goblets.

I ventured, "I noticed that the seven planetary metals are carved into the doors of your private quarters."

The knife in his hand hovered perfectly still over the cooked flesh as his eyes bore into mine. "What do you know about such matters?" When I hesitated, he frowned. "Answer me."

"I've read *Tesoro del Mondo*. The Florentine, Antonio Neri, describes the work of the Jewess, Maria Prophetissima. She was a brilliant alchemist. Have you heard of her?"

"Of course I have," he said before resuming the task of slicing and placing a piece of meat in his mouth. He sat back and glared at me while he chewed his food.

Blushing, I stammered, "You seem upset, my lord."

Setting down his utensils, he finally said, "You surprise me, Celeste. I imagined young girls who are raised in convents only concern themselves with history, lives of various saints, poetry, perhaps even music, but…"

"Not alchemy?"

"*Never* alchemy," he stated in a steely tone.

"Sister Assunta suggested fogging tents during the plague that raged through the city four years ago, thus preserving the lives of many nuns," I improvised. "Her knowledge of alchemy had prompted her to take action."

"Interesting."

"Do you have a laboratory?"

"I do."

"May I see it?"

"No."

I barely hid my disappointment. "Please? I've never stepped foot in a laboratory."

"I don't feel at ease with a wife who occupies her mind with subjects best left in the hands of men. While I recognize that there have been women who have contributed to the alchemic canon, I would prefer it if you focused on domestic matters."

Remember, Valentina, he married you because he thinks you're submissive, docile, obedient…

In my sweetest voice, I said, "I'm sorry you feel that way, sir. I certainly don't wish to displease you."

Soothed by my compliance, he said, "Nor do I wish to displease you, my lady, but there are rules governing the sexes and I feel these guidelines should be respected. Noble wives are required to maintain their chaste reputations by occupying themselves with female endeavors."

I would hardly consider my interest in alchemy as unchaste but I didn't dare argue with him. "What do you propose in the absence of alchemy?"

"Flower lore, of course. There are several books on the topic in the library that you might enjoy. There is also a well-tended herb garden outside the kitchen. I assume Sister Assunta provided you with basic knowledge of curatives."

I forced a smile. "Yes."

He waved his hand in a manner that settled the issue. "Donna Florinda has extra mortars and pestles, and you can make a list of whatever else you need. I'll have the servants procure the items in the city center. There are a few vacant storerooms on the ground level where you can work undisturbed. The servants can clean out one of them and we can furnish it to your liking. What do you think about having your own studio?"

A studio would offer me sanctuary and privacy. Perhaps, in time, I could create my own little laboratory far from my husband's prying eyes. I could even conduct some rudimentary experiments at first, and eventually become as daring as Maria Prophetissima. What if I discovered the secret to making gold? Dozens of ideas flooded my head as I entertained the possibilities of having a space all to myself.

"Celeste? What do you think about that?"

Ferrante's voice broke my reverie. "It would please me greatly, my lord."

"Consider it done."

"Thank you."

Once again, I was touched by Ferrante's generosity toward me—even if he didn't want me poking my nose in his laboratory. He drew my gaze several times during the meal. What would it take to make a man like him trust me?

Paola knew the secret.

As promised, he led me into the library at the meal's conclusion. Located on the ground floor, the enormous room boasted floor to ceiling shelves loaded with tomes. The frescoed ceiling depicted Santa Sofia, the Roman martyr of wisdom, and her three daughters—Faith, Hope, and Charity.

Ferrante leaned his shoulder against the doorjamb and crossed his arms as I ventured into the room.

I twirled in a slow circle. "Alexandria."

"What did you say?"

I met his gaze. "The Library of Alexandria in Egypt, which got destroyed—"

"I know the story. Perhaps I should call you Hypatia."

I smiled at his attempt at humor. "As long as you allow me the freedom to read your books, I will respond to whatever name you wish to call me."

His lips twitched. "I'll keep that in mind, my lady."

I ran to the nearest bookshelf and began skimming various titles. Ferrante sauntered into the room and took a seat in a leather chair. I made a mental note of where the alchemy books were located, but selected Shakespeare's *Hamlet.*

Clutching the book to my chest, I looked at him expectantly. "May I select another one?"

"You may borrow as many as you wish."

I took Dante's *Inferno* and *Meditations* by Marcus Aurelius.

"Eclectic choices," he commented drily.

I blushed and stopped at three. "This is enough for now."

He stood. "You are free to come and go as you like here."

"Thank you, Ferrante."

"You're welcome." Glancing at his pocket watch, his expression sobered. "Now, I must bid you goodnight."

"So soon?" The manner in which he looked at me prompted me to add, "I thought that perhaps we could sit and talk…Or play a game. Do you like cards? Dominoes?"

"Forgive me, but I am feeling rather unwell this evening."

I regarded him dubiously, for he glowed with health and vitality. To my chagrin, I realized that he simply didn't wish to be in my company. "I see. Well, goodnight."

"Goodnight Celeste."

His eyes burned into my back as I reluctantly exited the room. I could have sworn that I heard a woman's soft giggle as I ascended the stairs.

CHAPTER 9

I set out the next day to transform one of the ground floor rooms into my studio. Donna Florinda's muscular arms were elbow-deep in gooey bread dough when I entered the kitchen. She was about to stop her task when I put my hand up.

"No, please continue."

"What can I do for you, Signora Celeste?" she inquired cheerfully while kneading the dough.

"My husband told me that I could take one of the rooms on this level."

"Signore Ferrante did mention that to me. He instructed the servants to summon Sandro for the task." Turning her head toward a girl coaxing the embers in the hearth, she added, "Carla, go and fetch the valet."

"Thank you, Donna Florinda. I'll be out by the garden."

She nodded. "I'll send him out to you."

The well-tended herb garden boasted a wide variety of healthy shrubs and plants. Fat bumblebees buzzed around fragrant rosemary and lavender bushes as high as my waist. Butterflies fluttered amid the basil, oregano, foxglove, and goldenseal root. Parsley, fennel, thyme, and chives filled the air with their fresh scent.

The sound of footsteps alerted me of Sandro's approach. I had seen the neatly dressed man on a few occasions but had yet to speak with him. Light blue eyes sparkled within a pleasant face, and his sparse reddish hair was brushed back and secured with a plain black ribbon.

I took a few steps toward him. "Sandro?"

"At your service, my lady. Signore Ferrante has already apprised me of the situation and instructed me to show you two rooms that he feels would be best suited for the purpose."

"Very well."

I followed the valet from one room to the next and opted for the latter. Not only was it more spacious and sunlit, its location afforded privacy. Glazed red tiles covered the floor, two large windows looked out onto the lawn, and a rose marble mantle graced the small fireplace. The low timbered ceiling signaled that this section of the house was the oldest, and had remained untouched for over a century.

"This will be my studio," I said, wandering around the space and absorbing its pleasant energy.

"A wise choice, madam. In winter, this room gets more sun to help keep you warm."

That afternoon, the servants swept and cleaned the old room before outfitting the space with a long wooden table, a pair of cushioned arm chairs, an oak desk and a small pine cabinet painted in shades of green and red. Donna Florinda had already set aside bowls, mortars, pestles, and glass bottles for me.

At one point, Sandro brought me an old chaise longue in need of reupholstering due to a stain. "This was in one of the store rooms and I thought you might like it."

"The brocade is still in good condition," I said, examining the piece. "I can easily hide the stain with strategically positioned pillows. Do you think you can have the servants muster a few for me?"

He nodded, then returned a few minutes later with an armful of pillows in various shades and textures. I placed them on the chaise longue, then pushed it toward one of the windows to create a reading nook.

"Thank you, Sandro."

He inclined his head at me and left me to my work. I ventured out into the garden with a pair of shears and began snipping the stalks of plants and flowers. I soon found myself humming in contentment, for I now had my own space in which to do whatever I pleased.

Ferrante came to the studio at sunset and found me binding stalks of lavender. He lifted his gaze to the rafters where I had already secured various bunches of fragrant herbs for the purpose of drying them.

Wiping my hands on the white linen apron Donna Florinda

had lent me, I said cheerfully, "Hello."

"You've been busy, I see," he said, crossing his arms and leaning against the doorjamb.

"I have, my lord."

"I admire your efficiency, madam."

"Thank you. Come in, please."

His face lit up as though he found the idea appealing, but he shook his head. "No, thank you."

"You won't disturb me, I promise. I would welcome the company, actually."

"I have matters that require my attention."

"Oh."

"I'll see you at supper."

I stared after him in mild disappointment before returning to my task.

***

I turned eighteen the following week. Naturally, I informed no one of this since Celeste's birthday fell on the first week of December.

After taking a morning stroll, I found Lisa in my room placing several dolls on the bed. Each white fabric effigy sported a pretty dress.

"There you are, Signora Celeste," she said with a smile.

My gaze fell upon the dolls. "What's all this?"

"The seamstress will be here this afternoon. One of her apprentices stopped by earlier with these samples. Aren't these styles lovely, madam?"

"May I ask your age, Lisa?"

"Seventeen."

"How long have you been serving at this household?"

"Since the age of thirteen."

"You were here when Lady Caterina was alive, which means that you've seen many stylish people here at the villa. I'm afraid my sense of fashion may not be up to the high standards of my husband or his peers. I'm going to count on you to help me make some selections. Do you mind?"

Lisa's face lit up. "I'd be happy to oblige, Signora Celeste."

There were twelve dolls on the bed, so I opted to pick three. "Which one do you like best?"

Lisa glanced at my hair and figure, then picked up a doll wearing a gown of lovely peacock blue brocade shot through with silver thread. Due to the fabric's elaborate nature, the style was simple. Snug bodice with low rounded neckline.

"Gorgeous," I said while picking up a deep yellow silk with floral embroidery along the hem and elbow-length sleeves. "What of this one?"

"It will bring out the highlights in your hair. Good choice."

Lisa's last selection was a pea green velvet with generous lace adorning the sleeves.

The color reminded me of spring. "Perfect."

Donna Teodora arrived at the villa in a finely-cut gown of red and white striped linen. Her assistant was clad in a neat gown of violet cotton. Lisa brought them up into my chamber.

The seamstress said, "Signora Celeste, it's delightful to make your acquaintance. Shall we get down to business?" At my nod, she added, "I need you to remove your gown."

Lisa stripped me down to my sheer cotton shift.

"Hand me my measuring string, Anita," Donna Teodora said while extending her hand.

Anita offered me a shy smile before obliging her mistress. Donna Teodora measured my breasts, waist, torso, and hips, as well as my arm and body length. Anita jotted down the numbers on a scrap of paper with a piece of charcoal.

Lisa helped me dress afterward. I then handed the three dolls I had selected to the seamstress.

Donna Teodora made a face while indicating the other nine dolls on the bed. "You don't approve of those styles?"

"I love them all," I replied.

Holding up the three dolls, she said, "I don't understand."

"Those are the ones I've selected from the choices offered."

"Signore Ferrante must not have made his wishes clear to you, my lady. Your husband has commissioned *all twelve gowns* for you, assuming they meet your approval."

I glanced at the dolls, stunned. "Twelve?"

The seamstress nodded and smiled. "He is very generous."

"He most certainly is."

One of the gowns was fashioned from black silk and she pointed to it. "This one is a mourning gown, which every lady is required to own."

"I see."

"May I proceed with the commission, madam?"

"Yes please."

The apprentice gathered together the dolls, measuring strings, and notations. Donna Teodora assured me that she would begin creating the garments tomorrow. I thanked her and saw her out of the villa.

Twelve new gowns!

I could hardly believe it as I watched their hired carriage take off down the drive. Venturing into my studio, I decided to read for the remainder of the morning. Lisa knocked on the door half hour later.

"Come in," I said, placing my finger on the page so I wouldn't lose my place.

"Excuse the disturbance, my lady. There is an elderly nun waiting in the salon to see you."

Masking my distress, I inquired, "Has my husband returned from riding?"

"Not yet. Shall I have the servants send in refreshments?"

My first impulse was to say no but that would appear suspicious. "Yes," I said before rushing into the salon.

Sister Assunta stood by the window wringing her gnarled hands. She came over to me the moment I closed the door. "Oh Valentina—"

I grabbed her arm and led her across the room, far from the door. "Hush! Are you mad? Why are you here?"

The nun's face crumpled as tears streamed from her eyes. "It's Celeste, she's disappeared…"

"*I'm* Celeste," I reminded her coolly. "Remember that while you are in this house."

She nodded distractedly. "My precious ward disappeared a few days ago. No note, nothing. I'm desperate."

"Did she tell you about the monk?" Sister Assunta's vacant stare answered my question. "Obviously, she didn't trust either of us with the truth."

"What truth?"

"She is pregnant—"

"Impossible!"

Glancing at the door, I snapped, "Keep your voice down."

The nun shook her wimpled head. "There's no way…"

"Signora Livia told me everything. Celeste has a lover, a monk from the monastery across from Santa Patrizia. She's pregnant with his child. If she has disappeared, it's because she's gone to live with him."

Sister Assunta covered her face with her hands and wept.

The servant arrived with the tray and set it on the table.

"You may go," I said, shifting my body so that it hid the nun.

The girl curtsied and said, "Signora Livia's carriage has pulled up the drive. Shall I send her in here?"

"Yes."

The servant's head leaned sideways to get a better view of the nun.

I shooed the girl from the room and whispered to the nun, "Remember where you are and what's at stake."

Footsteps echoed on the marble corridor and then the door flew open.

Livia entered the room with purpose, cringing at the sight of Sister Assunta. "What the devil is going on here?"

"Celeste ran away," I replied quietly.

Livia peered down at the old nun and sighed tiredly. "She is carrying a monk's child."

"I've already told her," I said.

Sister Assunta lifted her head and tossed me an accusatory look. "You're a wicked girl to keep such a secret."

Recoiling from the accusation, I protested, "I didn't know, I swear."

She shook an angry finger at me. "Celeste told you everything. You two were as close as sisters."

Livia gently pushed me aside and grabbed hold of the nun's

shoulders. "Imagine my surprise when this girl here married my nephew instead of your ward. I know you were behind this charade, and you're lucky I haven't alerted the authorities. What's done is done. Ferrante is now wed to our lovely *Celeste*. You will never again refer to her by any other name. Do you understand?"

Sister Assunta appeared genuinely frightened as her head bobbed up and down.

Livia pointed to the window. "My carriage is outside. Come along, my driver will take you wherever you need to go."

Sister Assunta gazed at me with eyes full of remorse. "Valentina, I—"

Livia's sharp slap stunned the nun into silence. "Did you not hear me? I said *never again*."

Overwhelmed with pity for the old woman, I offered, "I'm sorry it has to be this way, Sister Assunta."

She shook her head sadly while adjusting her wimple. "I'm the one who put you up to this. I pressured you to save my beloved girl…She has betrayed us both."

I watched as Livia and Sister Assunta vacated the room.

***

Although I had initially agreed to marry Ferrante for reasons of convenience and material comfort, I found myself drawn to him. In my former life, I had spoken to boys at church and in the neighborhood, but none of my acquaintances had been *men*. Ferrante oozed raw masculinity, strength, and the kind of seriousness that only came with maturity. My heart raced whenever he was near me, and I often wondered what it would be like to kiss his lips.

My desire to get to know my husband prompted me to always engage him in conversation during supper. He politely obliged me but always excused himself after the meal, leaving me to my own devices. On the nights that Livia dined with us, he remained at the table until his aunt went home. Since she retired early, it made little difference.

We were dining alone one evening and I asked, "Do you play the harpsichord?"

Ferrante swallowed the food in his mouth. "My father insisted that I learn an instrument."

"Whenever I'm in the salon, its red color draws my gaze."

"It is a lovely piece, so I'm not surprised."

"Will you play for me tonight?"

"I wouldn't put anyone through that torture," he replied with a deprecating chuckle before taking a sip of wine.

"I think you're being modest."

"My father purchased that harpsichord during a trip to Vienna. He had it shipped to the house so that my mother could play it for his pleasure. Maybe I'll play for you someday."

"Why not now, when we're done eating?"

"I have a matter to attend to, Celeste."

I pushed my peas from one side of my plate to the other with the tip of my fork. "It's rather late. What sort of matter can't wait until morning?"

Ferrante's eyes grew cold. A clear signal that I had crossed the line. "That's none of your concern."

"I am your wife."

"Are all nuns so willful and bold?"

"I'm not a nun, sir."

Wiping his mouth with his napkin, he stood. "If you'll excuse me, I must bid you goodnight."

I watched him go with regret. Ignoring the man and enjoying his wealth would have proved infinitely easier, but I couldn't allow myself to be dissuaded by his aloofness. Beneath that cool exterior existed an alchemist with secrets—a man who piqued my curiosity.

In the days that followed, I spied on Ferrante from windows and shadowy corridors to learn his habits and moods. Uncouth as it was, I couldn't help myself. Sometimes, I caught him staring into the distance with a stony expression on his face. I tried to guess his thoughts on such occasions, for he seemed to be somewhere far away. Somewhere unpleasant.

Days turned to weeks, and I arrived at the conclusion that my husband was a tortured soul. Who existed beneath those thorny layers? Of one thing I was certain: I wanted to find out.

I took comfort in other aspects of my new life. Livia's presence during suppertime served as entertainment, for she and *Ferrino* bickered in a comical manner.

Nadia also proved a source of unexpected joy in my life. Despite Ferrante's admonition to keep her indoors, I made sure she got at least an hour of playtime in the sunshine before he returned from his morning rides. Admittedly, I felt a bit guilty breaking my promise and sneaking behind his back.

We were playing on the back terrace one morning when Nadia took my face into her hands and patted my cheeks.

I laughed at her, then something struck me. "Berta, when does my husband visit his daughter?"

"Signore Ferrante visits before she goes to bed."

Nadia stared at Berta, then at me.

I grinned at the child. "Does Papa tuck you in at night and give you a goodnight kiss?"

The little girl nodded in a solemn manner.

"Do you like that?"

She nodded again but failed to smile.

"Papa loves you very much."

Nadia only stared at me with serious eyes that seemed out of place in such a youthful face.

"Time for your nap," Berta said, taking the child's hand.

"Did you hear that, Nadia? It's nap time. I'll visit you tomorrow."

At that, Nadia's face broke into a smile. I returned the gesture before planting a kiss on her smooth brow.

I partook of the midday meal in solitude, then went into the library to inventory Ferrante's books. I made a list of the tomes that dealt with science, then broke them down into categories: anatomy, chemistry, astronomy, botany…

To my delight, I found copies of the same books I had left behind with Aunt Gloria. The thought of her made me pause. I missed my aunt and vowed to see her soon. I wasn't certain how I would accomplish this feat, but I would think of something.

Later that evening, Lisa helped me into a yellow silk gown and tied my hair up with matching ribbons. I descended the stairs to the dining room to join Ferrante for dinner.

He stood gazing out the window. "Celeste."

"Good evening."

Taking a seat at the head of the table, he motioned for the servants to bring out our supper. "It appears that my aunt has a cold and won't be joining us this evening due to a headache."

He said nothing more as we ate the first course. Silence stretched between us, tense and uncomfortable, during the second course too. Something obviously troubled him.

I ventured, "Are you all right, Ferrante?"

Ignoring my question, he said, "Did you visit Nadia today?"

"Yes," I replied while watching him slice into the rare steak on his plate. The bloody juice oozed from the meat and settled beneath a pair of boiled potatoes.

He was about to place the morsel in his mouth, then stopped. "Do you visit her every day?"

I nodded. "Sometimes twice a day."

"You're fond of her?"

I offered him a heartfelt smile. "Oh yes…Very much so."

"Does my daughter return your affection?"

"I believe she does," I replied cautiously, my smile wavering in the face of his stoicism.

The dripping piece of beef hovered inches from his mouth, yet he inquired, "Does she smile at you?"

I nodded. "Often, in fact."

The ferocity in which he snapped the meat from the fork startled me. His brows knitted together in a pensive frown as he chewed. I couldn't determine if he was annoyed, angry, or both. Did he resent me for having bonded so quickly with Nadia?

I stared at my plate and picked at the rare meat while these thoughts flitted through my head. Ferrante's dark mood unsettled me, causing me to lose my appetite. Throughout the meal, I felt his eyes on me many times.

I wanted to say something appeasing, to soothe him with kind words, but I couldn't think of anything. At one point, he reached out to take a piece of bread from the basket and I couldn't help admiring the thickness of his wrists or his long, tapered fingers. What would those hands feel like upon my skin? Turning his head, he captured my gaze as the wicked thought popped into my head. My cheeks burned with shame.

A moment later, he cleared his throat and stood. "I have a matter that requires my attention. Please excuse me."

I looked up. "Wait. Will you share the midday meal with me tomorrow?"

"No. I cannot."

"It's rather unpleasant to eat in the dining room alone."

"The servants can bring a plate to your room."

Summoning my courage, I confessed, "I would prefer to dine with *you*, Ferrante."

"I'm afraid I'm busy," he replied, staring into the contents of his goblet before draining it in one long gulp.

Defeated, I poked at a bit of congealed fat on my plate with the tip of my knife. "Of course."

Setting the vessel on the table, he said, "Goodnight."

He headed toward the library, leaving me alone.

***

The last day of April dawned warm and clear. I broke my fast then went downstairs in search of Sandro. I found him in the kitchen speaking with Donna Florinda. The servants stopped what they were doing to incline their heads at me.

"Good morning everyone," I said. Turning to Sandro, I inquired, "Has his lordship returned?"

I had not seen my husband for two nights. According to his valet, Ferrante had descended into the city.

Sandro cast a wary glance at Donna Florinda, then replied, "He returned at dawn and went out hunting."

"Thank you," I said, being sure to keep my head high as I turned my back on them and walked away.

Whispering broke out among the servants the moment I vacated the kitchen.

Despite the disturbing thoughts roiling inside of my head, I visited Nadia then went outside to enjoy the glorious weather. Crossing the expanse of the terrace, I headed for the vibrant green lawn. The wind caressed my hair as I inhaled the fragrant spring blossoms. The gorgeous weather inspired images of the goddess Flora dancing amid the wildflowers.

Distant barking made me pause mid-step. Listening carefully, I discerned there was more than one dog. Every muscle in my body coiled with fear as my eyes scanned the rim of the forest. A big brown dog burst through the bushes with Ferrante's black mastiff at its heels. Wild-eyed and foaming at the mouth, the mangy beast headed straight for me.

Lifting my skirts, I ran through the grass in an attempt to escape. Stumbling in my panic, I uttered a silent prayer to God. The ground sloped slightly but I was going too fast to compensate for the abrupt shift. I tripped over my skirts and fell onto the grass.

The dog stopped a few feet away from me, threatening me with a growl. The sunlight revealed various sores and scratches on the beast's powerful legs. Saliva dripped from its menacingly sharp teeth.

My hand patted around the ground for anything I could use as a weapon. Finally, I found a rock and threw it at the dog. "Go away!"

Angered by my action, the beast charged me. A sharp pain on my leg made me cry out. The deranged creature had bitten me through the layers of fabric and seemed intent on doing it again. I scooted away from the animal as the sound of thundering horse hooves filled the air.

"Don't move!"

I froze at the command an instant before a whirring sound zipped past my face. An arrow pierced the dog's torso, causing it to collapse onto its side. The animal whined in agony while its legs flailed in panic. A second arrow struck the animal in the eye, putting it out of its misery. I caught sight of Ferrante atop his horse with a bow in his hand. The black mastiff came over to sniff me and I cringed in fear from the great beast.

"Sampson!" Ferrante shouted.

I sagged with relief when the dog ran back to its master.

"My lady!"

I glimpsed Sandro racing across the lawn. He reached me

before my husband did and helped me to my feet. My knees felt as if they were made of pudding and my whole body shook uncontrollably.

Sandro craned his neck to look past me. "She's in a state of shock, my lord."

Ferrante came over and scooped me up in his arms without saying a word. I felt weightless within a cocoon of hard muscle. Pressing my cheek against his shoulder, I clung to his thick neck. A soft sob escaped my lips, compelling him to hold me tighter.

"You're safe now," he whispered before pressing his lips to my temple.

Several servants had gathered in the foyer to witness the scene. Setting me down on the nearest chair, he demanded that the people disperse to give him space. Lifting my skirts to my knees, he took hold of my injured limb and yanked down the stocking to examine the extent of the damage. Thankfully, Lisa came over to stand beside me in order to block the sight of my bare legs from the curious servants.

"It didn't break the skin, thank God," Ferrante said, relieved. Finally, he looked up at me. "That dog was rabid."

Too stunned to speak, I merely stared at him with glistening eyes. His expression softened in the face of my distress.

"Does it hurt?" At my nod, he placed a gentle hand over the wound. "Get her ladyship something for the pain."

Donna Florinda nodded and scurried into the kitchen.

Ferrante slowly pulled up my stocking before lowering the hem of my gown to cover my legs. I had never been touched so intimately by a man. To my chagrin, and despite the harrowing circumstances, I enjoyed it. The feel of his strong warm hands on my bare skin evoked foreign desires.

Offering me his hand, he asked, "Can you walk?"

I stood and he accompanied me as I took a few tentative steps. Although the bite caused soreness, I walked with ease.

Donna Florinda emerged with a tonic laced with herbs, and I drank the bitter liquid to the very last drop.

Ferrante waved a hand at the servants. "Leave us, all of

you." The moment we were alone, he continued, "I hate to think what would have happened had I not arrived when I did."

"That makes two of us, my lord."

"From now on, I don't want you wandering too far from the house." I was about to protest but he put up his hand to silence me. "We live in a remote area. From time to time, animals stray onto the property. Today it happened to be a rabid dog. You need to be more careful."

"I will…and thank you."

He offered me a curt nod before going outside to tend to his horse. I watched from the doorway as he led the animal toward the stables.

I spent the remainder of the day resting and reading. That night, Ferrante seemed more pensive than usual when I joined him for dinner.

Placing a hand on my arm, he asked, "How is your leg?"

"Better. My maid applied an unguent and wrapped it as a precautionary measure."

"A prudent thing to do."

"Has Signora Livia arrived?"

"My aunt won't be joining us. She's caught a chill."

"She sent a note?"

He nodded. "If you're feeling up to it tomorrow, perhaps you can mix a curative since you were trained by a healer. I'm referring to Sister Assunta, of course."

My lie had already come back to haunt me. "Oh yes…I'll be happy to do so. I'll take it over to her in the morning."

"I'm sure my aunt will appreciate your endeavor."

I sat down at my husband's right hand. While the servants ladled steaming chicken broth into our bowls, I ventured, "I missed you at supper last night."

"Oh?"

"As well as the night before that."

Visibly irritated, he paused and set down his spoon. "If you're trying to make a point then I ask that you get on with it. My soup is getting cold."

"You were gone for two nights."

Ferrante's eyes turned cold. "And?"

Confused by his aggressiveness toward me, I stammered, "I…I didn't know where you were."

"Well, that's not surprising since I didn't tell you."

The nasty tone puzzled me. "Why are you being like this?"

He heaved an irritated sigh before concentrating on his soup. "I don't like being nagged, Celeste."

"I don't mean to nag—"

"I'm not in the habit of explaining myself to children."

Mortified, I hung my head and said nothing else. I tried forcing down some of the soup, then set aside my spoon. "I'm sorry but I have no appetite. Will you excuse me?"

"Are you feeling unwell?"

Averting my gaze, I stood and replied coolly, "Nothing that a bit of rest can't cure."

He stood too. "Do you want some tea?"

"No, thank you," I said before turning my back on him.

"Celeste."

I paused but did not face him. At his hesitation, I continued briskly to the stairwell. His sigh reached my ears as I took the first step.

Lisa came into the room to help me undress and I told her about Livia's cold. Thankfully, she knew an easy cure that included a blend of lemon, ground olive leaves, oregano, brandy, and honey.

"Donna Florinda makes batches of this for everyone during the winter. It can heal the worse chill and even help abate fever," she explained while combing my hair. "I know where Donna Florinda keeps all of the ingredients. I'm happy to make some for you."

"That's very kind."

She vacated the room and I got into bed.

Still offended by Ferrante's careless words, I wondered if he would ever foster affection for me. I recalled how safe I felt in his strong arms when he had carried me away from danger. He had even kissed my temple as one would a child.

A child.

Is that how he saw me? A stupid, silly girl? Maybe that's why he avoided my bed.

I slept fitfully that night due to convoluted dreams that made no sense in the light of morning.

Lisa came in to help me dress and handed me a small bottle. "The curative for Signora Livia."

I removed the cork and sniffed the liquid. "Thank you."

I dressed quickly, paid Nadia a brief visit, then headed downstairs. The sight of Ferrante waiting by the door caused me to slow my steps.

"I've decided to accompany you," he explained.

I hid my surprise and opted to remain aloof. Peering past him, I inquired, "Where is the carriage?"

"It's such a fine morning that I thought we could ride there together. My aunt's villa is not very far and the scenery is pleasant." My apprehension prompted him to add, "What's wrong?"

"I've never ridden a horse," I confessed, embarrassed.

Now Ferrante would have yet another reason to dislike me and chide me for my lack of experience.

Indicating a stable boy leading a pretty tan mare by the reins, he said, "I had Pina saddled for you. You can't outrun a dog, but a horse can. Riding is safer than walking around here."

I cast a nervous glance at the animal. "Please…I would prefer to walk."

"Are you frightened, Celeste?"

"I am."

He waved away the stable boy. "You'll ride with me today in order to rid yourself of the fear of being in the saddle."

Eyeing his stallion warily, I took a step backward. "What if your horse throws me off?"

"Achille won't do that, I promise."

The mighty white stallion snorted loudly and stomped his hoof against the ground, kicking up dirt in the process. The animal appeared angry and I wanted nothing more than to put some distance between us. Before I could protest, Ferrante lifted me effortlessly and set me in the saddle. He hoisted himself up and sat behind me, placing a protective arm around my ribcage.

So much for maintaining my aloofness.

Pulling me against his hard chest, he placed his lips to my ear. "Are you still frightened?"

Gooseflesh erupted along my neck and arms. I was so breathless that I couldn't speak, so I shook my head. Something moved to my right. I turned my head in time to catch half of a face peeking at me from behind the drapes. It vanished in a flash.

"Who is that?" I demanded.

Following my gaze, he replied in an unconvincing tone, "Probably one of the servants."

We both knew it was a lie.

Ferrante urged the horse forward. The warmth and strength of his body so close to my own heightened my awareness. Nestled between his arms, I felt safe.

"I grew up here and know every inch of this land," he said, pointing to the forest. "There are a few paths and even a pond through those bushes there."

Rather than remain silent and angry, I decided to give him a chance to make up for last night. "I saw a pair of foxes and a ferret a few days ago."

"Do you like animals?"

"Very much."

"Yet you fear horses?"

"I once witnessed a man falling from a horse. I was only a little girl but I remember the scene quite vividly. He broke his neck and died."

Ferrante's arms tightened around me. "I won't let you fall, I promise. Pina is sweet and calm, so if you ever feel inclined to learn how to ride…"

"I'll give it some thought."

"It would please me. We could ride together."

Surprised by his suggestion, I assured him, "I would like that very much, my lord."

He pressed his nose behind my ear and inhaled deeply.

"Mmm, you smell sweet."

Warmth radiated throughout my chest and my heart fluttered. I lifted my hand to touch his cheek. "Ferrante…"

Catching himself, he cleared his throat and straightened in the saddle to place a bit of distance between us. "Forgive me."

His tone was crisp. *Formal*. The abrupt change made me feel like forbidden fruit instead of his wife. Awkwardness followed.

We eventually arrived at a charming villa surrounded by lemon trees. I admired the small fountain gracing the front lawn as I dismounted with Ferrante's help.

Once inside the villa, I glanced around the rooms filled with vibrant paintings and porcelain vases brimming with fresh flowers. We found Livia resting on a chaise longue. The scene reminded me of Aunt Gloria during one of her bouts.

Livia's face beamed with pleasure. "Ferrino, you've come to see me. Is it true that Celeste was attacked by a dog?"

"She was bitten by a rabid dog," Ferrante replied with a look in my direction. "Fortunately, it didn't break the skin."

Livia crossed herself. "Thank the Madonna."

"Your nephew saved me." Handing her the bottle, I added, "I've brought you something to make you feel better. It's Donna Florinda's special recipe."

Livia removed the cork and took a sip. "Ah yes, her curative helped me two years ago. Thank you."

"Are you feeling any better?" Ferrante inquired.

"Dr. Bernardo examined me yesterday. My lungs are clear." She coughed, then added, "I would love some tea. Ferrante, would you please find my maid? I instructed her to air out the linens in the guestroom."

"Of course," he replied, already walking across the room.

Livia whispered, "I hoped you would come alone."

"Ferrante insisted on accompanying me."

"Things are good between the two of you?"

I shrugged. "I think so."

"Hopefully, you've already conceived. When was your last monthly?"

The heat of shame exploded in my cheeks. "Ferrante and I

have not…We don't…" At Livia's confused frown, I finally blurted, "I'm still a virgin."

"What?"

"Don't you remember? He said he wanted us to become mutually acquainted."

She cocked an eyebrow. "We are already in May. The fact that you haven't yet consummated your union is shocking to me—especially given what's at stake."

"Do you think it's because of what Camillo told him about my health?"

Livia's mouth formed a hard line as she shook her head in a disapproving manner. "Something else is keeping my nephew from performing his duty. Think, girl."

"Paola Colombo?"

"Who else?"

Everything became painfully clear in that moment. Ferrante's loyalty to his mistress verged on religious fanaticism. My earlier thought about me being forbidden fruit wasn't so farfetched after all. "I saw someone at the window when we were leaving to come here. In fact, I often feel as though I'm being watched."

Livia glanced over her shoulder to make sure Ferrante wasn't there. "You probably are. That scheming trollop has sunk her claws into my nephew deeper than I had imagined."

I did my best to hide my shock at her words. "Ferrante was gone for two nights. He came home yesterday morning."

She cursed under her breath. "He and Paola sometimes head off into the city for pleasure. They visit the salons of dubious socialites after supping together in fashionable cafés."

"I thought you said Ferrante tolerated few people."

"Paola whines until he gives in to her desires. I'm sure she's pitching quite the fit now that you're here. For starters, you're younger and prettier than she is. What's more, Ferrante genuinely likes you and it's obvious that he's attracted to you."

"Do you really believe that?"

"Oh yes. One of the reasons he is avoiding you is because you terrify him. Don't you see? With you, he is vulnerable."

"What would you have me do, Signora Livia?"

"For now, nothing."

Our conversation ceased at the sound of my husband's footsteps in the hallway.

"Forgive the delay, Aunt Livia. Your maid wasn't in the guestroom. I eventually found her in the kitchen gossiping with your cook," Ferrante explained while taking a seat. "What topic were you two discussing?"

"Flowers," Livia improvised with a smile. "I'm thinking of adding hydrangeas to my garden. Celeste here advised me to plant daffodils because she likes their bright yellow color."

Ferrante looked at me. "I'll have the gardener plant some daffodils for your pleasure, my lady."

Livia and I exchanged glances.

We drank tea together and chatted over mundane things for a little while.

At one point, Livia said, "Celeste, my dear, I wish to have a word with my nephew in private. Do you mind?"

I stood. "Not at all."

"The roses and irises have bloomed in the garden. Why don't you go and take a look? Snip off a branch if you like."

***

Noticing the determined look on his aunt's face, Ferrante braced himself.

Livia waited for Celeste to close the door before pinning her nephew with a hard stare. "You are forsaking your husbandly duties and I demand to know why."

"Is that what Celeste told you or did you pry the information from the girl?"

"I merely commented that she may have already conceived and she confessed to still being a virgin," she replied matter-of-factly while setting down her tea cup. "Again I ask you, why?"

Ferrante ran his hands through his hair, disturbing the neatly combed style. "I want to but…"

"Is she not to your liking?"

"Not to my liking?" he repeated, shaking his head in disbelief. "She's…she's more than I ever expected. Celeste is pretty and clever—she even loves Nadia."

"From what the servants tell me, Nadia is extremely fond of her stepmother."

"It's true."

Silence filled the space between them.

Livia studied him with knowing eyes. "It's Paola isn't it?"

He sighed in irritation. "Partly, yes."

"The time has come for her to go."

"I can't kick her out onto the street like a dog simply because I've fall—" He stopped himself and said nothing more.

Livia gaped at him, so he paced the room in a feeble attempt to escape her scrutiny.

"You love her," she deduced, pleasantly surprised.

He scowled. "That's ridiculous."

"Celeste is a kindhearted young woman who exudes humility and grace. Why would loving her be ridiculous?"

"She's a *child*," he snapped, throwing up his arms in frustration. "She knows nothing, has seen nothing. I should never have married her. You were right—selecting a bride from a convent was a mistake."

"So, you don't love her?"

He hesitated. "I can't allow myself to love her."

Livia cocked an eyebrow. "I see."

"I should have married someone older…less naïve." *Less pure, less innocent, less enchanting…*

"Like Paola?"

He stopped in his tracks. "Stop it."

"Who said you can't have both women?"

"Now you're baiting me."

She shrugged, her face a neutral mask. "If you see Celeste as a mere child undeserving of your love, then what do you care? Fulfill your duty and be done with it. Plenty of noblemen use their wives solely for the purpose of producing heirs while satisfying their lust elsewhere. My late husband certainly did that…*and so did your father*."

"My father was an honorable man who loved my mother."

"I'm not denying that, Ferrino. I'm sure Luciano loved his

wife in his own way, but I knew my brother better than anyone. By the age of seventeen, his voracious appetite where women were concerned had garnered him a reputation among certain circles. Trust me when I tell you that he was not loyal to your mother. That didn't stop him from performing his duty and siring an heir. I'm advising you to do the same since you seem incapable of banishing your mistress."

"It's not that I'm incapable, it's just..."

Ferrante went over to the window and watched as Celeste bent over to inhale the fragrance of a rose. The sunlight played on her rich brown hair, infusing the strands with a coppery sheen. Her skin was akin to fresh cream and her lips...*her lips*...

There's no way he could ever use Celeste's body merely for bearing children. A woman like her deserved better. As for her body, he fantasized about worshipping her flesh. He wanted her so badly that it hurt, but he couldn't find the courage to knock on her bedroom door.

How does a beast approach an angel?

Besides, she didn't love him. How could she? She had been yanked from the only life she knew, forced to wed a stranger, and live on a remote hillside...What the hell had he done?

"Celeste has a certain way about her," Livia said, coming to stand beside him. "She's different."

His eyes never wavered from his wife as he said, "She's pure and innocent—untouched by the scheming, false, sycophantic members of our aristocracy."

"That's an accurate description."

"There's nothing contrived about the girl."

"*Young woman*," she corrected.

Ferrante's gaze rested on the tantalizing cleavage of Celeste's firm, ripe breasts. *Goddamn it*. To his chagrin, the mere sight of her perfect flesh caused a stirring in his loins. His lust was immediately doused by a pang of guilt. There was another woman in his life. A woman who had been by his side for years.

As though reading his mind, Livia said, "I know how much Paola means to you, but the time has come for you to put your feelings aside and be a husband to your wife. Heaven forbid if anything happens to you. Your cousin Ruggero would inherit everything. We cannot let that happen."

"This isn't easy for her."

"If Paola truly loved you, she would understand your precarious position and encourage you to consummate your marriage. Instead, she plays upon your guilt by throwing fits of jealousy. Can't you see through her pettiness by now?"

"Stop, Aunt Livia. It's not like that. Paola understands and even gave me her blessing when I began my search for a wife."

"While that may be true, Paola never expected you to select a young, desirable bride." Ferrante's silence confirmed Livia's suspicion. In a softer tone, she continued, "Your wife has every right to annul this marriage, you know."

He heaved a tired sigh. "Celeste believes that I dislike her."

"Can you blame the poor thing? You *are* aware that your servants talk to mine on a regular basis."

"What do you mean by that?"

"They tell me what goes on in your household, Ferrino. I know about you shutting yourself away for most of the day while your wife dines alone and reads in her bedroom. I know how you run to Paola's arms each night after dinner rather than spend time getting to know your wife." Pointing to Celeste, she added, "She's not dull-witted. I'm sure that she can sense your rejection. She's probably frightened of you too. God knows how you love to stomp around like an angry ogre."

"I was giving her time to settle in," he said icily in the face of her criticism.

Livia shook her head sadly. "Do you really know so little about women? Can't you see how Celeste looks up to you as someone older, wiser—a protector? She is most likely starved for your attention and affection. She grew up in a cold dreary convent without the comforting touch of parents…Now, her own husband avoids her. Imagine how she must feel."

Ferrante studied Celeste with renewed interest. "The last thing I want is to hurt her."

"Then don't. The choice is yours."

CHAPTER 10

Ferrante's deafening silence during the ride home made me uncomfortable. Whatever topic he had privately discussed with his aunt rendered him pensive. Almost melancholic. He descended from the saddle when we arrived at the villa, then helped me to dismount.

"I'm going into the city," he said distractedly, his hands still cupping my waist.

"May I go with you?"

"Not today." Heaving himself back into the saddle, he gazed down at me with an unreadable expression. "I'll be back late."

I watched him go with disappointment.

Later that evening, I requested that a tray be brought up to my bedroom and supped alone. I ate sparingly, then went upstairs to play with Nadia for a bit. After kissing her goodnight, I returned to my room in order to prepare for bed.

Lisa brushed out my long hair, letting it trail down my back. It felt wonderful to wear it loose. She bade me goodnight and left the room. Since I wasn't sleepy, I decided to read. Having finished *Hamlet* and *Inferno*, I began leafing through *Meditations* and stopped. I had already read the wise emperor's words a few years ago and wanted to experience something new. On a whim, I crept downstairs to the library in my shift and bare feet.

I selected a book by Robert Boyle and was about to return to my room when the front door opened and closed. Ferrante entered the villa and I panicked. A soft woman's voice alerted me that he was not alone. Quickly, I blew out the candle in my hand and slipped out of the library. It took my eyes a moment to adjust to the darkness. Pressing myself against the wall of the corridor, I shuffled toward the sound of their voices. Risking a peek, I saw them both standing within a pool of candlelight in the foyer.

Paola's blonde curls were piled high on her head and she gazed up at my husband with dreamy eyes. Her low-cut gown exposed a generous amount of cleavage, making me feel inadequate. She pulled on his hand as though trying to persuade him into following her somewhere. To her room, most likely. A surge of jealousy shot through me. How dare she attempt to seduce my husband? To my immense relief, he shook his head, prompting her to pout. Throwing her arms around his neck, she attempted to rub against him. Ferrante pushed her away more than once. This went on for a few minutes before Paola frowned in anger, turned on her heel, and stormed in the direction of Ferrante's private quarters. Was her room among those in which I was not allowed entrance?

I studied Ferrante's tired, irritated expression. Sighing, he went over to the sideboard and helped himself to a drink. Rather than retire to his bedroom, he headed in my direction. I retreated down the hall and rounded the corner just before I heard his heavy footsteps entering the library. Thankfully, he closed the door behind him.

Holding my breath, I silently tiptoed past the library door and raced to my room with feather light steps. My heart pounded in my chest as I turned the lock, then got into bed. The disturbing scene played itself over and over again in my head as I leafed through the book.

I read for the better part of an hour before I heard something. Straining my ears, I picked up the faint sound of someone weeping. Could it be Paola? Cautiously, I opened the door and determined that the sound was the unmistakable cry of a child. Without a second thought, I rushed to Nadia's quarters. I found the toddler weeping in her bed. Seeing me, she pointed to her belly. Alarmed, I struck flint to light a candle and pulled up her night shift in order to examine her torso.

Not seeing anything, I said, "Wait here, sweetheart."

Nadia shook her head and put out her arms. I picked her up then went in search of Berta. I found the servant dozing in a chair with a pair of stockings in her hands. She must have fallen asleep while darning.

"Berta, wake up."

The woman's eyes flew open and she shot upward in the chair. "Signora Celeste! Nadia! What's wrong?"

"She's not feeling well."

"Oh little one, does it hurt again?" Berta asked, gently touching Nadia's belly.

Nadia nodded, so I asked, "Does she often suffer from stomach aches?"

"I'm afraid so," Berta replied, moving past me to open a cabinet. Taking hold of a brown bottle and a spoon, she added, "Nothing that a bit of gripe water can't fix."

I could smell the potent liquid from where she stood. "Good Lord, what's in that?"

"I make it myself by allowing poppy leaves to soak for days in brandy. Then I distill it."

Nadia's face twisted when Berta held out the spoon.

"Come on, girl," the servant prompted.

"That gripe water is potent. It will cause her to sleep deeply but it won't remedy what caused the stomach ache in the first place," I pointed out.

Nadia swallowed a spoonful, then another.

Berta replaced the bottle and spoon. "She's a fussy child, Signora Celeste. Won't eat this or that. Doesn't listen to me."

I gazed on the little girl with pity. Motherless and daughter to a distant father, it was no wonder that she proved difficult. Nadia was most likely sad too.

Berta reached for her ward. "Here, I'll put her to bed."

"I'll do it," I said, holding Nadia a bit closer.

"What's all this commotion?"

We turned around and saw Ferrante sauntering down the corridor with a scowl on his face. Nadia's arms tightened around my neck at the sight of her father.

Having never seen me with my hair down, he couldn't tear his eyes from my long dark mane. My face burned as I realized that I was wearing only a thin cotton shift that verged on transparent.

Oh Lord...

"Nadia has a bellyache," Berta replied.

Ferrante's eyes roamed over my scantily clad body and bare feet before meeting my gaze. "What are you doing here?"

I glanced at Berta, then replied, "I heard Nadia crying so I came to check on her."

Berta hastily added, "I was in the privy and couldn't hear the child, my lord."

The servant and I locked eyes. I didn't call the woman out on her lie but wondered why she would do so in the first place.

Ferrante moved to take Nadia but she wouldn't let go of me. I discreetly tried to pry her little hands from behind my neck but she only burrowed her face into my shoulder.

"Come," he said, placing his hand at the small of my back and urging me toward Nadia's room.

Berta remained behind wringing her hands.

I gently placed Nadia on the bed and whispered, "You need to let go of me, dearest. Papa is here to tuck you in and kiss you goodnight."

Her big green eyes slid from me to Ferrante. I took advantage and distanced myself from the bed to allow my husband access to his child.

Taking Nadia's hands, he said, "Do you feel better now, my angel?"

She nodded, her eyes filling with tears.

"Don't cry, my love," he said before gathering the little girl to his chest.

I stared at Ferrante, entranced. It was the first time I had seen him lower his guard to display vulnerability. Touched by the love and tenderness he exhibited toward his daughter, I vacated the room in order to grant them privacy.

Berta crept toward me and whispered, "Thank you."

"Why did you lie?"

"Signore Ferrante has a mean temper and I didn't want to be on the receiving end of it."

"You need to be more attentive in the future."

"Yes madam."

"Go on and get some rest."

She inclined her head at me and slipped into her room. After she closed the door, I headed toward the stairs.

Ferrante emerged from Nadia's room. "Celeste, wait."

I paused to allow him to catch up to me. His eyes rested on my breasts so I crossed my arms in modesty.

"Thank you for helping Nadia," he said, his tone sincere.

"Is she asleep?"

"Yes."

"I'm sure she'll feel better in the morning." I paused, then ventured, "You're so gentle with her."

"She's my life."

"Yet Nadia fears you." My comment hardened his features and prompted him to clench his jaw. I hastily amended, "What I mean to say is—"

"Stop."

"Forgive me if I spoke out of turn."

"Nadia fears me, yes. There's no reason for her to do so because I would kill for my daughter. I would *die* for her too."

The words, spoken with such conviction, moved me. "I have no doubt of that, my lord."

I turned to go and he placed his hand on my arm. "I have been unchivalrous toward you. As you know, I can be boorish and coarse at times."

Glancing down at his hand, I retorted coolly, "You've shown me nothing but generosity and kindness since my arrival. You even saved me from a rabid dog. I won't impose on your goodwill, for the last thing I want to be is a burden to you. Goodnight."

He appeared stricken. "Wait…don't go."

I stared at him expectantly. "My lord?"

"You're not a burden, Celeste. I *want* to know you…The age difference between us is considerable, but it's not so great that it prevents us from enjoying each other's company. Wouldn't you agree?"

Realizing that it wasn't easy for a man like Ferrante to express himself thusly, I replied, "I do, sir. There's something else you need to know. I'm not a child, Ferrante."

"I know you're not." Gentle fingers traced the curve of my cheek before he leaned forward and pressed his lips to my forehead. "You're every bit a woman."

He looked like he wanted to say more, so I prompted, "But?"

Shaking his head. "Get some rest."

I went to bed that night with my head full of thoughts. After having witnessed Ferrante and Paola in the foyer, I didn't know whether or not to believe him. The abrupt change in my husband's demeanor toward me was nothing short of baffling. I slept fitfully and rose from my bed the next morning with a headache. I removed the gauze my maid had applied to my leg and examined the ugly bruise on my shin. Patting the tender skin, I winced. It hurt less than it did yesterday, which served as a good sign.

The day began with a morning stroll, a visit with Nadia, and then a lonely lunch. According to Sandro, Ferrante had departed at dawn and wouldn't be back until supper. A message arrived from Livia stating that the curative had worked wonders. She would join us for dinner that evening.

Later that afternoon, I heard my husband's arrival while reading in my room. Going to the window, I pulled aside the drapes. His high black boots were caked with dust from the ride. He glanced up at the window and tipped his tricorn hat at the sight of me. Embarrassed at being caught spying, I inclined my head. I heard him ascending the stairs before he stomped into his bedchamber, which was located down the hall from mine.

Livia arrived an hour before dinner. Ferrante still hadn't emerged from his quarters, so she and I retreated to the terrace to speak privately. The balmy evening offered a lovely twilight sky streaked with gold and vivid rose.

My gaze tracked a cluster of plummy clouds drifting low on the horizon. "Why didn't Ferrante marry Paola instead of me?"

Startled, she clutched at the pearls around her neck. "Why do you ask?"

"I saw them both last night after they had come home from an evening out together. Paola tried to seduce Ferrante but he refused her advances."

Livia heaved a sigh. "First of all, she's a bastard. Paola's father was a nobleman and her mother, a whore."

"Who is her father?

"*Was*. My late husband."

I gaped at her in shock.

She laughed derisively. "I can see that you didn't expect that answer. This family is full of secrets. Paola's mother died of syphilis when she was only six so, at my husband's insistence, his bastard came to live with us. Paola was the only child he ever sired. The servants kept the girl out of my sight but every year that passed without legitimate heirs prompted him to lavish money and affection upon his daughter. It was his way of spiting me for being barren."

I listened with empathy. "It must have been hard for you."

"It wasn't easy, that's for certain. I was relieved when my husband found a successful merchant for Paola to marry, given that no respectable nobleman would have her. She and her husband lived in the city center, far from me. Those were good years. Tranquil."

"Until she came back to be a lady's maid to Caterina," I deduced, recalling what Livia had previously recounted.

"Correct, and she hasn't left since. Paola is now a thorn in your side as well as mine."

Behind us, the door opened.

"There you are, Ferrino." Livia smiled sweetly, her black silk gown reflecting the last golden rays of light as she went to kiss her nephew's cheek.

I inclined my head at him but remained distant. Where had he been all day? With Paola, perhaps?

"You look much better, Aunt Livia," Ferrante commented.

Livia slipped her hand into the crevice of his elbow and urged him toward me. "I feel better too. Feast your eyes upon your lovely young wife. Her curative made me good as new."

"I was happy to oblige, Signora Livia," I said, deliberately avoiding my husband's gaze. Their combined scrutiny made me uneasy.

Ferrante said, "Celeste, it's chilly and the fabric of your

gown is too thin for you to be out here without a shawl."

"I'm not an invalid, husband," I said with far more aggression than I intended.

"Your uncle—"

"—is an old fool," I snapped, finishing his sentence.

Livia shook her head slightly in warning.

I amended, "My uncle exaggerates."

Livia added, "Dr. Bernardo stated that Celeste was perfectly healthy. Look at those rosy cheeks."

Ferrante urged us toward the door. "I still think we should retire indoors. Dinner will be served soon."

The meal turned out to be a pleasant affair despite my sour mood. I couldn't help but wonder if Ferrante would have married Paola had she been of noble blood.

Livia talked of the operas planned for the spring and summer season, and that lifted my spirits, for I loved music.

"Some of the nobility open their homes as venues for theater performances and concertos," she explained.

"Even the prince?" I inquired.

"I'm sure Raimondo has all sorts of wonderful events planned. You will love his home and the entertainment he provides."

I grinned in excitement. "I'm sure I will."

Livia then went on to describe the amazing works of art and sculpture owned by the prince. I was sad when she announced that it was time for her to return home.

"Stay a while longer, won't you?" I prompted. "We could play cards."

She shook her head. "I'm still recuperating, my dear. I need my rest. Perhaps Ferrante will entertain you this evening."

Casting a hopeful glance in my husband direction, I whispered, "Will you be joining us for dinner tomorrow?"

"I'm afraid not. I'll be dining with an old friend."

We escorted her outside to her carriage and watched it disappear down the drive into the night.

Turning to me, Ferrante said, "I thought I could play the harpsichord for you tonight, if it please you."

"I would like that *very* much, my lord."

We retreated into the villa and I froze. Sniffing the air, I made a face. A familiar, sickeningly sweet perfume permeated the space around the front door. Paola had been spying on us. Ferrante smelled it too, for his face expressed a mixture of guilt and irritation. He turned to look at me and I pinned him with an icy stare.

"Celeste," he began, his face apologetic.

I turned my back on him and stormed off without so much as bidding him goodnight. I locked the door the moment I was in my bedroom. My overwhelming jealousy shocked me. Not only that, I felt shame for having given into it in front of Ferrante. To have his mistress living under the same roof was bad enough, but to know that the woman spied on us was more than I could bear. In an attempt to calm down, I told myself that I was being irrational.

I went to bed that night with restless thoughts.

Storm clouds eclipse the sun and the world grows ominously dark. I open my eyes and stand on shaky legs. Tall grass brushes my fingertips but I don't dare move. Celeste and Sister Assunta rush toward me, their expressions serious. They each tear off their face as easily as one removes a mask. I can't stop screaming. Two sets of hollowed eye sockets stare back at me...

I awoke to the sound of my own scream.

Lisa poked her head into the room. "My lady, are you ill?"

"I'm fine," I replied as I wiped my tearstained face.

Footsteps pummeled down the hall and Ferrante's tall frame loomed behind my maid.

He barged into the room holding aloft a candle. Peering at me, he said, "You were screaming."

"I had a nightmare," I explained sheepishly.

Glancing at Lisa, he said, "Fix her ladyship a draught."

My maid exited my chamber to obey his command, leaving me alone with my husband.

He regarded me coolly. "What ails you?"

What could I possibly say? My nightmares stemmed from the fact that I was an impostor. If ever discovered, I feared prison as well as Ferrante's wrath. To make matters worse, I fostered a strong emotional attachment with a man who loved another woman while openly rejecting me.

He continued, "Something is causing you distress. I can see it in your eyes. This isn't the first time you've been plagued by nightmares."

"I'm sorry if I've inconvenienced you, sir."

Sitting on the edge of the bed, he gently patted my forehead and neck as a parent would a child. "You don't feel feverish."

I placed my hand over his, pressing his palm to my cheek.

His eyes darkened. "What are you doing?"

"Is it wrong for a wife to crave her husband's touch?"

Withdrawing his hand, he stood. "You are unwell, my lady."

"Why are you acting like this?"

"Like what?"

"Cold, distant."

"Don't be ridiculous."

"Oh, I see…I assume your mistress is not ridiculous." No sooner had I said the words than I regretted them.

"That's not your concern," he said in a deceptively soft tone.

I bit back an angry retort, remembering my place. "You're right, my lord. Nothing in your life is my concern."

We stared at each other through a layer of ice.

Lisa rushed in with a cup and placed it in my hand.

"Thank you," I said, deliberately avoiding Ferrante's gaze.

He watched as I drank the contents, then waited for the servant to vacate the room before addressing me again. "I should summon the physician."

"There's no need."

"Celeste, I know things haven't been easy for you—"

"Goodnight, my lord," I rudely interjected.

He stared at me, then left. I watched him go with mixed feelings. I suspected Paola to be the source of his aloofness toward me and felt a surge of hatred for the woman. A long time passed before I fell asleep.

***

The next day passed without incident. My husband kept to

his quarters and barely spoke to me during supper. I remained distant and kept my expression neutral as I picked at my food.

"The weather is changing," Ferrante said, setting down his fork. "Livia's gardener predicts a vicious storm in the coming days, and the old man is seldom wrong."

Pushing the food around my plate, I didn't bother looking up at him. "Why are you telling me this?"

"To prepare you." He stood, adding, "You won't be able to spend time outdoors and I know how much you enjoy that."

Deliberately keeping my eyes on the plate, I nodded slightly in response to his words. When he hesitated to convey something else, I stood and asked to be excused. Disappointed, he bade me goodnight.

I went for a long walk the following day. Ominous clouds pregnant with rain hovered over the Naples Bay. The sky behind Vesuvius resembled gray wool. By the time I returned to the villa, the wind had gained considerable force. A few of the servants were transferring small potted plants from the terrace to the foyer in order to spare them from the powerful gusts of wind.

I claimed a headache and requested that a tray be brought up to my room for supper. There was nothing wrong with me. I simply didn't wish to face Ferrante.

I had barely finished my meal when the tempest finally rolled in from the sea. The storm proved so severe that it rattled the shutters. It felt good to be reading in a warm cozy bed as Mother Nature raged outdoors. The rhythmic sound of the rain eventually caused me to doze.

One of the shutters came loose during the night and began banging against the outer wall. The loud noise woke me up and the book slid off my chest as I sat up in the darkness. The candle had melted down to its stub. Groaning, I threw back the covers and opened the window in order to secure the shutter.

The driving rain pelted my face, arms, and chest like icy needles. A blinding white vein of lightning illuminated the sky accompanied by a deafening crack. I gasped aloud in fear as I jumped away from the window. Sure enough, I spied smoke coming from the woods where the lightning struck a tree.

"Santa Madonna," I whispered.

Each time I grabbed hold of one of the wet handles, the powerful wind pushed the wooden panel so hard that it slipped from my grasp. The shutters were big, which made it hard for me to reach the handle in the first place. Drenched and breathless from the effort, I finally called out to my maid in the antechamber.

The door opened behind me as I tried to grasp the handle. "Hold on to me, Lisa. I'm going to lean further out the window."

"You'll do no such thing," Ferrante said sharply.

I staggered backward in surprise. "It's you."

Ignoring my reaction, he reached out and took hold of the handle and brought the shutters together. His movements were effortless as he locked them. "Why didn't you wake me? Or at least Sandro?"

"I didn't want to bother anyone," I said through chattering teeth as I rubbed my arms for warmth. My shift was thoroughly soaked through with cold rainwater.

"You need to get out of that wet garment and get into bed lest you catch cold. Shall I wake your maid or can you manage by yourself?"

Shivering, I shook my head yet made no move to undress.

"You don't wish for me to call you a child yet you behave like one," he said, taking hold of the hem of my shift.

I said nothing as he gently pulled the garment over my head. With the shutters closed, the dark room hid my naked body from his sight. Despite this, his breathing grew heavy and a thick silence filled the space between us. I felt the heat from his body rolling off of him in waves and my body responded by coiling every muscle.

In that moment, I wanted nothing more than to wrap myself in the comforting warmth of his arms. Unlike Paola, I didn't know how to seduce a man. I took a tentative step forward and he instantly retreated as if I were a leper.

Taking hold of my arm, he guided me to the bed and urged

me to get beneath the covers. Pulling the blanket up to my chin, he leaned over to kiss my forehead. "Get some sleep."

My hands shot out to cup his face. "Stay with me."

His eyes glistened in the darkness as he said hoarsely, "You don't know what you ask."

My hands dropped and I said nothing. He exited my room as stealthily as he had entered it, leaving me feeling utterly alone.

Throwing open the shutters the next morning, I inhaled the fresh sweet scent of wet vegetation. Memories of last night flooded my mind as I visually tracked a stray storm cloud scuttling across the sky. I dressed hastily and rushed upstairs to fetch Nadia so that we could enjoy a bit of playtime outdoors before it rained again.

The little girl flicked flowers with her chubby fingers, then laughed when last night's rain sprayed the ground in a shower of tiny droplets. It amazed me how children could find pleasure in the simplest things. At one point, the water sprayed onto Berta's shoes and Nadia couldn't stop giggling. Her adorable laughter made us laugh too. The toddler squealed with pleasure as I chased her in a circle on the wet terrace.

"Celeste!"

I stopped at the sound of Ferrante's angry voice. Not only had he returned from his ride earlier than usual, but we were making too much noise to hear his approach.

He dismounted and stormed onto the terrace. Pointing a finger at Berta, he bellowed, "Take Nadia upstairs. *Now.*"

Nadia clung to my skirts. "It's all right, sweetheart. I'll go and visit you later. Go with Berta now."

Cringing inwardly, I watched as Berta snatched the child and ran inside without so much as a backward glance.

Taking a deep breath, I faced my angry husband. "Ferrante, please—"

"If Achille hadn't thrown a shoe, I would never have known what you were up to behind my back. How long have you been disobeying my orders?"

Orders? "I take Nadia out in the mornings but only for a little while. Berta and I are with her at all times."

"Nadia has a tendency to stray. She could get hurt or lost. My God, Celeste, you were recently attacked by a rabid dog. Have you no sense of responsibility?"

His words were an affront but I maintained my composure. "There were two adults supervising your daughter."

"You obviously don't see the danger, do you?"

I breathed deeply to calm myself, then said in the most reasonable tone that I could muster, "She spends most of her life up in the attic."

His eyes flashed in outrage. "It's not an attic. There is a solarium and two balconies on the upper floor so she receives more than enough sunshine."

"She needs to run and feel the fresh air on her face."

"Who are you to give me such advice?

"Children need grass, trees, butterflies…Think of your own childhood, will you?"

"You are not a parent!"

Balling my hands into fists, I retorted, "Given that I'm still a virgin, how can I ever become one?" Stunned by my own vehemence, I covered my mouth with my hands.

He regarded me in a manner that chilled me to the core. "Addressing me in that unpleasant tone won't change your current predicament."

Turning on his heel, he marched back to his horse. I trembled in the wake of his anger, unsure of what to say or do. This was not at all how I wanted things to be between us.

I went about my day in a distracted haze, feeling bad about what happened on the terrace.

Ferrante and I were forced to dine alone in his aunt's absence. I could tell that he was still upset with me for my rude outburst. Throughout the first course, he barely looked at me.

Finally, I said, "Please accept my apology for this morning."

Motioning for a servant to refill his wine goblet, he said, "You'll learn the rules of the house soon enough, and I'll expect you to obey them."

"What I said to you was disrespectful...It's not my place to tell you how to raise your child. What do I know?"

The cold mask slipped from his face. "I'm sure you mean well where my daughter is concerned."

"Did you not say that you expected me to aid in her upbringing?"

"I did convey that, yes. That doesn't mean you have the freedom to do as you see fit."

"Understood, my lord."

Servants came out with the second course.

In an attempt to lighten the mood, he picked up his goblet and said, "I saw that you've already replaced the books that you borrowed. May I inquire what you're reading now?"

"*The Sceptical Chymist* by Robert Boyle."

Ferrante almost choked on his wine.

"The Englishman proposes interesting theories," I added casually, hoping to draw him into conversation about alchemy.

My husband stared at me as if had grown a second head.

I continued, "According to Boyle's law, the volume of a gas decreases as the pressure on it increases, and vice versa. He also elaborates on the transmutation of the elements, claiming to have changed gold into mercury. Do you believe him?"

"Did I not explicitly tell you to avoid alchemy?

"You said I could borrow any of your books…"

Leaning in closer, he speared me with a pointed look. "Novels, plays, poetry, religious works...I thought I had made myself clear."

I swallowed the lump in my throat. "I don't see the harm in allowing me to pursue a topic that interests me."

"You may not see it but I do."

"What do you mean? I'm not harming anyone."

He smacked the table top in irritation. "You're naïve and it is my duty as your husband to guide you. Why are you being so difficult?"

"That's not my intention, I assure you."

Reaching for his goblet, he took a long sip then said, "I want you to return the book to the library first thing in the morning."

"Why?"

He stood, his eyes flashing in anger. "Because I said so,

Celeste. Santo Cristo, you try my patience."

Ferrante stormed off, leaving me alone at the table. I picked at my food as my eyes filled with tears.

One of the servants approached me and quietly inquired, "Would you like me to take the rest of your dinner to your room, madam?"

"I've lost my appetite. Thank you."

The young man's eyes were full of empathy, which only made me feel worse. "Shall I have Cook prepare some tea?"

I shook my head and offered him a teary smile.

"Goodnight, Signora Celeste," he said before removing my plate and vanishing behind a screen.

Deeply saddened, I stepped out onto the terrace. A sliver of moon cast its light upon the potted fruit trees. The rain had chilled the air, causing me to shiver. I heard rustling coming from the line of trees bordering the lawn and wondered what sorts of animals lurked in the darkness. A hooting owl answered my question. Not wishing to dally outside for too long, I prudently retreated to my room. It was still too early for Lisa to help me undress. My eyes slid to the bedside table where the "forbidden book" reminded me of my husband's angry behavior during supper.

It's his house and his book, Valentina.

With that thought in mind, I decided to return the book to the library at once. Why wait for the morning?

I crept downstairs and noticed that the servants had already cleared the table and extinguished many of the candles. The villa looked creepy at night as I made my way to the library with silent footsteps. Throwing open the doors, I found Paola Colombo sitting on my husband's lap. Wearing nothing but a red corset and white linen skirt, she held a book in her hands. She stopped reading aloud and coolly regarded me. My heart sank when I glimpsed victory in the woman's eyes.

Ferrante followed his lover's triumphant gaze to where I stood blushing in humiliation. We stared at each other for a tense moment and I thought I saw a flicker of regret in his eyes. Willing myself not to cry in front of them, I clutched the book to my chest and fled.

I locked myself inside of my bedroom. Overwhelmed by conflicting emotions, I finally gave in to tears. Fortunately, they had dried by the time Lisa came in to help me undress. Sensing that I was upset, she performed her duties with quiet efficiency and left me alone with my book, which I read with rebellious delight. Eventually, my eyes grew heavy. I was beginning to doze off when footsteps in the corridor startled me. I sat up in bed with a jolt. The abrupt movement caused the remaining flame in the candle stub to sputter. Eerie shadows danced across the walls. Someone stood outside my door. The latch turned first to the left, then to the right.

A wave of relief washed over me when I remembered that I had locked the door. I didn't want Ferrante barging into my room whenever I had nightmares or needed to close my shutters. The last time he came into my room, he stripped me of my clothing and rejected me. I wasn't going give him the chance to make me feel bad again. Especially not after tonight.

The scene in the library caused my fury to boil inside me like soup in a cauldron. The victorious expression on Paola's face summoned the bile to my throat. I could never compete with a woman like that.

A soft scratch on the door made me hold my breath.

"Celeste?"

Ferrante's whisper compelled me to remain perfectly still and not make a sound. He tried the door once again.

"Celeste, please..."

Tense silence.

Finally, he gave up and walked away. Every muscle in my body relaxed as I sagged against the soft pillows.

What would have happened had I not locked the door?

CHAPTER 11

I woke up much earlier than I usually did the next day. The outrage I had felt at having been chastised by Ferrante last night for merely reading a book, only to catch him with his lover in the library, created a fresh wave of resentment toward him. In truth, the incident had offended me. *Deeply.*

Had he knocked on my door to apologize?

At that point, I didn't care. I rose from the bed in the grayish blue gloom and padded to the vanity where I studied my reflection in the mirror. Dark circles stood out in a pale face.

Paola's face loomed in my mind, her eyes mocking me.

Ferrante loved a woman of loose morals yet criticized me for being curious about science. A strange heaviness settled around my heart at the thought of him enjoying the evening with his mistress…*the intimacy they shared.*

Worldly and sensuous, Paola had known my husband her entire life. What's more, she had carnal experience with men. How could I ever compete for his affection? At this rate, I would never succeed in getting Ferrante to fall in love with me. How was I supposed to provide him with an heir if another woman tempted him into her bed instead of mine? Then a thought struck me: maybe I didn't want to bear his child.

Maybe you don't want to remain here, Valentina.

I paced the room with racing thoughts as an idea began taking shape in my head. Marrying a stranger had been a mistake. I should never have allowed Sister Assunta to persuade me. I stopped in my tracks at the thought of not having Nadia and Ferrante in my life. In truth, I had grown fond of them in my short time at the villa.

Fond? You feel more for him than that, Valentina.

The voice in my head was right, of course. Nadia already had me wrapped around her pinky. As for Ferrante, my feelings for him expanded daily. I never planned on falling in love with my husband. Even admitting it seemed irrational, especially since he only cared for Paola. Had she been born of noble blood, the wedding ring would be on her finger right now and not mine. Bitterness consumed me. I slid the gold band off my finger and placed it atop the Bible on the bedside table.

What prevents you from running away?

The question crept into my head with wicked stealth. The answer came just as quietly: *nothing.*

With the exception of Livia, nobody knew my real identity. I could return to my Aunt Gloria as Valentina Gaetani. *Unscathed.* She would understand, especially since my marriage had never been consummated.

The more I entertained the possibility of my freedom, the more appeal it held for me. Before I could change my mind, I donned the plainest dress in the armoire and tied my thick mass of hair at the nape with a ribbon. I found a dark cloak in the armoire and threw it over my shoulders. A glimpse in the mirror's reflection revealed a frightened girl with heightened color in her cheeks. Quiet as a cat, I descended the stairs and crept out the front door. No one stopped me as I opened the main gate and picked my way down the pebbled drive.

The moment I cleared the villa, I exhaled a huge sigh of relief. I imagined sitting at the table with my aunt and Natalino later that evening. I would tell them of my adventure over a bottle of decent wine, which I deserved at this point. Maybe even two bottles. I had saved Celeste *and* myself from a horrible life with a cold, selfish man.

I forced my thoughts on the downhill path, the birds singing in the crisp morning air, and the pale sun rising over the Naples Bay. My racing heart began to slow as I took note of various plants and flowers. A fox poked its nose out of a bush to greet me, and I smiled. *I was free.*

I managed to walk for over half hour before I spotted a horse trotting uphill. I knew instantly that it wasn't Achille, which made me sag with relief. Squinting, I noticed that the rider sported a red riding jacket and a black tricorn hat with fabulous ostrich plumes. The chestnut stallion's gleaming coat testified to the beast's excellent health and breeding as it came to a stop in a cloud of dust several feet from me.

The rider waved. "Signora Celeste."

I automatically curtsied. "Your Highness."

"What are you doing up at this unholy hour?"

"I couldn't sleep," I improvised.

Raimondo took in my plain clothing and messy hair with an appraising eye. When his gaze settled on my hands, he afforded me a knowing look. "Did you lose your wedding ring, my lady?"

Feigning surprise, I cried, "Oh dear, I must have left it in my room. My maid applied some cream to my hands before bed."

"Women and their beauty secrets," he said drily, unconvinced by my performance. "Where are you headed?"

Shrugging, I replied nonchalantly, "Ah…I'm taking a leisurely stroll."

"You appeared determined a moment ago." When I quietly stared down at my feet, he added, "The views up by the house are far more pleasant."

I wrung my hands nervously. "You're right, my lord. May I ask what you're doing here so early in the morning?"

"Ferrante invited me to meet with him. We're to ride together and discuss an event that I'm planning—*one that I hope you will attend.*"

His tone caused my cheeks to redden. Unable to meet the man's eyes, I merely nodded.

Raimondo dismounted and held out his hand. "Why don't I accompany you back to the house, Signora Celeste?"

"You're very kind, but…"

Gently, he prompted, "Come, before you do something you'll later regret." Seeing the sheen in my eyes, he added, "Here, let me help you into the saddle. Better to ride on Perseo than to trek uphill."

Staring at the horse with wide eyes, I took a step backward. "I prefer to walk."

Realization lit up his features. "Don't be frightened. He's well trained."

Reluctantly, I allowed him to heave me up into the saddle. He then sat behind me, as Ferrante had done when we went to see Livia. Thankfully, Perseo made no protest to the added weight on his back. After a few paces, I relaxed a bit.

"I told him that you would feel isolated up here," Raimondo said, his lips so close that I could feel his breath on my nape.

"My lord?"

"Ferrante is a stubborn man—and I say this as his dearest friend and mentor."

Astonished by the ease in which the prince spoke to me, I held my tongue and listened.

He continued, "A young woman needs a bit of excitement after a life of confinement. I told him that too."

"The villa is lovely and everyone has been so kind…"

He chuckled softly. "I'm sure they have, but that doesn't make things any easier for you."

"No, Your Highness, it does not," I finally confessed.

"I beseech you, give him a bit more time before making any *permanent* decisions. Ferrante is in the process of transitioning from one life to another. I daresay you're undergoing the same."

I understood his meaning but refrained from commenting.

Raimondo continued, "May I confide something?"

"By all means, my lord."

"I strongly suspect that he loves you, which is no small feat for a man with Ferrante's past. He's distrusting, possessive, suspicious, and jealous. He's known to be aggressive at times. Despite these faults, he's the best man I know. A kinder, more generous spirit you will not find in this city or elsewhere—of that, you have my word."

"I believe you."

We rode in silence for several paces.

"Do you love him, Celeste?"

Raimondo's question caught me off-guard. Glancing at him over my shoulder, I nodded.

His eyes softened. "Then give him time. Remember what I told you on your wedding day?"

"You advised me to be patient."

"That's right. Promise me you will try to do that."

"I promise."

"Good girl. This conversation is best kept between us. What say you?"

"I agree, my lord."

He paused, then changed the subject. "I take it that you're enjoying Alexandria."

"The library is my favorite room in the villa."

"What are you reading right now?"

"The book I'm reading has recently earned me a harsh chastisement from my husband, so it's best if I not say."

Raimondo laughed heartily. "You're full of surprises, aren't you? The curiosity is killing me."

"Robert Boyle's *The Sceptical Chymist.*"

He sobered instantly. "Why are you reading that?"

I couldn't reveal that my late father was a chemist so I stated the truth. "I find the topic fascinating."

"Have you read anything else on the topic of alchemy?"

"*Tesoro del Mondo* and some works by Sir Isaac Newton." Peering at him over my shoulder, I added, "Did you know that Boyle corresponded with Newton?"

"I did, yes," he replied, frowning. "You're an odd young lady and I mean that in a good way."

"I wish Ferrante saw me like that too."

"Take heart, Celeste. Things will improve."

The villa loomed before us, compelling me to be silent. Ferrante exited the front door as Raimondo and I passed through the gate. My husband's worried expression signaled that my disappearance had been reported by the servants.

Raimondo said with forced joviality, "I found your wife wandering the grounds and offered to accompany her home. I believe she was lost."

Ferrante's eyes never left my face. In a deceptively calm tone laden with steel, he said, "Please alert the servants if you're going out, Celeste. You had the entire household in a frenzy."

His gaze roamed over me, stopping at my hand. I saw anger and disappointment in his eyes at my lack of a wedding ring.

Raimondo dismounted from the saddle then helped me to do the same. "See? I told you my horse is well-trained."

"Thank you, my lord."

"My pleasure, madam." Looking to Ferrante, he added, "I was hoping to get your opinion on the artworks I'll be exhibiting at my upcoming soirée. I've acquired a new and exciting piece."

I lowered my gaze. "Please excuse me, gentlemen."

The men waited for me to walk away before continuing their conversation. I ascended the stairs, sickened by the thought of facing my husband later on that day. Would he scream at me in anger? Punish me for trying to leave him? I stood at the window and watched as the men engaged in discourse.

Nadia would surely lift my mood, I thought. The child always made me smile. I found her and Berta in the solarium. At the sight of me, the child squealed.

I greeted Berta, then scooped Nadia up in my arms and spun her around in a circle. She made gurgling noises and sounds that sounded like short vowels. There was nothing wrong with her vocal cords or her hearing, so why couldn't she speak?

"Can you say Nadia?" I asked in a sweet voice.

The joy vanished from her face and she pouted.

"One little try?" I prompted.

"Nah."

Berta and I exchanged surprised glances.

I sank to my knees to be at eye-level with the toddler. "Very good. *Nah-dee-ah.*"

Nadia shook her head and refused to comply.

"That's all right. You don't have to talk if you don't want to. Only when you're ready."

I stood, happy to have made a bit of progress. 'Nah' was better than nothing.

I spent the afternoon in my studio, pouring over books that offered any insight on muteness.

Later, I went down to dinner and found my husband on the terrace with a drink in his hand. He stood with his broad back to me and I couldn't help but admire his fine physique. We hadn't seen or spoken to each other since this morning. Bracing myself, I opened the French doors leading to the terrace and stepped into the coolness of twilight.

He turned around and pinned me with a hard stare. "I wasn't expecting you to join me."

I closed the doors behind me and walked to where he stood. "Would you prefer to dine alone?"

"No, but I imagined you would."

I hesitated. "This morning—"

Holding up his hand to silence me, he averted his gaze. "I know you've witnessed certain things that have no doubt caused you offense, but you can't simply storm off like that."

"Why not?"

"You're my wife, that's why."

I deliberately shrugged to provoke him. I knew I shouldn't, but I couldn't help myself.

He clenched his jaw. "You disappointed me this morning."

I shrugged again, making his eyes darken with fury. "The marriage hasn't been consummated and can still be annulled, if you wish."

He stared at me aghast, making me almost regret my words.

Moving past me, he said, "I'm famished. Let's go inside."

I tracked him at a prudent distance and quietly took my seat at the table. Servants began spooning stew from a tureen and setting out bread and wine. The same young man who had spoken kindly to me last night offered me a slight smile. I returned the gesture, only to receive a sharp look from my husband. The silence between us became palpable, causing the servants to cast nervous glances in our direction.

Ferrante cleared his throat. "Raimondo sought my opinion on some artwork he plans to display."

I blinked at him. Was this to be my life? Engaging in banal conversations to mask the festering problems underlying our union? Playing along, I replied flatly, "I'm sure he appreciates your help given that your taste is impeccable."

"At least in artwork, yes." Recognizing the possible offense to me, he hastily amended, "I didn't mean—I'm not referring to you, Celeste."

I regarded him squarely. "I'm aware that I'm naïve and not up to your *sophisticated* standards when it comes to women…"

"I don't expect a girl who grew up in a convent to possess any level of sophistication."

I pretended to smooth the linen napkin on my lap to hide the pain caused by his comment. "I imagine that a worldly man such as yourself must find my company quite dull."

He sighed. "Celeste…"

My fingers trembled as they repeatedly rubbed against the unbleached fabric. "Perhaps Paola Colombo can teach me how to curry your favor since I'm incapable of doing it on my own."

Upon hearing my words, the servants wisely retreated behind the screen to afford us privacy. For the life of me I don't know what made me say that. Perhaps it was my feisty spirit, the mischievous girl that I had suppressed in my attempt to become Celeste Carducci.

He eyed me frostily. "How dare you?"

"You're right, of course. This is your house and you can do as you wish with whomever you wish." I threw the napkin on the table and stood. "I'll spare you the tediousness of my company, Ferrante. That way, you can meet with Paola earlier than your usual time."

Gripping the table's edge, he glared at me. "You will sit down and finish your meal."

"I'm afraid I've lost my appetite. Goodnight, my lord."

I took a few steps, then heard the scrape of chair legs. His hand clamped down upon my arm. "Don't go."

I spun around and said with far more vehemence than intended, "Why not?"

"I want you to stay."

Despite the sincerity in his gaze, I yanked my arm free from his grip. "You barely speak with me. When you do, it's either to criticize my choice of books or scold me for playing outside with Nadia. I can't do anything right in your eyes, so I'll stay out of your sight until you deem it fit to sire a child upon me. After all, that's the only reason I'm here, isn't it?"

The shock on his face was so great that I didn't know whether to be frightened or laugh aloud. I doubted anyone had ever spoken to him in such a blunt manner, least of all a woman. I headed for the stairwell. To my astonishment, he kept pace behind me. Being young and fit, I raced up the stairs. He pursued me with serious intent. Would he strike me if he caught me? Punish me for my sharp tongue?

Reaching the door of my bedroom, I hastily turned the latch. I managed to open the door a crack but his big hand reached past me and slammed it shut in my face.

Crowding me with his tall frame, he breathed heavily against my ear. I turned around to find his face inches from my own. Pressing my back against the door, I stared at him defiantly.

"Your uncle lied to me, for only someone with robust health in the prime of life can race up a flight of stairs that fast," he whispered, his gaze resting on my mouth.

"Or someone who wishes to run from you."

"Is that what you want, Celeste? To run from me? Like you did this morning?"

"What woman wouldn't in my situation?"

His brow creased into a frown. "Do you think life mimics the novels of which you are so fond? Did you and your young friends at the convent sit around daydreaming of love and the dashing husbands you would someday marry? Poor, silly girl."

"Forgive me for believing that husbands and wives should actually love each other and foster mutual respect."

"I'm no hero."

"No, you're not. You're an adulterer."

He flinched, instinctively raising his hand as if to strike me. Dropping his arm, he hung his head. "I deserve that."

The sheer size of him made me feel vulnerable. His nearness caused my body to respond to his in unfamiliar ways. Flustered, I hid my excitement with anger. "You're right to call me a poor silly girl, my lord. Why waste another precious moment on me when Paola awaits you with open arms?"

His head snapped up and he studied my face. "If I didn't know any better, I would say that you're jealous."

"What if I am?"

Surprised, he emitted a humorless chuckle. "*You*, jealous of *me*? Surely, you jest." When I remained silent and serious, he took hold of my chin and tilted my head back in order to stare into my eyes.

I drowned in his green gaze.

To my astonishment, his eyes reflected fear. "You're telling me the truth." Letting go of my chin, he took a step backward. "You can't possibly love me."

"Why not?"

"I fail to treat you as you deserve."

"You're still a good man, a generous provider, a loving father. People say horrible things about you because they don't know you."

"Do you think you know me?"

I shook my head in answer to his question. "I *want* to know you. Sometimes, I catch glimpses of the real Ferrante behind the prickly barrier you've constructed to keep everyone out."

He searched my face. "You're not at all what I expected."

"Is that good or bad?"

In response, he stared at my mouth for a long time and then inclined his head toward mine. He smelled of leather and the forest. My eyes fluttered shut as his lips pressed against my own. He pulled back and I met his puzzled gaze. Cupping my jaw in his big hand, kissed me again. This time, his tongue demanded entrance and I granted access. I had never kissed a man before so I mimicked what he did, coiling my tongue along his tongue. I had once watched a pair of slugs mating as a child and the image popped into my head as my husband slowly devoured my mouth.

A deep moan escaped his lips as he moved to nuzzle my throat. I felt his hands in my hair, impatiently yanking the ribbons that kept my tamed locks in place. A mane of coppery brown silk strands cascaded to my shoulders and spilled around my face. Grabbing a fistful, he brought my hair to his nose and inhaled deeply.

"Oh God," he whispered.

I heard the soft click of the door and found myself inside of the room, locked in his powerful arms.

Pulling me hard against him, he said, "I want you."

He kissed me, his hands caressing my shoulders then cupping my breasts. With expert fingers, he untied the back laces of my garment so that it fell to the floor. Next, he helped me out of my corset and skirt. I shivered in my lace-edged shift as he removed his own clothing. My eyes were glued to his chiseled hairy chest the moment he stripped of his linen shirt. As his garments continued to come off, I admired his flat stomach and muscular thighs. Having never seen a naked man, I stared at him, transfixed.

Following my gaze to his engorged member, he demanded, "Are you frightened?"

"Yes," I admitted.

At this, he chuckled. The low sound vibrated at the base of his throat, causing my pulse to quicken.

"Take off your shift."

I maneuvered out of the garment and stood before him in nothing but my thigh-high stockings, which were held up by satin garter ribbons. Circling me slowly, his eyes roamed over me with obvious approval. Slowly, he untied the garter ribbons and removed each stocking with touching tenderness.

When I stood completely naked, he backed away in order to see all of me. His pupils dilated, deepening the color of his eyes. Motioning toward the bed, he whispered, "Lay back."

Just smile and lay still. Your husband will know what to do.

I obeyed Ferrante's command with Camillo's words echoing through my head. He took his time admiring me, then explored my body with his mouth and hands. An involuntary moan of pleasure escaped my lips when he cupped my buttocks and suckled my breasts.

"Do you like that, Celeste?"

"Yes…"

He touched my most private part, making me gasp. "Do you want me? Do you want *this*?"

"Yes…"

Kneeling between my thighs, he forced my legs apart and smothered me with his weight. Although he moved slowly and gently, I yelped when he claimed my maidenhead. He kissed my brow and stroked my cheek while whispering loving words into my ear. It didn't take me long to learn how he wanted my body to respond to his movements. His breathing grew louder, heavier. His thrusts deepened. We cried out at the same time, clutching at each other's damp bodies.

The experience was unlike anything I could have imagined, and I already looked forward to doing it again.

He raised himself on his elbows to plant kisses on my face and neck. "So sweet..."

"Like you."

"*I'm* sweet?" When I nodded, he laughed in a deprecating manner. "I've been called many things in my thirty years. *Sweet* has never been on that list."

"You're like honey."

"You're serious," he said, eyeing me dubiously.

I sniffed his neck. I loved his scent. "Why wouldn't I be?"

"I didn't expect a girl like you to...I never thought..."

When he trailed off, I prompted, "What do you mean a girl like me? Speak plainly."

"Young, innocent, beautiful...*so beautiful*," he whispered, touching my bottom lip with his fingertip.

In an attempt to lighten the mood, I inquired, "Would you prefer that I call you bitter instead of sweet?"

"I deserve to be called that after the way I've treated you."

"Stop," I said, wrapping my arms around his neck and holding him tightly.

He returned my embrace with a sigh of relief. "I've wanted you from the onset but I couldn't bring myself to touch you."

"Because of my uncle's account of my health?"

"That was merely an excuse."

"What's the real reason you waited so long?"

"How does a beast approach an angel? I feared your rejection—more precisely, your revulsion." He stroked my cheek while studying my face. "The portrait your uncle gifted me didn't do you any justice, you know. Usually artists compliment their subjects. In your case, it's the opposite."

I didn't respond to his unkind speculation of Celeste's physical appearance.

He continued, "I only hope that you find me half as comely as I find you."

"You're quite handsome, my lord."

This amused him. "Now I'm sweet *and* handsome?"

"Correct."

"Most of Naples would disagree with your assessment."

"To hell with them."

His eyes widened in disbelief. "Are nuns usually so opinionated when it comes to members of the opposite sex?"

"I've told you before, I'm not a nun."

"Thank the Lord for that!"

We laughed simultaneously. For the first time, I experienced a sense of true intimacy with Ferrante.

His expression sobered. "There's something you need to know."

Pressing my fingertips to his lips, I admonished, "Don't ruin this perfect moment, my lord. *Savor it.* In fact, you should make love to me again."

Ferrante readily obliged my request, only this time the act proved more tender than lustful.

Afterward, as we held each other, I inquired, "What did you want to tell me?"

"It's about Nadia and my late wife. We can talk of it another time."

"Tell me."

He hesitated, searching for the right words. "Caterina neglected our daughter. She was a selfish woman who only cared about her vapid friends. Shortly before she took ill, Caterina was outside with Nadia one summer morning and she sent the servants on some frivolous errand. Assuming the child would be safe with her mother, they left the pair alone. Caterina fell asleep beneath the shade of a tree and Nadia was gone by the time the servants had returned. It was almost dark when we found her by the roadside, a quarter mile from the villa."

Leaning up on my elbow, I gazed at his face. "How terrible."

"My daughter had been wandering through the woods alone for all those hours," he said, his eyes glistening.

"She must have been so frightened."

"Caterina wasn't allowed to be alone with her after that. I strictly forbade it. I'm telling you this so that you'll understand why I'm protective of Nadia."

"That's why you were so angry with me for playing with her on the terrace."

"Yes."

"I will never be careless with your daughter. More than that, I already love her as my own."

"Thank you," he said before kissing my forehead.

"Please allow me to take her outside in the mornings. Nadia loves it, and Berta and I will watch over her at all times."

"Permission granted."

I laid my head on his shoulder and caressed his chest. "See? Like honey…"

CHAPTER 12

I awoke alone, twisted in the sheets. At one point last night, my husband had sought his own bed. Memories of our lovemaking prompted me to smile as I stretched like a cat.

Lisa entered my room and, seeing the look on my face, offered me a shy smile. The knowing look in her eyes made me blush. Naturally, she knew what had finally transpired.

Handing me a dampened, perfumed cloth, she said, "Good day, my lady. His lordship awaits you downstairs."

I sat up, puzzled. "Whatever for?"

My maid's eyes twinkled. "It seems you're going on a trip, for the carriage is being readied as we speak."

Throwing back the covers, I swung my feet off the bed and ran to the window. Sure enough, a fine black carriage stood outside our front door.

"Did my husband say where we're going?"

"No, madam."

"Hurry, help me dress."

I descended the stairs and found Ferrante in the foyer.

His features lit up at the sight of me. He kissed my lips softly, then said, "Good morning. Did you sleep well?"

"Yes…Where are we going?"

"I prefer to surprise you, if that's all right."

I grinned, excited. "I've never been outside of Naples."

"Today, we'll remedy that."

"How long will we be gone?"

"All day."

I could hardly believe it. We sat across from each other as the vehicle took off downhill. Unable to temper my eagerness and excitement, I smiled until my face ached. My elated mood served to lift Ferrante's spirits, for he chuckled.

Patting the seat beside him, he said, "Come here."

I snuggled beside him without hesitation.

His eyes turned soft. "I know you don't like being compared to a child, but you should see your face right now."

"I'm happy."

Inclining his head toward mine, he gently took hold of my throat. "You're so soft," he murmured.

I touched his cheek and he leaned forward to claim my lips. Deepening the kiss, his hand moved from my throat to touch my breast.

I pulled away. "Ferrante, someone may see us."

He closed the velvet curtains at once. "Better?"

"Yes…"

In the privacy of our carriage, I welcomed my husband's fevered kisses and love play.

After an hour or so, the carriage stopped and I gasped in surprise the moment I realized where we were.

I scanned the ancient city. "This is Herculaneum, is it not?"

"Correct. Named after Hercules who, according to the legend recounted by Dionysius of Halicarnassus, founded the city in 1243 BC. Although some scholars believe the Etruscans founded the city."

"I've only seen this place as a drawing in a book," I confessed, reaching for his hand. "It's incredible."

He brought my knuckles to his lips, then said, "Shall we?"

Ferrante led me through the wide stone streets and we paused frequently to admire the neat, frescoed houses the ancient Romans referred to as *domus*. Some had furnishings inside of them, and I even spotted the remains of foodstuffs in the kitchen.

Ferrante led me to the city's theater and said, "Prince Emmanuel Maurice ordered a well to be dug in this area in the year 1707. The workers discovered several chunks of marble statues and a theater wall."

"So they discovered the theater while digging," I deduced, taking in the massive structure.

"Exactly. Can you imagine, Celeste?" Spreading his arms, he turned in a circle. "All this was buried under several feet of mud, dirt, and ash."

"Vesuvius devastated this entire region in ancient times," I commented, recalling what I had read about the tragedy of 79AD.

Ferrante's eyes took on a distant look. "Each time I come here, I try to imagine the panic those poor people must have felt. The sheer dread of knowing the end was imminent."

I shivered at the disturbing thought.

"I've frightened you," he said gently.

My eyes traced the line of Vesuvius in the distance. "Do you think it will erupt like that again?"

"Only God can answer that question." Leading me into the cool space of the excavated theater, he continued, "Prince Emmanuel began excavations shortly after the initial discovery but the work eventually ground to a halt. Unfortunately, treasure hunters stripped the city of many things. In 1738, Charles III of Bourbon employed a Spanish engineer to continue the work. They discovered Pompeii ten years later."

"How thrilling it must be to make a discovery like this," I said, moving toward a frescoed wall in order to admire the impressive details.

"Five years ago, Accademia Ercolanense was established."

"Did Prince Raimondo have a hand in that?"

"He has a hand in everything."

We walked past various buildings, each flaunting evidence of its former use. There were places to purchase food, wine, oil, meat, and even a brothel. The fresco on the wall depicted men and women copulating in various poses. A flush of warmth spread through my insides as I studied their fleshy pink bodies. Ferrante came to stand behind me with his hands on my shoulders. I averted my gaze out of respect and modesty.

Seeing this, he took hold of my chin and said, "Don't look away. It's *art.* Raimondo brought me here a few times when I was a boy. This was my favorite building besides the theater."

I giggled. "Wicked boy."

"Come, there is so much more to see."

We spent hours exploring courtyards and homes. I pictured husbands and wives eating dinner, mothers in the kitchen while children played in courtyards. I closed my eyes and tried to imagine the sounds and smells. Did they decorate the city to honor their pagan gods on feast days? Sing and dance in the streets with unabashed exuberance?

"You must be hungry," Ferrante said, glancing at his pocket watch. "It's almost two in the afternoon."

"I've been so absorbed with exploring that I haven't even thought about food. Now that you've mentioned it, yes, I'm quite hungry and thirsty."

Taking my hand, he led me up a grassy slope.

Confused, I pointed in the opposite direction. "I thought the carriage was there."

We cleared the crest and I froze. A picnic awaited us, complete with wine, fruit, cheese, bread, and sweetmeats. A blanket had been laid over the soft grass so that we could eat while enjoying the view of the ancient city.

"I wanted to surprise you," Ferrante said, helping me to take a seat on the blanket. "Are you pleased?"

"Oh yes. Thank you," I said before kissing his cheek.

The transformation of my husband from reclusive man to affectionate lover was nothing short of a miracle. He poured some wine for us and set about placing the food on small plates. We shyly fed each other fruit and bits of cheese between kisses.

We returned to the villa in the late afternoon. Although we were both tired, we bathed and dressed for supper and enjoyed a quiet meal together before retiring to our separate rooms.

A note had been slipped under my door while I was downstairs. The parchment reeked of a familiar sweet perfume and the red wax seal bore the imprint of a *colombo*, a dove. I read the scrawled message: *We now share his body but his heart will always be mine.*

My triumph at having finally consummated my marriage and winning over Ferrante's affection was, unfortunately, short-lived. The humiliation and anger I felt in that instant caused me to curse under my breath. I was about to throw the letter onto the smoldering embers in the fireplace when a thought struck me. I sat down at my desk and penned a reply.

I said nothing to Ferrante about the note. Instead, I went about my business the next day as usual, relishing my husband's newfound joy and the attention that accompanied it. To my immense delight, he played the harpsichord for me after supper.

Clapping my hands, I said, "Wonderful, thank you."

"Does it merit a reward, my lady?"

I kissed him and he pulled me onto his lap. The sound of a door slamming shut startled us both and broke the kiss. He scowled, his eyes fixed in the direction of the sound.

Gently pushing me off his lap, he said, "I'll be upstairs shortly."

Although I was tempted to speak, I remained quiet and went upstairs to my room. Lisa entered a moment later to help me with my evening toilette.

"His lordship will be joining me shortly," I informed.

Smiling impishly, she set out a sheer rose peignoir with black satin ribbons at the neck. She also procured some scented rose oil to rub into my skin. No sooner had I slipped into bed and propped myself against the pillows than Ferrante entered the room. My provocative garment must have stoked his desire, for his gaze reflected lust.

"What are you wearing?"

"Do you like it?" I inquired coyly.

The question earned me a devilish grin. "You're about to find out, my lady."

He divested of his clothing and joined me in bed. Ferrante's lovemaking was passionate yet tender. He whispered my name in his final thrust and held me tightly afterward.

"You please me more than I could have hoped, but I fear that admitting this to you will be to my detriment," he confessed, his breath tickling my neck.

"On the contrary, my lord. Your honest proclamation tempts me to be yours in mind and heart, as well as body."

Leaning up on his elbows, he studied my face with a serious expression. "Are you telling me the truth, Celeste? For I hold honesty as the highest of moral traits."

Glimpsing fear in his eyes, I replied, "Do I strike you as the type of woman who would toy with a man's heart?"

"No, at least not deliberately."

"I know you've been wounded in the past."

"Don't—"

I stopped.

"I want my past to die and for my life to begin anew with you." When I nodded in agreement, he kissed my cheek. "I'll leave you to your rest now."

"Stay," I purred, running my hand along his chest.

"Another night," he said, throwing back the covers.

I scrambled out of bed too.

Puzzled, he demanded, "Where are you going?"

I went over to the desk and held out the letter I had written last night. "Take this with you."

His eyes lingered on my naked body before accepting the sheet from my hand. "What's this?"

"My reply to your mistress."

He appeared stricken. "Reply?"

I held up Paola's note. "She slipped this under my door while we supped last night, so I'm hoping you will entrust my response into her hands."

Ferrante read my words aloud. *"I have never made but one prayer to God, a very short one: 'O Lord make my enemies ridiculous.' And God granted it."*

Silence ensued as he gaped at me wearing an unreadable expression. Was he shocked? Angry? Had I gone too far?

To break the tension, I shrugged and said lightly, "Voltaire's wisdom never fails."

At that, he laughed slightly then sobered. "The situation with Paola is complicated and I ask that you be patient."

Closing the gap between us, I reached up and placed my hand against his cheek. "I know better than to make demands on a man like you."

He kissed me hard on the mouth then left the room.

***

I sat reading peacefully in the formal garden the following morning until a noise caused me to glance up from my page. I spotted a woman in a large straw hat several feet away. Recognizing her at once, I stood and braced myself for the inevitable confrontation.

Clad in a floral gown boasting several layers of lace, Paola Colombo came to a stop before me. She drew herself up to her full height, which was just short of my own. Arranging my face into a neutral mask, I took in her plump figure and blonde curls. Although her plain features were cleverly enhanced by cosmetics, I judged her to be at least ten years older than me.

Adjusting the costly lace at her sleeve, she said pleasantly, "Signora Celeste, good day. I received your message and I believe the time has come for me to introduce myself."

"Save yourself the trouble."

Dark blue eyes regarded me with disdain. "In that case, I'll be brief. I've known Ferrante for most of my life and he cares for me more than you can imagine."

"I don't doubt that."

"If you're intention is to pry him away from me, don't waste your time."

"I may lack experience, Signora Paola, but I'm no fool. Ferrante is a powerful man, as you well know, whereas I'm only a girl. I can't control anything *my husband* does, so you can rest assured that whatever decision he makes where you are concerned will be of his own accord."

She fixed me with a cold stare. "You seem quite self-assured for one so naïve in the ways of men."

Recalling my husband's sweet kisses from the previous night, I smiled dreamily. "Ferrante has given me every reason to feel the way I do."

Paola narrowed her eyes at me in jealous anger. "*Everything is fine today, that is our illusion.* As you can see, I am also quite capable of quoting Voltaire. In time, perhaps even *you* can develop enough wit to formulate your own words instead of stealing them from the lips of others."

"I am eager to learn from *elders* such as yourself."

"How dare you?"

"You ask that question of *me*, madam?"

"I'm curious as to what kind of convent would produce such a sharp-tongued shrew."

Setting my book on the bench, I stood. "The kind that enforces God's laws, such as abstaining from fornication and adultery. Now, if you'll excuse me, I wish to enjoy my morning in peace."

I turned my back on the seething woman with a racing heart and headed toward the villa. My words had rushed from my lips without prior thought. Would they come back to haunt me?

Livia took me aside later that afternoon when she came over to the villa to dine with us. "How are things between you and my nephew?"

"Wonderful," I gushed.

"I'm most relieved."

"He took me to Herculaneum."

"I know. Who do you think suggested that little outing?"

"Thank you, Signora Livia. We enjoyed ourselves."

She smiled. "That's good. My nephew needs to have a bit of fun once in a while because he works hard. Maintaining a fortune isn't easy, you know. Ferrante owns various properties with tenants who work the land and care for his many animals. There are investments to oversee, supplies to be ordered, repairs to be made, allegiances to be forged…"

"I assumed he hired people for those tasks."

Her eyes widened. "Oh he does, but as master of a great estate, he must go over every single document. Nothing is done without his knowledge and consent."

"Hopefully, he'll delegate some tasks my way."

"Why would you desire such a tedious task, my dear?"

"I love him and wish to help him in any way that I can. Isn't that what a good wife is supposed to do?"

Her gaze softened in the wake of my confession. "That gladdens my heart, for he deserves the love of a good woman."

"I hate to bring up an unpleasant matter, but I must tell you what happened this morning. Paola Colombo confronted me."

Her eyes instantly hardened. "What did she say to you?"

I repeated word for word the exchange in the garden.

"The fact that you stood up to her could be interpreted as a challenge," Livia concluded.

"Wouldn't the best solution be to find her a husband?"

"Without a doubt. I've recommended that option to Ferrante on several occasions." She turned her gaze to the window. "Paola is a willful, petty creature. *Be careful.*"

"Should I tell Ferrante about this?"

"Most definitely. In fact, if you don't then I will."

When Ferrante came to my bed that night, I told him about my confrontation with his mistress.

"Damn it," he cursed. "I'm sorry."

"There's no need for you to apologize, my lord. We were strangers until recently, and it would be foolish of me to believe that you didn't have a life—*and love*—before me."

"Paola and I grew up together. She is like one of the family. She was there for me when I had no one else. I never want to offend you, but I don't want to hurt a loyal friend either."

"Be kind," I urged, toying with the hair on his chest.

His brow creased. "I thought you were jealous of her."

"I am, but I would hate to be the cause of anyone's pain—even Paola's. Honestly, I can't blame her. She's in love with you and I've turned your head. If I were I in her shoes, I would fight to keep you too. Any woman would react like that."

"You are wise beyond your years, Celeste, which only makes you more desirable in my eyes. Also, you've done much more than merely turn my head."

"Whatever I know I've learned through reading books."

Grinning wickedly, he positioned his naked body over mine. "Books, you say? Have you read torrid novels?"

I replied breathlessly, "A few, yes."

He pried my legs apart. "And now you're the protagonist."

My arms slid around him. "Oh Ferrante…"

Burying his face in my neck, he confessed, "I love it when you say my name."

CHAPTER 13

I convinced Ferrante to allow me to visit the Convento of Santa Patrizia accompanied by Livia. It was only a pretense, of course, for my intention was to see my Aunt Gloria. Livia played along with my ruse with the implicit understanding that these outings would be few and far between.

Aunt Gloria was surprised to see me and offered her best curtsy to Livia. Donna Pasqualina was asleep in her room and Natalino wasn't home, affording us a private visit. My aunt poured her best liqueur for our pleasure. Livia said little as her eyes discreetly took in the humble home.

Conversation was limited to our health and the practical domestic wisdom shared between married women. I wanted to tell her about Celeste's betrayal and pregnancy, but I didn't want to discuss those things in Livia's presence. Why ruin the visit? To my immense delight, Aunt Gloria and Natalino were both enjoying marital bliss. I was too, for that matter. We stayed for only an hour and I squeezed Aunt Gloria tightly before returning home.

***

The seamstress completed the formal peacock blue gown in time for Raimondo di Sangro's soirée. Lisa took special care with my hair and applied cosmetics with a light hand to enhance my natural beauty. To my surprise, Ferrante entered my room while I was still at my toilette.

I stood from the vanity and twirled in a circle. "I love my dress. Thank you."

He presented me with a small box. "You look splendid, my lady. Here, I thought this would go nicely."

I lifted the lid and gasped at the exquisite sapphire and diamond necklace. "Oh."

"Do you like it?"

"It's gorgeous," I replied, throwing my arms around his neck and kissing his lips.

"Let me put it on you."

I shivered at the feel of my husband's fingertips against the bare skin of my nape.

"There," he said, turning me around to admire the necklace.

I went to the mirror. "It's perfect. You're so good to me."

Gathering me in his arms, he kissed me. Lisa discreetly left the room to afford us a measure of privacy.

Livia arrived at the villa shortly afterward. The moment she laid eyes on me, she plied me with lavish compliments.

The balmy evening held the promise of excitement as I entered the carriage with the help of my husband.

"This is your first social event as a married woman," Livia whispered in my ear as I settled beside her on the seat.

"I'm thrilled, Signora Livia."

The carriage sped toward the Palazzo di Sangro, a Renaissance-style palace facing the Gothic church of San Domenico Maggiore. Originally built in the sixteenth century, the stately palace was designed by Giovanni da Nola.

Livia said, "Everyone will be curious to meet you, Celeste. Don't worry, stay close to me."

Never having attended such a grand affair, I felt giddy. Ferrante sensed it too and winked at me as we alighted from the carriage. Several lanterns lit up the entryway leading upstairs to the main ballroom.

A highly polished parquet floor gleamed beneath the light of dozens of candles. Oriental vases brimmed with early blossoms, infusing the room with a fresh scent. Lords and ladies in their finery moved and chatted about the space, making me feel instantly self-conscious.

True to Livia's words, many sets of eyes were drawn to us as we entered the room. Raimondo and Carlotta greeted us at the door.

"Welcome to my home, Signora Celeste," Raimondo said before kissing my hand in greeting. To Livia, he added, "Signora, your presence lifts my spirits."

"Your Highness," Livia said with a curtsy.

More guests were arriving, so we made our way past the gracious hosts to mingle with others. Ladies studied my gown and newly-acquired jewels with piqued interest. Since most of them believed that I had been selected from a convent, I kept my eyes lowered out of modesty.

Ferrante stood conversing with Raimondo while Livia and I remained off to the side. The men spoke of finances and politics.

At one point, Raimondo glanced at me. "Celeste, do you enjoy sculpture?"

"Very much," I replied, grateful for his kind attempt to include me in the conversation.

"Then you must see the *Veiled Christ* that was created for me by Giuseppe Sanmartino."

"I'll be sure to show it to her," Ferrante promised while casually placing his hand at the small of my back. "What about the anatomical forms?"

"If you'll recall, I recently commissioned Giuseppe Salerno to place the male and female under glass domes," Raimondo replied.

"I remember, yes."

"He's completed the task and did a fine job of it too. I've planned an unveiling after dinner."

I had no idea what anatomical forms were, but I was eager to find out. To my irritation, Livia excused herself and led me away to introduce me to a few ladies. Peeking over my shoulder at the men, I longed to hear what they were saying.

"Signora Mirella has been dying to meet you, Celeste," Livia said.

I plastered a smile onto my face as she introduced me to a group of noble matrons. I prudently listened much and spoke little for the better part of an hour.

To my immense relief, Ferrante came over to me and took my hand. "Dance with me, for the love of God, or my aunt will never let me hear the end of it on the way home."

I giggled. "Is that any way to ask a lady to dance?"

"I hate dancing."

"I've never danced."

Glancing at the couples twirling in the center of the parquet floor, he said, "This dance is simple. Come. Let's show my aunt how it's done, shall we?"

He led me toward the center of the room and I did my best to mimic his movements under Livia's watchful eye. I found that it wasn't as difficult as I thought. Before long, I was laughing and having fun.

We eventually stopped after several tunes and I noticed many sets of eyes tracking us across the room.

"Where is my aunt?" Ferrante inquired.

"There. She is engaged in conversation with a group of old women."

"Stay close to me and you'll be spared the same dreary fate."

I found his wry humor refreshing. Slipping my hand into his, I said, "I'll remain *very* close."

"Now you're being wicked, my little temptress."

The buffet dinner provided by the prince offered lobster, oysters, shrimp, fish, broiled pheasant, stuffed guinea fowls, and tender roast beef. Delicate pastries, luscious cakes, airy soufflés, and fine wines delighted the palate.

People whispered and stared as my husband and I giggled between nibbles.

"I think we're being watched," I pointed out.

He didn't even bother to look. "No one has ever seen me so happy. In fact, I'll wager that the majority of the people here have never witnessed me crack a smile. I've even heard that I wear a permanent scowl. Didn't you know? I'm a monster."

I took a piece of lobster meat from my plate and fed it to him. He bit my fingers lightly, causing me to gasp. Taking my hand, he kissed my fingertips while eyeing me in a manner that almost caused my knees to buckle.

"Rumors will fly after tonight, my lady."

"I don't care," I shot back, my eyes glued to his.

Later that evening, Raimondo led us to a private room that he referred to as the *Apartment of the Phoenix*.

Standing before the closed door, he turned toward his guests and said, “As many of you know, I purchased Giuseppe Salerno’s male Anatomical Machine four years ago, then hired him to create a female version. I have also commissioned two glass cases, allowing for public viewing.”

Everyone began speaking at once and someone hushed the crowd into silence.

With a dramatic wave of his arm, Raimondo opened the door. “Behold! *Macchine Anatomiche.*”

People gasped aloud in shock as they rushed into the space. Two human skeletons, one male and one female, stood erect behind giant glass panes. Their veins and arteries, as well as their organs, were preserved and on display for everyone to see. A tiny fetus in the open placenta rested at the feet of the female form, connected by the umbilical cord.

One woman fainted.

Ferrante watched me carefully as my eyes traced the blood vessels of the male’s head to those of his tongue. “Are you all right, Celeste?”

“Who are they?” I whispered.

Placing his lips to my ear, he replied, “The remains of two of Raimondo’s servants.”

“They’re amazing…”

Livia clicked open her fan to hide the disquieting forms from her view. “Dear God, how dreadful.”

The more I stared at the anatomical forms, the more intriguing I found them. “The veins and organs appear to be solid, as if coated in wax. Look at the preservation of the heart…it’s incredible. How is there no decomposition?”

The prince fixed me with a surprised look. “Excellent question, Signora Celeste. Tell me, do you like them?”

“Very much, my lord.”

Raimondo chuckled. “See? Not all members of the weaker sex are prone to squeamishness.”

To my dismay, I noticed several women either hiding behind their fans or turning their eyes away from the anatomical forms. The men stared at me in a manner that made me uneasy, including my husband.

Raimondo extended his hand to me. "Would you care to come closer?"

I accepted his invitation without hesitation and stood before the figures so that I could better inspect them. In honesty, I longed to touch them too. The prince waited for me to say something.

In a voice meant only for his ears, I said, "Only surgeons and soldiers ever glimpse the innards of humans. This is a privilege…a peek at the divine. Thank you for this, my lord."

Raimondo eyed me incredulously. Feeling the fire in my cheeks, I lowered my head to study the bones of the female's foot. I admit, seeing a fetus disturbed me but only a little bit. My curiosity far outweighed any repulsion or fear.

"In answer to your initial question, Signora Celeste, I aided the surgeon who made these by developing a solution that could be injected into the veins to prevent decomposition."

Men began crowding around me to get a closer look, compelling me to retreat to Livia's side. Ferrante said nothing but I saw that his mouth formed a hard line. Clusters of women stood out in the corridor chatting with each other while their men remained in the *Apartment of the Phoenix*.

Livia nudged me. "Perhaps we should join the ladies."

"Yes," I reluctantly agreed, for I wanted to remain with the men and hear their observations.

The moment we stepped into the corridor, the women abruptly stopped talking and stared at me in horror.

Leaning close to Livia, I whispered, "I'm afraid I've made a spectacle of myself."

"Not necessarily. You displayed curiosity and an interest in science, nothing more. The prince approves of you and that's what matters, my dear."

Although her words seemed reasonable, I felt that I would be marked after tonight. Perhaps it was for the best given that I was an impostor. The less interaction with people, the better.

Ferrante eventually exited the room and joined us. Taking hold of my elbow, he said, "Raimondo insists on showing you his laboratory."

"Really?"

Livia smirked when she saw the look on her nephew's unamused face. "Don't keep the prince waiting, Celeste."

Ferrante's disapproving silence made me anxious as he urged me toward Raimondo. Several sets of eyes turned my way as the prince led me to a studded door. Whispers exploded behind my back as the three of us stepped into the room.

Raimondo closed the door and said, "Ignore them, madam. They're all jealous. Feel free to roam but I ask that you refrain from touching anything."

"Thank you," I said, awestruck by what my eyes beheld.

The men lagged behind as I closed in on a pair of long wooden tables. I marveled at the many glass vials and oddly-shaped bottles filled with a variety of foul-smelling liquids. Mortars, pestles, long-handled spoons, metal shavings, roots, and powders drew my curious eyes. One wall was covered with shelves holding books and a variety of specimens under glass. I went over to them in order to study the display of insects, small animals and birds, dried human organs, and a pair of human skulls. I froze at the sight of a human brain. Intrigued, I leaned in to better study the intricate patterns on the gray glob floating in murky liquid. I turned around to find Raimondo and Ferrante staring at me with a mixture of surprise and apprehension on their faces.

"Well?" Raimondo prompted.

"Fascinating," I declared.

He nudged Ferrante, whose eyes never left my face. "See? I told you." To me, he added, "Few women have seen the inside of this room. Those who have, fled in disgust. *Except you.*"

I shrugged self-consciously. "Is that a bad thing?"

"It makes you rather unique, which is never a bad thing. What do you think, Ferrante?"

My husband smiled wryly. "My wife is full of surprises."

"May I ask you a question, Your Highness?" I waited for him to nod. "Did you use zinc sulphate to preserve the veins?"

"In addition to other ingredients, yes." Raimondo chuckled and nudged Ferrante again. "Well done, my friend. How many men have an alchemist for a wife?"

Ferrante's wan smile prompted me to shake my head. "I know very little about alchemy, sir."

"Have you ever performed experiments, Signora Celeste?"

"No."

Raimondo eyed me indulgently. "No or not yet?"

The prince chuckled at his own joke.

"Don't encourage her," Ferrante murmured.

"Come, let's join the rest of the guests, shall we?" Raimondo said, indicating the door.

We left the room and I went straight to Livia's side.

She smiled wryly. "Your name is on everyone's lips."

"I think Ferrante is angry with me."

"My nephew hates it when attention is focused on him, and you are an extension of him."

"Oh dear…"

"Your innocence and naiveté are forgivable sins."

"I hope you're right, Signora Livia."

"Leave Ferrante to me."

We said our goodbyes shortly afterward. Tense silence filled the carriage as the horses pulled the vehicle in the direction toward home.

At length, Ferrante turned to me and said, "You certainly captured Raimondo's interest."

"It wasn't my intention," I protested.

Livia added, "Don't be unreasonable, Ferrante. Those anatomical figures were quite shocking."

"Other women didn't make spectacles of themselves," he shot back.

"No," she agreed. "They've had *years* of practice at being artful deceivers. Your wife is refreshingly honest."

"I'm sorry, Ferrante," I offered.

He sighed, then gripped my hand and brought it to his lips. "No…I'm sorry. My aunt is correct."

I smiled at him. "The last thing I ever want to do is cause you displeasure, *my darling*."

He kissed my hand again at the sound of my endearment.

The carriage dropped Livia off at her front door before taking us home. Our late arrival to the villa prompted Ferrante to bid me goodnight and go straight to bed. Tired, I went straight to my room too.

***

My visit with Nadia proved brief the next day, for the child was fussy due to an earache. Armed with a pile of books, I went to my studio to try and whip up a curative. I spent the remainder of the morning reading several entries on the probable causes of earaches and the remedies conducive to easing pain.

After the midday meal, I collected what I needed from the garden and returned to my studio. I began grinding various roots into powder.

At the sound of a knock, I stopped. "Enter."

Sandro poked his head into the room. "Forgive the disturbance, my lady."

I regarded him expectantly. "Yes?"

"You have a visitor." At my frown, he added, "A young woman wishes to speak with you privately and refused to give her name or be announced."

My stomach sank. "Where is she?"

"By the front gate. She wouldn't come inside no matter how much I tried to persuade her." He glanced over his shoulder. "If you'll excuse me, I am needed in the kitchen."

"Of course."

I rushed outside and found a cloaked figure lingering by the gate. Thankfully, she was hidden by a row of old cypress trees.

Throwing back the brown hood covering her head, Celeste gaped at me. "Look at you!"

I stared back at her, stunned. "What are you doing here?"

"Is that any way to greet a friend?"

"Forgive me." I embraced her, then said, "It's good to see you but you shouldn't have come. If Ferrante sees you—"

"Marriage has obviously agreed with you," she interjected, her eyes sweeping over me with a hint of envy. "You look well, Valentina. Radiant, in fact. Does he treat you kindly?"

"He's generous and solicitous toward me."

"So, the rumors about him aren't true?"

"For the most part, no."

"In that case, I've done you a great service."

"While that may be true, it is I who did you the great service," I gently reminded her. "Fate smiled upon me."

Celeste's eyes filled with tears. "And frowned upon me."

"What do you mean?"

"Luigi…"

When she trailed off, I said, "He's the father of the child growing inside of you, is he not?"

Her eyes grew wide. "How do you know?"

"Livia told me everything. Sister Assunta knows too."

"What?"

"She came to the house in a desperate state to inquire if I had received word from you. The poor woman was so distraught. Why did you lie to us, Celeste?"

Her expression turned guilty. "Luigi swore me to silence."

"Sister Assunta loves you like a daughter. She said that you ran away in the middle of the night."

"How could I possibly have told her the truth?"

"You could have told *me* the truth. I'm your best friend, remember?"

Taking my hand, she whimpered. "I wanted too…I really did. I'm so sorry."

I shook my head sadly. "What have you done?"

"I fell in love."

"Love comes with a price."

"Do you love Ferrante?"

"Yes."

Letting go of my hand, she frowned. "It certainly worked out for the best in your case, didn't it?" She waved her hand toward the villa. "Behold your fine home, your gown and costly jewels…I did you a favor, Valentina. The least you can do is repay me."

I bristled. "Exactly how would I do that?"

"Help me." Rubbing her slightly swollen belly, she added, "Luigi and I have to find a home in which to raise our child.

We've been staying with his sister but…"

"I don't have any money."

"Your husband does," she snapped.

"I don't have access to his funds."

"Can't you ask him for some?"

I stared at her incredulously. "You're placing me in a difficult position, for I'll need to come up with a convincing lie in order for him to give me money."

"You're already lying to him every day so what's one more act of dishonesty?"

The callous manner in which she said this stung me. "I can't, Celeste. I'm sorry."

"Can't or won't?"

"Ferrante is no fool."

Her eyes shifted from my face to my ear. "Those silver earrings are lovely. Heavy too. I'm sure they would fetch a tidy sum if you tried to sell them."

"Aunt Gloria gifted these to me on my wedding day."

She quirked an eyebrow. "You mean *my* wedding day."

Appalled by her comment, I said nothing.

She continued, "Please Valentina, I beg you. I only need a little bit to get us through the next few weeks, and then he'll find work. Luigi is a good and honest man. You would like him if you met him."

Not wishing to argue, I removed my earrings and placed them in her hand. "Here. Now go before someone sees you."

Celeste hugged me and kissed my cheek. "I knew I could count on you, my best and dearest friend! I hope our paths cross again soon under better circumstances."

"I hope so too."

Placing the hood over her head, she waved at me and picked her way down the drive. I held my breath until she was out of sight, then made my way back to the studio. I pinched my bare earlobes, saddened by the fact that Aunt Gloria's gift was now gone forever.

I tried to occupy my mind with work but Celeste's visit kept coming back to haunt me. It was the first time during our entire friendship that she had made me feel uneasy. Hopefully, the money from the earrings would help her and Luigi make a decent start.

Will she be back for more? What if she resorts to blackmail?

The mere thought brought me to the verge of panic.

By mid-afternoon, I had created a curative for Nadia that I hoped would work. I was in the process of cleaning up when a shadow fell over the surface of the table. Raising my head, I found Ferrante staring at me from the open doorway. I had left the door open earlier in order to rid the space of the foul smell caused by the boiling of various roots.

"Busy, busy," he commented.

"I've been creating a curative for your daughter. She complained of an earache."

"She gets them often."

"Stomach aches too."

"I'll summon the physician."

"Let me try this first," I suggested, holding up the bottle I had filled a moment ago.

"Very well." He entered the studio, closing the door behind him. "You seem to enjoy this space."

"I do. Thank you again for letting me have it."

His gaze swept over me in a provocative manner. "I think you should show me your appreciation."

Accepting the challenge, I slid my arms around his neck and pecked his lips. "You are the most generous husband in the world. Handsome and sweet too."

Ferrante angled his body toward mine and gave me a proper kiss. I soon felt my husband's mounting desire through the layers of my gown. We staggered toward the table, our lips locked together. Lifting me by the waist, he sat me on top of the table with my back to the windows. Slowly, he raised my skirts and slid his hands up the insides of my thighs. I gave myself to him eagerly, matching his passion with my own.

Clinging to me afterward, he whispered into my ear, "You drive me mad, woman."

"Is that a bad thing, my lord?"

"As long as you truly love me, the answer is no," he replied before holding me close.

His sincere reply revealed his vulnerability. In that instant, I was overwhelmed by guilt. How would this man react if he knew the truth about me? Would he cast me aside? Pushing the disturbing thoughts to the back of my mind, I returned his embrace. "I love you, Ferrante. Of that, you can be sure."

No sooner had I said those words than a brick crashed through one of the windows. Glass shards exploded onto the tiled floor, making me cry out in fear.

"What the devil?" Ferrante cursed, untangling himself from my embrace and adjusting his clothing.

I slid off the edge of the table as my husband threw open the door. "Be careful!"

I ran outside to where he stood scanning the area. A faint trace of sweet perfume lingered in the air. We both knew who threw that brick.

"Damn it," Ferrante said.

I placed my hand on his shoulder and said nothing.

He took my hand and squeezed it. "I will resolve this problem as quickly as possible, I promise."

"I know you will," I assured him in the most convincing tone I could muster.

CHAPTER 14

Ferrante surprised me the next day by joining me for the midday meal.

Taking a seat at the dining table, he said, "The servants are fixing the window of your studio this afternoon. In the meantime, I have a surprise planned for you."

"Will you give me a clue?"

"You will be very pleased."

After the meal, he led me upstairs to the door with the seven alchemic symbols. I could barely contain my excitement.

Opening the door, he said, "My lady."

I ventured into the brightly lit space and turned around in a slow circle. Although smaller than Raimondo's laboratory, it was no less impressive. Windows overlooking the hillside and Naples Bay lined one wall. The rest of the walls hosted shelves containing books, bottles of various specimens, vials of liquids and solids, skulls of humans and animals, old-looking scrolls, and plenty of plants.

I picked up one of the skulls. "Ape?"

"Chimpanzee, yes."

I set it down and placed my hand atop another. "Crocodile?"

"Correct."

Ferrante moved to stand behind me and his nearness distracted me. "What are you working on now?"

"Oh, this and that," he replied cryptically.

Not wishing to pry, I refrained from asking questions. I noticed an open journal on the table and attempted to discreetly read the neatly jotted notes. Seeing this, Ferrante casually shut the book and led me to a shelf full of plants.

"Feel free to take what you need for your curatives," he said, handing me a pair of shears.

I glimpsed chamomile and aloe vera, so I helped myself.

Unfortunately, we didn't dally long in his laboratory

because he had work to do. I left him alone and went downstairs to my studio where I placed the plant snippets in water. Tomorrow morning, I would plant them in the herb garden.

***

In an attempt to transform base metals into gold, Boyle wrote that one of history's first alchemists had discovered how to isolate the element of phosphorous by distilling vast amounts of horse urine. My interest in alchemy stemmed from my love of nature, philosophy, and spirituality. Alchemy encompassed mysticism with physics, and medicine with art. The secret of purifying base metals into gold could lead to the purification of the human soul. The ultimate goal, however, was to procure the elixir of life, or rather, immortality.

Naturally, my goals were not as lofty since I considered myself a mere aficionada of the subject—not an expert.

I was contemplating these matters during my morning toilette when Lisa mentioned that Genaro Biancatesta was expected to dine with my husband later in the evening.

At my blank expression, she inquired, "You've never heard of him?"

"No."

"Captain Biancatesta owns a merchant ship. He's wealthy but his reputation is questionable."

Meeting her eyes in the mirror's reflection, I demanded, "Why is he coming here?"

"May I speak freely, madam?"

"Always."

"I overheard Donna Florinda speaking with Sandro about tonight's dinner preparations. It seems that his lordship is attempting to arrange a marriage between Signora Paola and the captain."

Relief swept over me. "That's good news."

"I thought so too, Signora Celeste, if you don't mind me saying so."

"I don't mind at all."

I went to see Nadia a bit later, only to discover that the child was suffering another stomach ache.

I was in my studio by mid-morning, crushing fennel seeds with my mortar and pestle. To my surprise, Raimondo passed by the window. Seeing me, he smiled and opened the door.

I set down the pestle and curtsied. "Your Highness, good day. What a delightful surprise to see you."

Touching his plumed tricorn hat, he smiled. "My lady."

"My husband has not yet returned from his morning ride, but he should be back soon. Was he expecting you, my lord?"

"No," he replied, wandering throughout the space and surveying everything with keen eyes. "Ferrante mentioned that you now have your own laboratory."

"Studio," I corrected.

"I stand corrected. He did indeed use the word *studio*." Coming to a stop behind me, he peered down over my shoulder. "What's in the mortar?"

"Foeniculum vulgare."

"Fennel seeds," he said, interpreting the Latin words. "I'm sure one of the servants would grind that up for you."

I shrugged. "I don't mind. Nadia has been complaining of stomach aches so I'm making a tonic. Berta has been giving her gripe water. Poor child."

"Have you grown fond of Nadia?"

"I have."

Raimondo smiled. "I'm sure she is fond of you too."

"I believe so."

"I've brought you a gift," he said, extracting a book from the pocket of his fine coat.

I accepted the small book bound in dark green fabric. "What a fine gift, thank you."

"Are you familiar with Paracelsus?"

I nodded as my brow creased in thought. "If my memory serves me well, he was German. Correct?"

"Swiss, fifteenth century. He was a surgeon who became the first toxicologist."

"I see," I said, examining the book with renewed interest.

"Paracelsus had an interesting theory. Mercury, sulfur, and salt are the three controlling substances that must be balanced.

He believed that our bodies, our organs, worked in an alchemical manner, separating the pure from the impure. He called this maintenance of balance the *tria prima,* and insisted upon it for good health."

"Interesting. I look forward to learning about him and his theories."

"Normally, I gift books of prose and poetry to the ladies whom I admire. You do more than curry my admiration, Celeste. You pique my curiosity."

"You flatter me, my lord."

The door opened and Ferrante stood in the doorway. He looked from me to the prince, then said, "Raimondo, how long have you been here?"

"I arrived only a moment ago, my friend." Indicating the book in my hand, Raimondo added, "I also wanted to gift your wife a book from my library. Remember Paracelsus?"

Ferrante's eyes met mine. "I'm sure Celeste will enjoy it."

Raimondo kissed my hand in parting. "As always, it's been a pleasure, my lady."

I watched him go with my husband. Ferrante would never object to my reading choices now that Raimondo has shown his approval of me. The prince had done me a great service, one that I would never forget.

I worked throughout the remainder of the morning and went inside before noon. The dining room was empty, so I turned to one of the servants. It was the same young man who had been kind to me in the past.

I inquired, "What is your name?"

"Riccardo, madam."

I couldn't help noticing that one of his eyes was half gold and half gray. Obviously accustomed to female attention, he made no attempt to avert his gaze. "Will his lordship and the prince be joining me for luncheon today?"

"No, madam. They left for the city center a moment ago. Your husband instructed me to relay a message to you."

"Go on."

"His lordship will be back by suppertime with a dinner

guest, but has requested that you remain in your quarters. One of the servants will send a tray to your room."

Lisa was right, I thought. "Thank you for relaying the message."

"My pleasure," he said before serving my meal.

I supped alone that evening. After Lisa had helped me undress, I readied for bed and settled in with the book Raimondo had given me. Reading became an impossibility due to the raucous male laughter coming from downstairs. The gruff voice did not belong to my husband, but rather Genaro Biancatesta. Shutting the book, I decided to do a bit of spying. Holding a candle aloft, I crept out into the corridor and stood at the head of the stairs so that I could glean snippets of their conversation.

"My last wife died in childbirth."

"I'm sorry to hear it."

"I swore I would never marry again. Women are more trouble than what they're worth."

"I agree, but a man should have a wife."

"Having a bed companion is pleasant, I admit."

"What about children? Don't you want a family?"

"How old did you say Paola was?"

"She is still within her childbearing years.

"Like your bonny young wife?"

"Yes, only a tad bit older."

I frowned at my husband's lie, for Paola was at least a decade my senior. I reminded myself that he was trying to sell the woman to the ship merchant, whom I believed to be rather inebriated judging by his slurred words.

"When will I get to meet her?"

"Paola will be joining us in the salon later this evening."

Genaro lowered his voice then roared in laughter. I heard my husband's forced chuckle and concluded that his guest had said something crude. Cringing inwardly, I returned to my room and went to bed.

***

I awoke the next morning feeling less burdened. Perhaps it

was because Paola would soon be out of my life. *Forever.*

I left my bedroom after breaking my fast to find my husband standing at the head of the stairs. "Good day, my lord. Why aren't you out riding?"

"I wanted to share some good news with you. I dined with Captain Genaro Biancatesta yesterday. He has agreed to marry Paola at my behest. What's more, he lives in Sicily. She will be forced to move there with him."

"Excellent news. Has she agreed to this plan?"

He hesitated. "Not yet."

Not wanting to reveal that I had been eavesdropping last night, I inquired, "Did the captain get the chance to meet with his intended?"

"He did."

"Did she not like him?"

"She found him attractive and wealthy enough…"

"But…?"

"She has requested time to ponder his proposal."

"A woman of her age doesn't have the luxury of time if she wishes to bear children," I pointed out.

"I realize that. I will try to convince her to marry the man."

I refrained from asking details despite being curious as to when and where his conversation with Paola would take place. "I'm about to visit Nadia. Why don't you come with me?"

"I never visit her in the mornings."

"All the more reason to do so. She'll be surprised."

"I need to resolve this issue."

"You can spend the remainder of the day doing that." Taking hold of his hand, I tried to pull him toward me. Naturally, I lacked the strength. "A brief visit with your daughter will lift your mood."

He indulged my request and we both made our way to Nadia's quarters hand in hand. To our mutual astonishment, the toddler squealed in delight at the sight of us. First she ran to hug my legs, then she included her father's legs.

Ferrante scooped her up effortlessly into his burly arms and kissed her face. "Hello, my angel."

Nadia smiled at him, causing him to melt.

"She's never been so happy to see me," he said, perplexed.

"That's because she's never seen *you* so happy. Children are extremely sensitive to our moods."

He pecked my lips. "Maybe you're right."

My eyes slid to Nadia, who watched us intently. "Am I right, little one? Can you sense Papa's joy?"

"Papa."

Ferrante and I stared at Nadia in shock.

Berta, who stood off to the side, crossed herself. "Santo Cristo! She spoke!"

"Nadia, say it again," Ferrante prompted.

"Papa," she repeated.

He spun her around in a circle, causing the toddler to screech with excitement. Nadia then reached for me and patted my cheek with her plump little hand.

"Cewest."

I gaped at the child. "That's right, sweetheart."

Ferrante's eyes glistened, and the sight of his bliss brought tears to my own eyes. The fact that he was a loving father to his daughter made him even more attractive to me.

"Papa, Cewest."

"The Lord has answered my prayers," he whispered while holding Nadia close. "Thank you, God."

"Perhaps we should notify the physician," Berta suggested.

"A fine idea," Ferrante agreed, gazing at his daughter with wonder. "Summon him at once."

Berta turned to me and said, "By the way, my lady, that tonic is working wonders. No more stomach aches."

"Remember, only a teaspoonful."

We left Nadia a moment later, both of us feeling elated.

"She's not mute," I said once we were in the hallway.

Ferrante leaned against the wall and sighed in relief. "Thank you, Celeste."

"For what?"

"You're wonderful with Nadia and I believe you've brought her out of her shell. She's no longer afraid to speak."

"*You* prompted Nadia's words," I assured him. "You're a changed man."

"How so?"

"For one thing, you're not always scowling as you were when I first arrived here."

"Did I scowl often?"

"Most of the time, yes."

"You exaggerate."

"I do not. Nadia was probably afraid of upsetting you."

He pondered my words for a moment, then said, "I believed her muteness was due to the shock she had suffered from having been lost in the forest."

"That may have been part of it."

"The important thing is that she has the ability to speak."

I touched his cheek. "That's the only thing that matters. Today is a blessed day, my lord."

"It is, indeed." He kissed my forehead. "I shall see you later, my lady."

I watched him go, then went directly to my studio to distill some of the herbs that I had picked yesterday afternoon. Working quietly and efficiently, I was soon lost in my thoughts. Ferrante dominated them, of course. Like the moon, I revolved around his world. Each day revealed a different facet of him for me to explore.

While the boiled herbs cooled, I made a posy of dried lavender for Nadia. Tying it with a pink ribbon, I smiled to myself. Today would be a day of celebration. I would ask Donna Florinda to prepare Nadia's favorite meal and maybe bake a cake, then we would enjoy our luncheon together.

A fast-moving blur outside the window caught my eye, making me pause in my task. The door swung open abruptly, banging against the wall in the process. Sporting violet silk and pearls, Paola glared at me from the open doorway.

Eyeing her warily, I set down the flowers and demanded, "What do you want?"

"I bet you fancy yourself clever," she said, sauntering up to the table. "It was your idea to marry me off, wasn't it?"

"Actually, no."

"Liar," she spat, grabbing hold of the lavender posy and throwing it at me. "Getting rid of me won't be so easy."

I calmly picked up the tiny bouquet and set it back on the table. "As I've said before, I have nothing to do with Ferrante's decisions where you are concerned."

She sneered at me. "The sound of his Christian name on your lips repulses me."

"I'll remind you that he *is* my husband."

"Only because you are of noble blood. Otherwise, he would be mine."

Her words pierced my soul. Born of a noble father, Paola had a greater claim to Ferrante than I did. My peasant blood would never have landed me a man like him. In that instant, I felt lower than an insect.

You are a fraud, Valentina.

Seeing my guilty face, the astute woman narrowed her eyes. "You're hiding something from him, aren't you?"

Ferrante loomed in the doorway, startling us both. "Paola!"

"I'm having a lovely conversation with your wife," she said coyly with a sidelong glance in my direction.

He darted into the studio and took hold of her arm. "Come away. Her ladyship has nothing to do with this."

Blonde curls bounced as she whipped around to face him. "Oh no? Why are you sending me away?"

He sighed tiredly. "You know why."

"Let's discuss it openly, in front of your wife."

"No."

"Has she become so *precious* to you in this short period of time that you can't risk upsetting her?" Pointing at me, she added, "You believe she's an innocent angel due to her youth. You're wrong. You don't know her!"

"Neither do you," he snapped.

"She's keeping secrets, Ferrante."

He frowned in outrage. "How dare you?"

"A cloaked figure recently came to the villa. I saw your wife consorting with the person at the gate in a furtive manner. In fact, the two of them were hiding behind the tall bushes."

My heart raced and my face burned at her accusation.

Ferrante stared at me. "Is this true?"

Visibly offended, Paola interjected, "Must you confer with her? I have never lied to you, my darling."

"It's true," I replied. "One of my former companions from the convent came to see me. She's incredibly shy."

Paola laughed derisively. "Do you honestly expect us to believe that? Why didn't you invite your friend inside rather than lurk about?"

"I did invite her inside. She wouldn't enter the villa due to her vow of poverty. Displays of wealth are offensive to those who sacrifice for Christ."

As they both stared at me, I silently prayed that my lie was convincing enough to appease them.

Finally, Ferrante demanded, "Why didn't you tell me?"

I shrugged. "It slipped my mind. It wasn't important."

Paola narrowed her eyes at me. "She's lying."

Tightening his hold on her arm, he said, "You're forgetting your place."

She grabbed his coat collar. "My perception is as keen as a honed blade. You know I'm never wrong."

"This time, you are," he said icily.

Tears streamed down her face. "Don't send me away."

"Let's talk outside, shall we?"

Balling her hands into fists, she cried, "No!"

I spied Sandro outside watching the scene with a concerned expression.

Ferrante sighed. "Captain Biancatesta is a wealthy man who can provide—"

"I don't care!"

Paola screamed this last sentence in my husband's face while stomping her feet like a six year old.

"Stop it," he said through clenched teeth.

"You sought my bed like a stud in heat when Caterina was alive. Now that you have *her* you wish to cast me aside. It's not fair. You're *mine*."

The unmistakable contempt in her eyes when she looked at me evoked a shiver.

Seeing my shock, my husband grabbed the distraught woman's arm and marched her outside. Although he closed the door, I could still overhear their words.

"How can you do this to me, Ferrante? I thought you loved me...Oh God, I still love you!"

"We both need to move on with our lives. Biancatesta is a good man. Don't you want a family of your own? A home?"

"Not with him! Let me stay here with you, my darling."

"That's not possible."

"You've found someone prettier and younger, but she can't possibly love you as much as I do. What can that naïve girl offer you? She's practically a child!"

"Stop insulting my wife."

"You haven't visited my bed in a while..."

As sickened as I felt in that moment, I reminded myself that Paola and Ferrante had a long history together. My husband was doing his best to appease two women simultaneously, which was no easy task even under the best of circumstances.

Peering through the window, I glimpsed Sandro hovering by his master. The shouting no doubt drew him downstairs in case Ferrante required his services. I waved to get his attention.

Seeing this, Sandro slipped into the studio. "Madam, are you all right?"

"Would you please escort me inside?"

"It would be my pleasure," he said, holding out his arm.

The valet physically shielded me from the arguing pair, then led me into the house.

Once inside, I locked myself in my room and stood by the window where I could discreetly watch them. I couldn't hear the words, but I saw Paola unravel. She sank to the ground in a heap of tears and cried in desperation. In that moment, I felt a pang of guilt and asked God's forgiveness.

Chapter 15

The next morning dawned as gray as my mood. Ferrante and I had supped quietly the previous evening before retiring early to our separate quarters. Unsurprisingly, I slept poorly.

I slipped upstairs to spend some time with Nadia. The child lifted my mood and kept me distracted until it was time for her nap. I tried reading in my room but my mind refused to cooperate. Setting down the book, I walked over to the window. Tiny droplets of rain clung to the panes, blurring the world outside.

At noon I went downstairs expecting to eat the midday meal with my husband. I hadn't seen Ferrante the entire morning, so I assumed he had forgone his ride due to the inclement weather. When he didn't join me in the dining room, I grew curious.

Sandro emerged from one of the rooms, so I went over to him. "Did my husband go riding this morning?"

"No, my lady. His lordship rose early, dressed hastily, and left. He has not yet returned."

"Where did he go?"

The valet shrugged but his eyes revealed otherwise.

"Doesn't he normally tell you where he's going?"

He hesitated. "Yes, but…"

"Where do you think he is? You know him better than anyone else."

Averting his gaze, he said, "I'm sure he'll return soon."

"He's with Paola, isn't he?" When Sandro didn't reply, I added, "I'm not stupid. You saw what happened yesterday."

"Madam, you know my loyalty lies with the master of this house, but I would wager that you are correct in your assumption. Unfortunately, I don't know his lordship's whereabouts at the moment."

My stomach lurched. "Thank you, Sandro."

"Shall I summon Lisa to attend to you?"

I shook my head and wandered to the window. The valet lingered a moment longer, then left me alone. Rain came down hard and I visually traced rivulets on the glass panes.

Ferrante's distance yesterday during supper had been the culprit for my lack of sleep. A disturbing possibility popped into my head: *maybe he didn't go to his room last night.* What if Paola had succeeded in luring him back into her bed? That would certainly explain his avoidance of me today. Images of my lustful husband and his naked mistress frolicking amid twisted sheets plagued me. The thought of her kissing him, caressing his skin…

Overcome by a wave of nausea, I placed my hand on the wall to steady myself. What if Paola had managed to convince him to allow her to stay at the villa? Would I be forced to share my husband with another woman? I knew it wasn't uncommon, but I found it distasteful. Hurtful.

Humiliating.

Catching sight of Livia's carriage pulling up the drive, I ran to the front door and threw it open. She descended from the carriage and hastened toward me.

Ushering her inside, I said, "It's not wise to travel in this weather, Signora Livia. I'll have the servants prepare some hot tea to warm you."

Gripping my arm, she looked past me and shouted, "Sandro! Sandro!"

The valet rushed into the foyer. "Madam?"

"His lordship will be spending the night in my home and so will you. Gather his clothing. He instructed you to take his horse. Go."

Sandro nodded to the command and scurried off to fulfill it.

"What happened?" I demanded, alarmed.

"You must come with me. *Now.*"

She dragged me outside into the rain and forced me into the carriage. Only when I sat across from Livia did I notice her trembling hands.

"Tell me what's going on, please."

"Paola…She…she stabbed Ferrante—" A cry escaped my

lips and her hand shot upward. "He's fine. I've already dispatched a servant to summon the physician."

"Santa Madonna," I whispered.

"They had a huge fight yesterday, it seems."

"I witnessed part of it."

"My nephew went out of his way to negotiate a good marriage for that trollop and this is how she repays him!"

"Paola blamed me for her plight."

Livia shook her head in disgust. "She showed up at my doorstep at dawn and dragged me into this ugly affair. She even threatened to hire a solicitor in order to claim her birthright through my late husband, which is absurd. Everyone knows she is illegitimate...Paola demanded to be recognized as a noblewoman in order to marry Ferrante."

"A scorned woman gone mad," I whispered.

"Exactly," she conceded before rubbing her temples. "After listening to her screech for a half hour, I sent a servant to fetch Ferrante. I believed his intervention would ease the tension...I was so wrong. The argument between my nephew and Paola escalated quickly. When he finally confessed his love for you, she came undone. He tried reasoning with her all morning. Alternating between fits of rage and tears, she eventually calmed down and listened to him. We thought she had finally accepted her fate until she extracted a dagger from her bodice."

"Dear God!"

"She placed the blade to her throat and threatened to kill herself. Naturally, Ferrante tried to soothe her with words. When that didn't work, he attempted to wrestle the weapon from her grasp. She fought him like a hellcat and ended up stabbing him." I crossed myself and Livia added, "I don't believe it was intentional."

"Where is she now?"

"I don't know. She became hysterical once she saw what she had done. She ran off screaming."

"Paola probably believes that she killed him."

"That's what I think too. Ferrante feared for your safety, so I left him in the care of my servants and came here."

A dull pain formed in the center of my chest and radiated toward my stomach. I tried to staunch the mounting anxiety to no avail. The moment the carriage stopped, I jumped out of the vehicle and ran into the house. I found my husband in the salon surrounded by Livia's staff, stripped to the waist, holding a bloodied cloth against his chest.

"Oh my love," I said, kneeling before him.

"Only a flesh wound," he assured me while touching my cheek. "The doctor is on his way to stitch me up."

"I'll make a salve the moment I get home."

"I don't want you out of my sight."

Livia rushed into the room. "Still no sign of Paola?"

"No, my lady," replied one of the servants.

"We must find her," Livia said to Ferrante. "She may hurt someone else in her deranged state of mind."

Ferrante's eyes lingered on my face. "I'm sorry for this mess, Celeste."

"This isn't your fault."

Livia said, "Paola must be held accountable for her actions."

"Are you going to notify the authorities?" I inquired.

Ferrante shook his head. "This will be handled privately. There are enough rumors attached to our family. Besides, I don't want to blemish your excellent reputation."

Livia's brow creased. "I'll dispatch armed servants to make a thorough sweep of both premises."

Sandro arrived and was directed to take Ferrante's clothing to the downstairs guestroom.

A moment later, the physician was shown into the room. Seeing me holding Ferrante's hand, the man appeared confused and looked to Livia for clarification.

She waved him over impatiently. "Dr. Bernardo, hurry. My nephew has been stabbed and needs your attention at once."

Dr. Bernardo moved aside the bloodied cloth to examine the extent of damage. "Who did this to you, my lord?"

"It was an accident," Ferrante replied.

The physician cocked an eyebrow. "It's a nasty cut but you'll live. I'll try to make the stitches small." Pointing to a servant, he added, "You there, get me a damp cloth. Make sure it's clean."

I let go of my husband's hand and went to stand beside Livia in order to give the man room to work. I watched as he cleaned the wound, then stitched together the two flaps of skin and flesh. Throughout this unpleasant ordeal, Ferrante sat perfectly still with his eyes closed. Although he didn't make a sound, beads of perspiration formed on his brow. He winced in pain when the physician pulled a bit harder on the string to complete the last stitch.

"Shall I make a tonic for the pain?" I asked.

"That would be a good idea," the physician replied while mopping up some blood with a cloth. Studying my face, he added, "Signorina, have we met?"

Hearing this, Ferrante's eyes slid in my direction. The question in his gaze caused my heart to stop.

Livia hastily interjected, "Dr. Bernardo, you obviously don't recognize Signora Celeste Carducci without her wimple."

Reading the warning in Livia's eyes, the physician played along with the farce. "Ah yes, of course. The young lady that I examined in the convent. My apologies, madam."

This seemed to satisfy my confused husband.

I stood. "Please excuse me while I fix that tonic."

With the help of Livia's servants, I brewed poppy seeds and other ingredients that helped dull the pain.

Dr. Bernardo had already left by the time I returned to the salon. I saw that he had applied a salve to the stitched wound and dressed it with strips of clean linen.

"Does it hurt very much?" I asked, handing Ferrante the cup.

"Enough to merit your tonic," he replied before draining the vessel. He noticed a few bloodstains on the cushions and added, "I'm afraid I've ruined your settee, Aunt Livia."

"That's the least of my worries, Ferrino. Why don't you go on and rest a bit?"

Sandro, who had been lingering by the door, finally came forward. "My lord, I have brought a fresh change of clothes."

Ferrante nodded and allowed his valet to help him stand.

Together, the men went into the guestroom.

Sandro emerged several minutes later and came over to where Livia and I sat. "His lordship has fallen asleep."

"Thank you, Sandro," Livia said.

He inclined his head at us and walked away.

Livia and I waited for the servants to return and we were puzzled by their report. Paola was nowhere to be found.

"I think it's safe to assume that she had the good sense to run away in order to escape prison," Livia concluded.

"I hope you're right," I said, frightened by the thought of a spurned woman wielding a knife coming for me in my sleep.

"I'll have the servants scour my villa from top to bottom before locking the doors and windows."

I nodded in agreement to her words since one could never be too careful.

We supped together quietly as Ferrate slept. Exhausted from the events of the day, Livia retired to her room early. A tray was brought to the guestroom and I sat with my husband until he woke up.

Stroking his hair, I asked, "Are you in much pain?"

He replied with a lopsided grin. "That tonic you administered earlier was so potent that I still feel numb—it's almost as though I am drunk."

"I suppose that's not a bad thing. Better than pain, at least."

"You were worried about me."

"Of course. I still am."

His eyes caressed my face. "With the exception of my aunt, no one has ever worried about me."

"You scared me to death today." I stood and went over to the tray. "Are you hungry?"

His expression turned sly. "Not for food."

I chastised him with a look. "I'm sure Dr. Bernardo would insist that you be careful not to do anything that would open that cut and tear those stitches."

"Dr. Bernardo is not married to an irresistible woman."

I blushed and refrained from encouraging him. "Your aunt has retired for the night and the servants have sent us a tray.

Let's see, there's bread, broth, cheese..."

"Wine?"

"Given that you are under the influence of poppy seeds, are you sure you want some?"

"Dilute it with plenty of water."

I poured him a chalice of watered wine and he drank it thirstily. I then fed him some bread sopped in broth.

"I can easily get accustomed to this, Celeste," he said before accepting another piece of bread from my fingers. He studied me thoughtfully. "You'll make a good mother someday."

"I hope so."

"The thought of you bearing my children..." He trailed off with a satisfied smile.

"Hopefully, I'll be with child soon."

"That would make me very happy."

"Me too. I should let you rest now. I'll have the servants prepare a room near yours."

"Stay with me."

Eyeing his wound, I said, "Wouldn't you be more comfortable alone, given the circumstances?"

"No. I want you near me."

"As you wish, my lord. I'll need help undressing."

"Come here. Sit."

I sat on the edge of the bed with my back to him and he undid the laces of my bodice. The layers came off slowly.

At one point, he said, "Good Lord, can't they invent easier garments for you women to wear?"

"I share your sentiment," I said while letting down my hair.

Stripped down to my linen shift, I crept into bed and snuggled beside him.

"That's better. Now, kiss me."

I leaned toward him and kissed his lips. The moment his hands caressed my breasts, I pulled away and shook my head. "No Ferrante. Not tonight. You may hurt yourself."

"You would deny me?"

"For your own good, yes."

Stretching out on his back, he urged me to sit astride him.

"How about now?"

"I don't think we should risk it."

Eyeing me wickedly, he countered, "Oh but I do…"

I found this delicious new position potentially exciting, and immediately became an eager participant in our game of love. In fact, I liked it so much that I had to bite my tongue a moment later to keep from crying aloud.

"We don't want to wake my aunt," he whispered with a grin.

Satiated, we stretched out on the bed and gazed into each other's eyes. Eventually, we fell asleep.

I awoke the next day to find my husband watching me.

"Good morning, my lord," I said shyly, for I had never slept in the same bed with him.

He touched my hair and smiled. "You look like an angel when you sleep."

"How are you feeling?"

"I'm fine."

Pushing aside one of the linen strips, I noticed the swollen red skin. "That must hurt."

"It does," he calmly admitted.

Throwing off the covers, I said, "I'll be right back."

"Where are you going?"

"I have an ointment in my studio that might make the wound heal quicker."

"Have one of the servants get it."

"They don't know where it is and they'll disturb my things with their search. It will be easier and faster if I get it myself. Besides, I want to check on Nadia."

"I'm sure she's fine."

"Paola is unhinged…She may feel vengeful."

"She would never hurt my daughter or any other child if that's what you're worried about."

"Are you sure?"

He nodded, his face serious. "She lost an infant once…"

My heart sank before I ventured, "Yours?"

"No."

Despite a wave of relief washing over me, I pitied the

woman. My presence was the direct source of her suffering.

Ferrante demanded, "What's that face? Tell me your thoughts."

"This is all my fault."

"You're wrong. Paola knew full well that I had to marry someone of noble blood. Actually, she was fine with the idea. Neither of us expected that I would fall in love with my wife. So, if it's anyone's fault—it's mine."

"For falling in love with me?"

"*And* spurning my mistress in the process." Changing the subject, he said, "Have Sandro accompany you home."

Home. "I'll be back shortly."

"Give Nadia a kiss for me."

"I will."

Livia was already up when I emerged from the guestroom. I broke my fast in her company, then left with Sandro. I arrived at the villa to find every window shutter and door locked.

"I instructed the other servants to secure the house before I departed yesterday," Sandro explained while extracting a large key from his pocket.

"Good thinking."

Once he had unlocked the door, I went directly upstairs to see Nadia, who was perfectly fine. Before I left, I instructed Berta to bolt the door behind me. While descending the stairs, I glimpsed a splatter of Ferrante's blood on the hem of my gown.

Lisa helped me to wash up and change into a clean garment. My next stop was my studio. Sandro escorted me outside and waited while I unlocked the door with my key. I stepped into the room and screamed. The valet ran in after me and froze to a halt. Paola's feet dangled several inches from the floor, her complexion a sickening shade of pale gray. The noose that had snapped her neck hung from the same rafter where bunches of herbs had been set out to dry.

To my horror, her lifeless eyes bore directly into mine.

Sandro caught me in his arms when I swayed.

Grabbing a chair with one hand, he dragged it outside while leading me toward the door. "Sit down and catch your breath, my lady. Best if you avert your eyes from this nasty business."

"Oh God," I cried.

Sandro left me sitting by the door and ducked back into the studio. "There's a note."

"What does it say?"

"Signora Celeste, perhaps it would be best if—"

"Read it to me."

He hesitated. "His lordship wouldn't approve."

"Please do as I say, Sandro. His lordship is not here and I am the lady of this house."

Reluctantly, he cleared his throat. "It says, 'My death is on your head.' She signed it too."

Tears stung my eyes. Paola's suicide confirmed my guilt. The woman's misery *and* death were my fault, and all because of my lie. Surely, Satan was dancing with glee at this moment because I was bound for Hell.'

Sandro tried to help me up but I shook my head.

"Come inside, madam," he insisted.

"I need a moment."

Lisa emerged from the kitchen and hurried toward us. "My lady, I heard you scream."

Catching a glimpse of Paola's corpse through the studio window, the girl gasped in shock and turned her face away from the gruesome sight.

I stood and took control of the situation. "Have the servants cut her down, Sandro."

"Yes, my lady. I'll summon his lordship too."

"Lisa, let's go inside," I said, placing my hand on my maid's shoulder. "I'm going to my room for a bit and I don't wish to be disturbed."

"Yes, my lady."

In the privacy of my bedroom, I wept.

Ferrante came home within the hour, pale and in pain. Sandro lingered in the background as I greeted my husband.

After embracing me, Ferrante asked, "Where is she?"

Sandro stepped forward and replied, "In the storeroom, my lord. I've already cut her down on her ladyship's command."

"You have no idea how much I regret that you had to see that," Ferrante whispered to me.

I said nothing as he moved past me to see the corpse for himself. Several minutes later, he found me seated by the window in the salon.

Placing a reassuring hand on my shoulder, he said, "This is not your fault."

"In her note—"

"Stop. Paola's jealousy drove her to madness and that note served only to spite you. Remember, she stabbed me with a knife and ran away."

"I was the cause of her distress."

Shaking his head, he countered, "Her distress was due to the fact that I want her gone because I love you."

His comment only made me feel worse. Despite this, I was determined to put the matter behind me. What other choice did I have, anyway?

He continued, "We can arrange to move your studio to another room. Take your pick—even inside the villa, if you wish."

Would I be able to work in my studio and not picture Paola's corpse? I doubted it. Although I loved my sacred space, she had defiled it in a manner that made it no longer viable.

"I'll select another storeroom," I said.

"Good. Now, if you'll excuse me, I need to speak with my valet in order to take care of things."

"Yes, of course."

As I made my way to the door, he said, "It would be best if you stuck to your quarters today."

I read in my room for the remainder of the day as various people came and went from the villa. A uniformed official arrived on horseback in the late afternoon. By the time the shadows grew long, a cart arrived with a plain wooden coffin. Four male servants carried it into the villa. A moment later they carried it out and heaved it onto the back of the cart. I stared at the coffin with a mixture of guilt and relief.

CHAPTER 16

For centuries, alchemists have tried to produce a mythical substance known as the philosopher's stone. Based on what I had read, it resembled hard red wax and supposedly enabled *chrysopoeia,* the miraculous transmutation of lead into gold.

Ferrante no longer restricted my selection of books, so I studied them with reckless abandon in my quest to create the philosopher's stone. My current obsession served as a respite from my tormented conscience.

A month had passed since Paola's tragic suicide. My new studio was located on the opposite end of my old one. The servants had taken special care to set it up exactly the same way. Donna Florinda kindly provided me with a window box overflowing with healthy herbs since I no longer had the garden directly outside my door. Aside from this minor inconvenience, I liked my space and spent more time in it each day.

On an early June morning, I crept into my studio. In truth, I had been secretly conducting experiments. I poured some liquid from one glass vial to another and watched in awe as it changed color. A knock on the door broke my concentration.

Raimondo poked his head into the room. "Hello."

I grinned. "Your Highness, it gladdens my heart to see you."

"Likewise, my dear. Forgive me for not coming sooner. You did receive my letter, did you not?"

Raimondo had sent me an encouraging letter after learning about Paola's suicide.

I nodded. "Your kindness and wise words were a balm to my soul. For that, I will always be grateful to you."

"Her death was not your fault. Remember that." His gaze swept over the beakers and vials scattered on the table's surface. "Is Ferrante home?"

"Not yet."

"Is he riding?"

"He took up the sport again last week. Yesterday, he went hunting. He's almost as good as new."

"I'm relieved to hear it. I'm sure your healing concoctions sped up the process."

"I would like to think so."

"You're up quite early, and by the look of it I'd say you've been here a while. What are you working on?" Raimondo inquired, his eyes falling upon one of several open books.

"Nothing in particular…"

One page captured his attention. It featured the Squared Circle, an alchemical symbol illustrating the relationship of the four elements.

Pinning me with an accusatory stare, he said, "You're trying to create the philosopher's stone."

I shrugged. "Only for my amusement."

"No one has ever succeeded."

"Including myself," I said, adding a deprecating chuckle for good measure.

"That you would even make the attempt surprises me."

Pointing to the book he had gifted me, I explained, "I read that Paracelsus believed in the existence of a mysterious fifth element that he called *alkahest*."

"I gave you that book merely for entertainment…"

"I know, my lord. Please don't tell Ferrante."

"Men have gone mad in their quest to recreate the philosopher's stone and find the magical fifth element. I would hate to see you go down that same road. While I admire your intelligence and spirit, I must advise you to immediately cease in this fruitless endeavor."

"But, my lord—"

"At once, Celeste."

Mortified, I stammered, "Of course. I was only trying to—I will take your advice to heart."

With that, I closed the books and tore my notes under his watchful gaze.

Raimondo breathed a sigh of relief. "Good girl. I have seen my peers fly into fits of rage and plummet into melancholia due to their many failed attempts. Even I once went down that path in my youth."

"It was silly of me to try."

Raimondo surveyed the books scattered throughout the table and selected one. "Here, this will prove a far better use of your valuable time and talents."

I held the book of curative recipes to my chest and nodded in response to his words.

He went to the door. "I'm going to check if Ferrante has returned. Don't worry, I won't mention this conversation."

"Thank you."

After he left, I emptied the vials and bottles, then wiped them clean. Raimondo did well in pointing out the peril of chasing an impossible dream. I was neither an alchemist nor a chemist, only a foolish girl conducting experiments. I had been laboring for almost four weeks with nothing to show for my efforts. Determined not to waste any more of my time, I collected the alchemy books and stacked them on a shelf.

***

I thought about the episode with Raimondo for days. Once again, the prince's counsel proved prudent. I had been wasting my time on frivolous matters.

Lisa poked her head into the studio as I was measuring out some linseed oil for an unguent. "Signora Celeste, Donna Teodora is here for your final fitting."

"Oh dear, I completely forgot that she was coming today."

I removed my apron and wiped my hands before following my maid into the main house. The seamstress and her assistant awaited me in the salon. Raimondo's son's birthday would take place on the eighteenth of June. Donna Teodora had created a delightful gown in lightweight cotton for the celebration, which would take place outdoors in the form of a garden party. The azure fabric highlighted the warm tones of my hair and skin. Skillfully embroidered roses in delicate shades of apricot and pink adorned the bodice and hem.

As I stood on a stool with my arms extended, Ferrante walked into the salon. The women glanced at him before making the final adjustments to the garment.

Catching my eye, he smiled at me. "My lady."

I grinned. "My lord. Do you like it?"

"You're lovely in any color."

Donna Teodora hid a smile as she pinned a bit of fabric.

He continued, "I'm going into town and will see you later."

I watched him go with a full heart. Never had I imagined that I could be so happy.

I ate the midday meal alone in cheerful anticipation of Ferrante's return. Peering out the window, I caught sight of a figure loitering at the front door. The familiar brown cloak made my stomach sink. I stood and waved the servants away before rushing into the foyer.

Throwing open the door, I glared at Celeste. "What are you doing here?"

Leaning against a column with both hands on her swollen belly, she began to cry. "I'm desperate. Please let me in."

She sniffed and wiped at her tearstained face. I saw that her eyes were red and puffy, signaling that she had been weeping for quite some time.

I shook my head. "I'm sorry but I can't do that."

"You must!"

Stepping outside, I ushered her away from the door so that no one would hear her. "Calm yourself. We can talk at Signora Livia's house. She knows the truth so—"

"I hate that woman!"

Urging her toward the back of the villa, I led her directly to my studio and closed the door behind us. "What's wrong?"

"Luigi, he…he can't marry me."

"You're not married yet?" I demanded, surprised.

"Luigi's older brother has been ill since March. He died last week and now my beloved stands to inherit his father's palazzo. Don't you see? He can only wed a noble woman and you have stolen my name."

I gaped at her, stunned. *"Stolen?"*

Ignoring my reaction, she declared crisply, "I need to reclaim my true identity."

Tense silence filled the space between us as I continued to stare at her incredulously.

Finally, I found my voice. "Have you lost your wits?"

Celeste switched from piteous to righteous. "Am I to be a poor and disgraced woman because you refuse to tell the truth?"

"How you can even say that shocks me to the core."

"Ferrante is a good husband and you're happy."

"It happened to turn out well for me, but the opposite could have easily been true. I took a big gamble, risking a life of misery to spare you from living one."

"I've already expressed my thanks—"

"Yet here you are *again* forcing me into a compromising position."

"I could have gone straight to the magistrate. Instead, I came here to reason with you."

"What's there to reason?" I shot back, pacing the room in nervous agitation. "I'll be ruined and may even go to prison."

"Not necessarily."

I froze. "Have you thought about your uncle and what this will do to him?"

"He never cared about me so why should I care about that old fool?"

I shook my head. "You can't go back to being Celeste Carducci. Too many people will be hurt if you do."

"I don't care. I need to think of my unborn child."

"And *yourself,* as always."

Her eyes narrowed. "You've been given a taste of life that other women only dream of, including myself. Be thankful."

"I love him."

"Well, if he feels the same about you then he won't care if your name is Celeste Carducci or Valentina Gaetani. You're still the same person."

Admittedly, she made a valid point. I paced the tiled floor as my thoughts raced. Finally, I said, "I certainly don't want you to end up in poverty and disgraced. Why can't Luigi marry you, regardless?"

"His widowed mother forbids it. She has decreed that his

wife must be of noble blood to carry the family name with honor. It's bad enough we conceived the child in sin…"

"Your child will still be a bastard."

"Not if he is born while we're in wedlock."

I wrung my hands. "What if I refuse?"

"I will reveal the truth to the magistrate and you will be formally charged."

I blinked back tears. "You're blackmailing me."

"I'm urging you to tell the truth, nothing more."

"Celeste, please, I beg you. This will ruin my marriage."

"*My* marriage. I'm sorry, Valentina, but my child comes before you."

I nodded, defeated. "I will tell Ferrante when he returns."

"I'm not leaving until you do."

"Is that really necessary?"

"Yes."

The love I once felt for my friend soured in that instant.

***

Livia arrived later that afternoon to find Celeste and I seated in the salon waiting for Ferrante, who had not yet returned from the city.

Her face blanched. "What's going on here?"

"Celeste wishes to reclaim her identity," I replied flatly.

Livia's gaze shifted from me to Celeste. "I'm afraid that's impossible, young lady."

"I beg to differ," Celeste shot back.

Livia bristled. "How dare you? Leave this house at once."

Celeste crossed her arms. "I'm not going anywhere."

"I'll have the servants remove you by force, if needed."

"I'll go straight to the magistrate."

I sighed. "Both of you, stop."

Livia rubbed her temples. "Why are you doing this, Celeste? Did your monk abandon you?"

Celeste crossed her arms. "On the contrary. He stands to inherit and needs a noble wife, which is exactly what I will be once I can reclaim my name and my identity."

"This is a fine mess," Livia murmured.

The sound of horse hooves drew our collective gazes to the window. Ferrante rode through the gates in a cloud of dust.

Livia turned to Celeste. "Don't do this, I beg you. For the first time in his life my nephew is happy."

"What about *my* happiness?" Rubbing her belly, Celeste added, "What about my child?"

Balling her hands into fists, Livia retorted, "You should have thought of that before dragging your friend and my nephew into your scheme, you stupid selfish girl!"

Celeste's face registered remorse. "I truly regret causing any inconvenience." Looking at me, she added, "I mean that, Valentina. I'm sorry."

Torn between my friend's dire predicament and my own, I said nothing. A wave of nausea washed over me as the front door opened and Ferrante's footsteps echoed in the hallway. Bracing myself, I stood by the window at the farthest end of the room.

He opened the salon door, took in our serious expressions, and said cautiously, "Good evening. I see we have a guest."

Livia and I exchanged worried looks.

Neither of us introduced Celeste, which signaled to Ferrante that something was amiss. His eyes roamed over her simple clothing and swollen belly. "May I have the pleasure of your name, Signora—?"

"Carducci."

His brow creased. "What did you say?"

"I am Celeste Carducci, niece of Camillo Custozi."

Betrayed by my own best friend, I staggered to a chair and sat down. Ferrante's eyes searched my face begging for an explanation, but I refused to meet his insistent gaze.

He was beside my chair in a few quick strides. "Celeste, what's going on here?"

Lowering my head, I replied, "She speaks the truth."

Silence, heavy and tense, followed my words.

Grasping my arm, he yanked me out of the chair to face him squarely. "Look at me. If what she says is true then who the devil are you?"

The hurt and distrust reflected in his glistening eyes broke my heart. "I'm so sorry..."

Gripping my shoulders, he shook me. *"Who are you?"*

Celeste said, "Her real name is Valentia Gaetani."

He recoiled from me and strode to where his aunt stood. "Tell me this is a joke." At his aunt's guilty expression, he exploded, "What have you done?!"

Livia's hand trembled as she indicated the settee. "Sit down and let me explain." When he hesitated, she added, "Please."

Ferrante eyed the three of us with suspicion as he took a seat. "One of you had better start talking."

Livia said, "I had no idea that a switch had taken place until after you were married in the church."

Pointing at me, he cried, "You knew she wasn't Celeste and didn't say anything? Why?"

"I saw how you looked at her when we were in the carriage, Ferrante. I had never seen you look at a woman like that. The reason I refrained from revealing the truth is because I thought that, perhaps, this union had the potential to become a love-match—and I was correct."

"How could you let this happen?" Pinning me with a cold stare, he added, "Valentina? That's your real name?"

I glanced at him. "Yes, my lord."

"Dear God...Why did you do this to me?"

Livia replied on my behalf, "She loved her friend so much that she risked her own happiness by marrying you."

Throwing up his arms in frustration, he cried, "Am I such a monster that I deserve to be lied to and deceived in such a conniving manner?"

"In my eyes, yes," Celeste boldly declared.

Ferrante stood, enraged. "You dare say that to my face? Under my roof?"

"I already loved another when your aunt came to see me in the convent," Celeste explained, coming to stand by my chair. "I had no desire to marry you or any other man chosen by my uncle. Sister Assunta and I convinced Valentina to take my place. We've known each other since childhood, we're the same age—"

"And to men like you and Camillo Custozi, one girl is as good as the next," I said, finally finding my voice.

"Valentina married you so that I wouldn't have to," Celeste concluded.

Ferrante's eyes slid from Celeste to me. "Stupid girls! This is not a game. I am legally married to Celeste Carducci on paper yet *that one* shares my bed," he bellowed, pointing at me.

Cringing inwardly, I bowed my head in shame.

"Valentina is your true wife," Livia said quietly.

His eyes never left my face as he demanded, "Is she of noble blood?"

Livia glanced at me apologetically. "No."

He stood and began pacing the room. "I need to annul this marriage…Another scandal for the House of Spini."

"You can't request an annulment," Livia said, coming to place an arm around my shoulders. "Think of poor Valentina."

Ferrante eyed me coldly, as one would a stranger. "Did she think of me when she agreed to this farce? You know that I hate dishonesty above all else, Aunt Livia. That woman has been living a lie and making a fool of me for months—just as Caterina did." His eyes glistened with unshed tears as he sank into the nearest chair. Running his hands through his unruly hair, he lamented in a defeated tone, "Will I ever be immune to the treachery of women?"

In an attempt to remediate the situation, Celeste said, "Valentina loves you, my lord. That's no lie."

Ferrante fixed her with an icy glare. "Your uncle will be notified and you'll be exposed as the scheming fornicator that you are, young lady. I hope your lover's heart is true, for no man will want you by the time my solicitors are done with you."

Celeste's face crumpled and her lower lip quivered in the face of his threat.

Livia tiptoed to where her nephew sat fuming with rage. "Ferrante, you're in love for the first time in your life and Valentina loves you back. That's what's important, my boy. Money, title, inheritance—they pale in comparison to love and happiness. Trust me, you don't want to end up like me in life."

He shook his head vehemently. "The three of you have tricked me and now I'm in a compromising legal position—not to mention humiliated. Cristo Santo!" He froze, eyeing Celeste's belly with a calculating expression. "Aunt Livia, judging by how far along Celeste is, she would have been pregnant when your physician examined her."

Livia's red face revealed her guilt.

Realization dawned on him and he shook his head in disgust. "You would have had me raise a bastard if Valentina hadn't stepped in to take her place."

"I didn't want to risk the girl being barren like me," she finally confessed. "Celeste and the monk were virgins—"

Ferrante's face darkened with rage. "I want the three of you out of my house and out of my sight." When none of us moved, he shouted, "Get out!"

I sat beside him. "Don't cast me out."

"I can't even look at you," he spat, turning his face away.

"I love you, Ferrante," I insisted, reaching for his hand.

Recoiling from my touch, he spat, "To think that Paola took her life because of *you*—a liar!"

A knife in my chest would have caused less pain. Defeated, I stood on shaky legs and swayed precariously. Livia and Celeste rushed to either side of me. Together, they ushered me out of the room and down the hallway. Ferrante's heart wrenching sobs reached our ears as we entered the foyer.

Hearing him weep evoked my own tears.

Livia cast a fretful glance over her shoulder. "It's best if we leave him alone. There is no reasoning with him when he's angry. Let's go to my villa and sort this out."

The acute pain radiating throughout my chest made it difficult to breathe as we piled into the carriage. Celeste and I sat side by side and the older woman stared at each of us in turn.

"I hope you're satisfied with your handiwork, Celeste."

Shaking my head, I said quietly, "Leave her be, Signora Livia. She has no choice at this point…Celeste must think of her unborn child first and foremost."

Celeste gripped my hand tightly. "I'm sorry for everything, Valentina. I hope you'll forgive me one day."

I offered her a slight nod but said nothing.

The carriage came to a stop at Livia's villa and she exited the vehicle. "Celeste, my driver will take you back to the city. Come along, Valentina."

I remained in my seat. "I'm going with Celeste."

"You can't," Livia countered, her face confused.

"Ferrante cast me out. He can't stand the sight of me."

"My nephew is in a state of shock. He's hurt right now. You'll stay here with me until he comes around."

"Ferrante took a great risk in trusting me—*in loving me*—and I have betrayed him. He'll never get past this. You heard what he said. I caused Paola's death."

"I'm sure he didn't mean it. He's upset, that's all."

"Thank you for everything, Signora Livia. I'll never forget your kindness."

Livia's brow creased with worry. "Where will you go?"

"To my Aunt Gloria." It was a lie, for I had no intention of going there.

"As you wish, my dear." Livia's eyes filled with tears as she closed the door and banged on the carriage.

Celeste squeezed my hand in a reassuring gesture as the driver retreated from the villa and began its descent to the city. I kept my gaze on the Naples Bay in order to distract myself. The sun shone on the waves and gulls circled high in the sky. In that instant, I would trade places with one of them and fly somewhere far away.

We rolled past dwellings and palazzos in the city's heart. Children ran alongside the fine painted carriage, waving and smiling at us. I waved back at them before poking my head out the window and telling the driver to stop.

"This isn't where your aunt lives," Celeste pointed out.

"I know."

"Where are you going?"

"I need a walk to clear my head," I improvised.

"When will our paths cross again?"

“I don’t know.”

Celeste began to weep when I opened the carriage door. “Good luck, my friend.”

I stepped onto the street and regarded her squarely. “Goodbye Celeste.”

I closed the door, then watched the carriage until it disappeared from my sight.

Sighing, I studied the familiar scenes around me with a heavy heart. Piles of animal dung and rotten vegetables littered the gutters. Children played outside their homes and I glimpsed a few scraped knees. Above my head, linens drip-dried on poles protruding from open windows. I picked my way gingerly around the trash and filth, pausing to admire a magnificent fresco of Jesus Christ painted on the wall of a crumbling palazzo. The fading light bathed the city in a veil of burnished gold. I took in the beauty with great sadness, for I had never before felt so alone in my life. The mere thought of Ferrante evoked a sharp stabbing pain in my heart.

Unable to face Aunt Gloria, I went straight to the only place for a woman in my situation.

CHAPTER 17

I opened my eyes in the milky sunshine of early morning. The muted light revealed the crumbling walls of a tiny cell. A crude wooden cross, the only décor in the room, hung above a patch of black mold. Reality rushed over me as the final cobwebs of sleep dissipated.

"Ferrante…"

Tears stung my eyes but I held them at bay. Rising from the lumpy straw pallet, I rubbed my sore back. I had grown accustomed to fine cotton sheets and feather pillows. At least my new bed was vermin-free.

The terracotta tiles felt cold beneath my bare feet as I tiptoed across the room. Taking hold of a ceramic pitcher, I poured water into a small chipped basin. The rough damp cloth I used to wash myself smelled sour and scratched my skin. Closing my eyes, I pretended it was a rose-scented, soft linen cloth.

Peep peep!

My eyes snapped open and I almost smiled at the sight of a sparrow on my windowsill. The tiny bird puffed its chest and fluttered its wings.

"Hello little friend."

The sparrow hopped around in a beam of sunshine, then flew away. Sighing resignedly, I donned a gray robe and starched white wimple, being sure to tuck all of my hair into the fabric. I exited the room with heavy steps and headed for the chapel.

Crossing the cloister garden, I shivered in the chilly early morning air. Whispers echoed in the ancient sacred space as I took my place amid the nuns. Although I repeated the holy words along with them, my mind inevitably wandered.

Mother Clotilda had agreed to take me in after I told her that my employer cast me out for refusing to entertain his inappropriate advances. My lie had gained my admittance into the Convent of Santa Patrizia. I planned on living like a novice until I figured out what to do with my shattered life.

I kept to myself and spoke little. Mealtimes were difficult since some of the nuns tried to be friendly with me. I began making a point of showing up late, that way, I could select the most remote seat.

By the onset of the second week, the nuns left me alone. I volunteered to do the hardest chores during the day. Physical labor served as a distraction from the pain of loss. Night time proved far more difficult since there was nothing to do but stare at the darkened ceiling from the confines of my uncomfortable cot. My mind conjured images of Ferrante's face, his smile, his touch…I cried myself to sleep on most nights.

One morning, as I knelt in the dirt pulling weeds in the garden, a shadow fell over my hands. Craning my neck, I shaded my eyes from the blinding sun.

The abbess stared down at me. "It's rather early for you to be out here doing this."

I brushed the soil from my fingers. "I saw the weeds…"

"I'm worried about you, Valentina. You've been here for over a fortnight and each day you grow paler and thinner."

"I'm fine, Mother Clotilda."

"I dispatched a messenger to your aunt." When my eyes filled with tears, she added, "I'm sorry but I did it for your own good."

I said nothing. After she left me, I returned to my task with troubling thoughts. What would I tell my aunt?

Later that day, Aunt Gloria came to see me. She gasped in dismay at the sight of my sunken eyes and hollowed cheeks. After hugging me tightly, she inquired, "Ferrante discovered the truth, didn't he?"

"He did."

"I was surprised to receive Mother Clotilda's message. Why didn't you come straight to me?"

"I didn't wish to disturb you or Natalino."

"How can you even think such a thing? We love you and your place is with us. Unless…are you thinking of taking the vows and becoming a nun?"

"I haven't decided yet."

Her eyes darted around my dismal cell. "I don't think this is the life for you, my sweet girl."

"I don't know who I am anymore or where I belong."

"Oh Valentina…"

"My heart aches all the time." The tears I had been holding inside spilled down my cheeks.

Aunt Gloria pulled me into her arms. "Calm yourself, child. Take a deep breath…there, that's better. I need to know what happened."

I sighed and indicated the only stool in the room as I sat on the edge of the cot. "Celeste came to the villa."

"Why?"

"She's pregnant—"

"Pregnant?"

I recounted Sister Assunta's surprise visit, then the time I gave Celeste the silver earrings. I concluded with Celeste's threats of blackmail.

Aunt Gloria heaved a weary sigh when I was done. "The mess in which that selfish girl has embroiled you has cost you your happiness."

"And Ferrante," I reminded her.

"That scoundrel could have at least—"

"Don't!"

"Are you defending him?" She studied my face closely. "You love him," she deduced, her eyes widening in surprise.

"Hopelessly."

"Even after he threw you out of his house like a dog?"

"I lied to him…I betrayed his trust. He had every reason to cast me out." I shrugged before wiping away a stray tear. "At least I can be Valentina again."

Taking my hand into her own, she pleaded, "Please come home with me now."

"I refuse to be the cause of friction in your marriage, Aunt Gloria. This is my problem, not yours."

"We're family."

Giving her hand a reassuring squeeze, I said gently, "I

appreciate your offer, but I'm in no condition to be anywhere except here."

"I'll respect your decision but I don't like it. I plan on visiting you frequently." She reached out to touch my cheek. "Promise me that when you feel strong enough, you'll come and stay with us."

"I promise."

"Maybe Natalino can secure employment for you." She hesitated, then ventured, "No one knows about your fake marriage to Ferrante degli Spini. In time, you may decide to remarry. Natalino's cousin is an attractive young man—"

"Please stop."

"Forgive me. I'm only trying to make you see that this whole thing will eventually fade away like a distant memory. Soon, you'll go on with your life as if it never happened."

"*As if it never happened*," I whispered sadly.

"Exactly. All you need is a bit of time to heal and you'll be your old self again."

I forced a smile. "Thank you, Aunt Gloria."

She kissed my cheek and exited the cell.

After our conversation, my demeanor slightly improved. The fact that I had confessed the truth to her lifted some of the weight I carried on my back. Each day that passed in the convent proved less painful than the last. My appetite eventually returned and I began putting on a bit of the weight I had lost. I even made the effort to be friendly toward the nuns.

The eighteenth of June dawned warm and muggy. It was a difficult day for me since I had planned on attending the birthday party honoring Raimondo's son. I thought of Livia in one of her black gowns with Ferrante at her side.

I missed them both.

I dressed and went outside to find something—*anything*—that would occupy my mind and hands for most of the day. Two nuns across the way carried a shallow wooden crate filled with seedlings that needed to be transplanted into separate pots. I volunteered to do the work and they happily obliged me by leaving me alone.

I filled small clay pots of soil and hollowed out a space in the center of each one with my finger. Gently, I transplanted the first seedling. While I continued working, I wondered if my herbs were thriving back at the villa. Who was caring for the window box garden in my studio?

My studio.

"Stop it," I murmured as I patted down the soil.

I paused in my task and hung my head. Determined to get through the day without tears, I forced my thoughts toward alchemy and began creating possible formulations in my head for the Philosopher's Stone.

I washed the dirt from my hands when I finished the task, then went to the convent library. Losing myself in a book would hopefully prevent me from daydreaming about my former life.

***

A few days later, the abbess rushed into my cell without knocking. Alarmed by her flushed face and bright eyes, I shut the book I was reading and looked at her expectantly.

"His Royal Highness, Prince Raimondo di Sangro, is here to see you," she announced breathlessly.

Although I was surprised, I remained calm as I stood and set the book on a table.

The abbess blinked in disbelief. "Did you not hear me?"

"I heard you. Where is he?"

Puzzled by my unruffled demeanor, she replied, "He awaits you in the chapel."

I smoothed the creases of my garment and made sure my wimple was on straight before exiting the cell.

We hurried down the corridor and crossed the cloister garden to the empty chapel. Raimondo stood facing the altar. At the sound of our footsteps, he turned around and stared at me. I offered him a curtsy and waited for him to speak.

His eyes never left my face as he said, "Mother Clotilda, would you please excuse us? What I have to say to *Signorina Valentina* is meant for her ears alone."

"Certainly, my lord," she replied, casting a curious glance in my direction.

Since nuns were not allowed to be alone with men within convent walls, the abbess retreated to the cloister garden where she could see us through the open door but not overhear our conversation.

"So you already know the truth," I said, averting my gaze.

"Livia arrived at my home unescorted to celebrate my son's birthday. When I asked after you and Ferrante, she almost broke down in tears. She told me everything."

I lowered my head in shame. "Forgive me."

"Look at me."

Reluctantly, I raised my eyes to his. "Are you here to condemn me and send me to prison, my lord?"

To my surprise, he chuckled. "Someone who would willingly sacrifice her happiness for the sake of another doesn't merit prison. An unselfish act merits a reward."

I stared at him in disbelief. "You're not angry with me?"

"On the contrary, my dear. You transformed Ferrante from a miserable man into a happy one. He loves you."

"*Loved*," I corrected. "He values honesty above all else and I deceived him."

"His wounded pride and distrustful nature is the cause of his current distress."

"I wish I could believe that."

Raimondo rubbed his chin thoughtfully as he regarded me with a serious expression. "Did he ever mention that his father, Luciano, was my distant cousin?"

"Ferrante never spoke of his father."

"I'm not surprised...Livia is the only person who truly loved her brother. Luciano was a harsh man but she always saw the good in him. I can't blame her since Luciano defended her on many occasions against her husband's cruelty."

"Signora Livia mentioned that her late husband resented her for being barren."

"He hated her for it. That's why he rubbed Paola in her face. Luciano and his brother-in-law engaged in many a heated argument when they were alive."

"Was Luciano harsh with his son?"

"More than I care to admit. In fact, to describe him as 'strict' would be an understatement. Luciano had been a soldier in his youth and applied a military approach in the rearing of his son. Ferrante grew up under constant criticism and even corporal punishment. He eventually became reclusive and suspicious of everyone. Why do you think he has such a terrible reputation? Ferrante treats people in much the same manner that his father treated him."

I imaged Ferrante as a little boy suffering such abuse and my heart twisted in pity. "Why are you telling me this?"

"Because I love Ferrante and I hate to see him suffering."

"You speak as if I have any control in this matter, my lord. I'll remind you that I didn't leave Ferrante of my own accord."

Closing the gap between us, he reached for my hand. "I know. I'm here to offer a solution to the problem."

"I don't understand."

"My spinster aunt passed away last year at the ripe old age of ninety-six. Perhaps you've heard of the Countess of Marechiaro?" When I shook my head, he continued, "I'm not surprised. It's a tiny *borgo* by the sea."

"Sounds lovely."

"It is rather lovely, yes. My aunt left behind a crumbling villa in a state of disrepair and I'm considering refurbishing the place. Naturally, it will need an occupant."

I stared at him, still not comprehending how this story had anything to do with me.

He smiled and continued, "I want you, Valentina Gaetani, to be the new Countess of Marechiaro."

The air shot out of my lungs so quickly that I became dizzy. Staggering backward, I reached out my hand toward the rough stone wall for support.

Raimondo rushed forward to grasp my shoulders and steady me. "Are you all right?"

I nodded, catching my breath. "Why me?"

"Isn't it obvious?"

I allowed the excitement to settle, then thought for a moment. "If Ferrante wanted me badly enough, he would have already asked you to do this favor for him."

"He is far too proud to come to me. Remember, he didn't even apprise me of the situation. Livia is the one who requested that I grant you a noble title. In fact, she practically begged me. I'm happy to oblige. We both want to see Ferrante happy."

"While I appreciate the honor you are bestowing upon me, I want Ferrante to love me for who I am—with or without a noble title."

"Trust me when I tell you that he does love you, my dear. So much so that it terrifies him. I've never seen him like this. Neither has Livia." Reaching into the inner pocket of his fine velvet cape, he extracted a scroll flaunting an official seal complete with a golden tassel. "I've already had the papers drawn up. Take it. *Please*."

I accepted the scroll and broke the seal. My eyes widened in surprise as I read the words. I gaped at him.

"Regardless of your decision where Ferrante is concerned, as of today, you are Valentina Gaetani, Countess of Marechiaro. Your humility, chasteness, and strong spirit earned you that privilege."

I curtsied deeply in gratitude. "Your Highness, I swear to spend the remainder of my life living up to the honor you have bestowed upon me today."

"I know you will."

For the first time since I left the villa, a genuine smile stretched across my face. "Is Ferrante aware of this?"

"I plan to ride over there now and tell him. I didn't want to say anything until I knew you would accept my gift."

"What will Ferrante tell people? Celeste Carducci abruptly disappeared. He can't simply show up married to me, Valentina Gaetani."

"Why not?"

I stared at him blankly. "Won't people talk?"

"People always talk no matter what you do. They've been talking about me for years." Waving his hand in the air, he shrugged. "Look at all the scandals that have landed on my doorstep. Do you think that stopped me from pursuing my interests? Never."

"You're a *prince*, my lord—a man with immense wealth and power. You can do whatever you want."

Nodding slightly, he eyed me intently. "My position sets me on a public stage where I am pressured to live as society sees fit. Do you think peasants have to worry about their names being sullied by politicians or Vatican officials? I'll remind you that I've suffered the humiliation of being excommunicated. Don't think for a moment that powerful men don't have their worries—and that includes Ferrante."

"You've given me much to ponder upon, my lord."

"No one knows what has transpired except for us. Ferrante's servants are practical and trustworthy, as are Livia's. They won't say anything and neither will I. Hopefully, in time, this will all die down like every other scandal in Europe. Trust me, there have been far worse." Casting a glance at Mother Clotilda, he added, "I'm going to leave you now in the care of the good abbess. I expect you'll be hearing from Ferrante soon. He may come to fetch you immediately after I inform him. Who knows? You may be sleeping back in your bed in the villa by tonight."

I took the prince's hand and kissed it. "Thank you."

Raimondo smiled and left. I stared after him, stupefied by how my life had completely changed in the blink of an eye.

I spent the remainder of the day in a daze. *Countess Valentina Gaetani of Marechiaro*. In the privacy of my room, I spun around with glee as my heart filled with hope. Ferrante could now marry me without repercussion.

The following day, I took extra care with my grooming. Lacking access to creams, tonics, and perfumes, I had to improvise with a bit of aloe vera and lavender. I applied the aloe's milk to my face and hands, then rubbed lavender on my skin to make it smell nice. Since Ferrante hadn't come for me last night, I figured he would show up first thing in the morning.

I found myself humming as I broke my fast with the other nuns, then actually smiling as I worked alongside them in the garden. I even volunteered to alphabetize the books in the library to keep myself from giggling with joy.

The morning passed with no sign of Ferrante but I kept my hope afloat. Certainly, he would come to fetch me in the afternoon. I ate the midday meal, attended prayers, and retired to my room to read. By the time the shadows grew long, my hope had disintegrated to dust. The evening bells rang for prayer and I couldn't bring myself to go. Instead, I dragged myself across the cell and stretched out on the cot. Staring at the ceiling, I devised a dozen reasons for his absence.

That night, I cried myself to sleep.

Ferrante didn't show up the next day, either. By nightfall, I concluded that he wanted nothing further to do with me. Why else had he not come as soon as Raimondo informed him of my noble title?

Devastated, I made a decision. The life of a nun was not for me, and I said as much to Mother Clotilda after the morning prayers the next day.

It is time to get on with your life, Valentina.

I divested of the gray garment and donned the gown I had worn upon my arrival. Taking one last look at the cloister garden, I exited the main gate and ventured out into the busy street.

Chapter 18

I rose from the cot in the corner of the room that doubled as Natalino's work office. His accounting ledgers and various orders were scattered atop a faded wooden desk. As the best *macellaio* in the area, his meat was in high demand. Several noble families dined on his fine cuts of beef and pork, fowl and sausages. It pleased me that my aunt had married a hardworking man with good business sense.

I rubbed my eyes and sighed before readying myself for the day. Three days had passed since Aunt Gloria and Natalino took me into their home. I helped with caring for Donna Pasqualina and today I would start helping Natalino in the butcher shop.

Aunt Gloria had created a makeshift vanity for me complete with ewer and pitcher, a small bottle of vetiver, and a comb. She had even gifted me a necklace of red glass beads, which I wore around my neck for good luck.

I washed my face and donned one of my old garments, grateful that my aunt had not discarded my things. I felt like Valentina again, well, at least I looked like my old self. Being with Ferrante had forever changed me on the inside.

The small mirror Natalino had hung on the wall served me well as I combed my hair and coiled it into a neat bun at the base of my neck. After applying a bit of vetiver, I exited the room and joined the happy couple breaking their fast at the dining table.

"Good morning," I said, heading for the kitchen to make Donna Pasqualina's tray. Each day, I insisted on bringing it to her before breaking my fast.

"Good day, Valentina," Natalino said.

My aunt added, "Did you sleep well?"

"Yes," I lied. "I'm looking forward to helping in the shop today. It will be good for me."

They nodded in unison and I forced a smile before knocking

on the old woman's door. Donna Pasqualina offered me a toothless grin as I patted her pillows and helped to prop her up.

"Pottage, a bit of soft cheese, and a pot of tea," I said, placing the tray across her frail lap. "I'll be back to collect the tray in a little while."

"God bless you, my pretty," the old woman murmured.

We ate bread, cheese, and fruit and then I followed Natalino downstairs to the butcher shop. He handed me an apron and instructed me on what to do. Basically, my job was to greet customers, take their money, and hand them their purchases.

The heat of summer made it hard to keep meat fresh. In light of this, Natalino sold less of it. People preferred cured meats in the warmer months. Those who came in to purchase meat greeted me with smiles on their faces, asking me where I've been for so long. Aunt Gloria had instructed me to tell them that my previous employer had died. Lying had become second nature to me by this point, so the dishonest words slipped glibly from my tongue.

At midday, Natalino fed me a bit of smoked sausage and bread. I washed it down with heavily watered wine.

Later in the afternoon, Natalino glanced over at me and grinned. "You're doing a fine job, Valentina. The customers enjoy seeing a pretty face."

"I'm happy I can be of use to you, sir. It's the least I can do to show you my appreciation."

He stopped hacking into the rack of pork ribs to look at me, the big cleaver in his hand hovering over the meat. "You need to stop talking like that. You're family."

I smiled at him with heartfelt gratitude. In that moment, I counted my blessings.

"Natalino!"

We both turned our heads toward the attractive young man who stood in the doorway.

Natalino grinned. "Giovanni, what are you doing here?"

"Mamma wanted lamb chops, so I came to fetch some." The young man's eyes turned my way and he smiled. "Aren't you going to introduce me to your comely companion?"

I blushed at the compliment.

Natalino obliged the young Giovanni. "This here is Valentina, my wife's niece." To me, he added, "Giovanni is my cousin, and the most talented carpenter in the *quartiere*."

Blue eyes met mine. "A pleasure to meet you, Signorina Valentina."

"Likewise, sir."

Giovanni's decent clothing suggested that he was a man making some headway in this competitive world.

Natalino selected two of the finest lamb chops and refused to accept payment from his cousin.

Touched by his generosity, Giovanni said, "This is the second time you've given me free meat."

"Make me a chair," Natalino teased.

"Consider it done, cousin."

The young man left but not before tossing me a smile over his shoulder.

Natalino winked at me knowingly. "Good looking lad, no?"

"Yes," I agreed before picking up a cloth and cleaning the work area.

Later that night, as I helped Aunt Gloria set the table for supper, she asked about Giovanni. Instantly, I knew the entire encounter earlier that day had been planned for my benefit.

"He seemed nice enough," I said coolly before taking a tray to Donna Pasqualina.

Natalino and Aunt Gloria stopped whispering the moment I emerged from the old woman's room.

"What are you two going on about?" I teased as I took a seat across from them.

Aunt Gloria only shrugged and grinned mischievously when I shot her an accusatory look.

Natalino said, "Giovanni seemed to have liked you."

I forced myself to appear grateful. "I'm sure he's a wonderful young man but I'm not—"

"Don't you dare say it," Aunt Gloria warned. "What happened in the past must remain there. You need to go on with your life."

"I know but—"

"Valentina, *enough*."

My eyes widened in surprise, for my aunt had never before taken a harsh tone with me.

She continued, "I have watched you mope about and I won't have any more of it."

"This is exactly why I went to the convent," I reminded her in a gentle voice.

Natalino shook his head, his expression stern. "That's not the answer, either. You need to marry and have a life of your own. Giovanni makes a decent living with his trade. He can give you children, a home—that will make you happy. Don't you want those things?"

Yes, with Ferrante, I thought. "Natalino, the last thing I want to be to you is a burden but I must speak the truth. How can I marry your cousin when my heart belongs to another man?"

Aunt Gloria scowled at me. "You need to forget Ferrante. His bride must be noble, and that's something you will never be in this lifetime or the next."

I folded my hands on the tabletop and lowered my head.

She continued in a softer tone, "The sooner you accept reality, the easier it will be for your heart to heal. I say this because I love you."

"I know you do, Aunt Gloria." Raising my head, I met their eyes. "I haven't been honest with either of you."

Natalino frowned. "What do you mean?"

I rose from the table and obtained the scroll Raimondo had given me several days ago. "See for yourself."

Natalino studied the seal before showing it to Aunt Gloria. She unrolled it and they both read the elegantly scripted words. Simultaneously, they looked up and gaped at me.

"Prince Raimondo visited me at the convent a couple of days before I came here," I explained.

Aunt Gloria held up the document, shaking it slightly. "*Countess of Marechiaro*? Why didn't you tell us?"

I shrugged. "Prince Raimondo assured me that he would immediately inform Ferrante of my noble title. You can imagine my joy…I waited for Ferrante to fetch me the next day but he never came. When he failed to come the day after, I resolved to leave the convent. I didn't tell you because I felt humiliated."

She handed me the document and I quietly rolled it up. No one dared to speak.

Finally, Natalino said, "Marechiaro is a little fishing village by the sea. I went there once as a boy. Very peaceful."

"Perhaps I should go there," I said, looking at each one in turn. "Prince Raimondo said the villa is in a bad state of disrepair but at least it's a home."

"*Your* home," Aunt Gloria pointed out.

"*Our* home," I corrected.

They beamed at me.

Natalino said, "We can ride there after church this Sunday, if you wish. I'll hire a carriage to take us."

"I'd like that," I assured him as I stood to put away the scroll. A wave of dizziness caused me to falter so I placed my palms against the table top to steady myself. Chair legs scraped as my aunt and Natalino rushed to my side. Natalino's sturdy arms guided me back to the chair.

Aunt Gloria's face loomed before my eyes. "What ails you?"

Overcome by nausea, I covered my mouth.

My aunt said, "Quick, Natalino! The empty bowl on the table there."

Natalino placed the bowl beneath my mouth in time to catch the stream of acidic vomit that rushed from my lips.

I groaned and placed a hand on my clammy forehead. "I don't feel—"

I vomited again.

When I caught my breath, I leaned back in the chair and fanned myself with my hands. "Maybe it was the sausage."

"I ate the same thing and I feel fine," Natalino pointed out.

Catching the knowing look that passed between Aunt Gloria and her husband, my stomach sank.

She whispered in my ear, "When was your last monthly?"

***

The local midwife confirmed my pregnancy the next morning. Plagued by an onslaught of mixed emotions, I laughed and wept at the same time. The confused woman left the room without uttering a word but I knew her lips would be flapping the moment she hit the streets. Before sunset, everyone in our neighborhood would know that Valentina Gaetani was pregnant. I could only imagine the raucous stories that would no doubt be invented to explain my condition.

I couldn't be happier to be carrying Ferrante's child yet the thought of being unable to tell him devastated me. Putting on a brave face, I vowed to do whatever it took to be the best mother I could for my child.

At least my son or daughter would have a title and a home.

I donned my cloak.

Seeing this, my aunt demanded, "Where are you going?"

"It's Saturday, remember? I'm going to help Natalino."

"You're carrying a nobleman's child, Valentina. You can't simply continue with your life as before. You must send Ferrante a message at once."

I shook my head. "I want him to marry me for love."

"Swallow that pride of yours, girl. You've got your baby to think of now, and he will need a father."

He. I smiled at the thought of Ferrante's son growing deep within me. A lively green-eyed boy with black hair who scowls as easily as he laughs…

"Valentina, did you hear me?"

"Forgive me, Aunt Gloria. What did you say?"

She sighed. "If you don't send a message to that man, I swear I will knock on his door and inform him myself of your condition. I'm sure he'll be overjoyed."

"I'll tell him after our visit to Marechiaro this Sunday."

"I'm holding you to that promise."

The next day, everyone stared at me when I entered the church. Months had passed since I had attended Holy Mass at San Severino e Sossio. Whispers and snickers were deliberately aimed at me as we selected a pew. Given that most of the parishioners had known me since childhood, their cruelty offended me.

Keeping my head high and my eyes straight, I refused to give them the satisfaction of a reaction. With my stoic mask set firmly in place, I focused on the high altar and paid attention to the priest as he conducted the service.

Afterward, I paid homage to the Filomarino brothers by admiring their unique chapel. Somehow, I didn't derive the same pleasure that I once did. Everything looked and felt different. Then it struck me: the chapel hadn't changed…*I had changed.*

Aunt Gloria came to fetch me. "The carriage is here."

I followed her and Natalino out of the church and piled into the carriage with them. We rode along the coast until we arrived at a quaint tiny village.

"This is Marechiaro?" Aunt Gloria inquired, unimpressed.

Natalino gazed at the water, which hosted a few fishing boats. "I remember swimming here with my father. I've always wanted to be a fisherman," he admitted, much to our surprise.

"Why did you become a butcher?" I inquired, curious.

"My father was a butcher, as was his father," he replied, his eyes tracking a net being cast by two men on a boat.

The carriage climbed the soft swell of a hill and stopped outside a rusty gate boasting elaborate iron scrolls. We descended from the carriage and stood outside the gate in awe of the sheer size of the villa before us.

"Is this really yours, Valentina?" Aunt Gloria asked, her gaze fixed on the waterless fountain near the front door.

"Yes," I replied, urging them through the unlocked gate.

The lovely two-storey villa flaunted green window shutters. Some of the exterior's yellow ochre plaster had fallen away in chunks, revealing the pink faded brick beneath. Weeds grew everywhere and the garden needed tending badly. Wild roses grew along the front and wrapped around the sides of the villa.

Natalino tried the front door and found that it was unlocked. "Hello? Is anyone here?"

We entered the cool foyer and admired the marble intarsia floor. Above our heads, a dusty chandelier and a faded floral fresco graced the ceiling.

I went ahead and explored various rooms. Gilded mirrors and frames greeted me behind layers of dust and flecks of crumbling plaster. Some of the walls sported cracks.

"Earthquakes," Natalino said while examining a particularly long fissure that reached across two walls.

There were tremors in our kingdom due to Vesuvius, but nothing compared to the terrifying Great Lisbon Earthquake that had occurred five years ago. The mere thought of such a catastrophe made me shudder.

I left Natalino and my aunt, then ascended the stairs. So far, every room flaunted a stately fireplace and at least one fresco. While Raimondo's assessment of the place being in bad disrepair was true, it wasn't uninhabitable. There were no leaks in the ceiling and no mold on the walls.

Footsteps shuffled down the outside corridor and an elderly man poked his head into the room, startling me. I took in his red chapped cheeks and the tuft of gray hair still clinging to his scalp. Dressed like a liveried servant, the short stooped figure entered the room and studied me with an appraising eye.

"This is private property," he declared.

"Good afternoon," I said, attempting to be civil.

"You're trespassing and I suggest that you and your friends leave at once."

My eyes were drawn to the musket in his hands as I said, "I am Valentina Gaetani. This home was gifted to me by the prince."

His rheumy eyes lit up. "*Contessa, mi dispiace*," he said with a formal bow.

I accepted his sincere apology with a smile. "May I have your name, sir?"

"Timoteo, at your service, madam."

"You served the late countess?"

"Forty-one years," he replied proudly, his chest puffing out.

Natalino and Aunt Gloria joined me and introduced themselves.

Timoteo said, "His Highness's message arrived yesterday.

I'm sorry, my lady, but had I known you were coming so soon I would have spruced up a bit. No one has lived here in many years."

My brow creased in confusion. "I thought the countess passed away last year."

"She did, but she spent the last ten years of her life with her widowed daughter in Sicily. I've been here alone all this time keeping vandals at bay." Timoteo patted one of the walls as his eyes took in the frescoed ceiling depicting Venus. "It's a shame this villa is unoccupied."

"It won't be empty for long," I assured him.

"The workers are scheduled to arrive sometime this week."

Aunt Gloria motioned to get my attention. "That's good news, isn't it?"

"Very," I agreed.

Timoteo inquired, "How many servants should I procure, madam?"

I stared at him, embarrassed. "I'm afraid I haven't any money to pay them."

The old man frowned. "That's not what the message relayed. The annual allowance you are to receive is more than enough to hire a few servants and allow you to live comfortably."

"Annual allowance?" I repeated.

"That is attached to the title of countess," Timoteo said, surprised that such a notion would even have to be explained to me.

Raimondo never said anything about an allowance and I was too ignorant to have made my own assumption.

"How many do you think I should hire, Timoteo?"

The old man rubbed his chin. "Let's see…Cook, a couple of scullery maids and a gardener should do it for now. You'll need a lady's maid but I suppose you already have one of those."

I blushed and said, "Very well. I trust that you will hire good people who work hard."

"I always hire the best, my lady. When can we expect you?"

"How long will it take for the villa to be cleaned and the rooms aired out?"

Aunt Gloria patted the bed and a cloud of dust exploded from the coverlet. "These linens need to be washed and aired."

I added, "And the beds checked for vermin."

Timoteo said, "I can have everything ready in a fortnight."

Satisfied, I left Timoteo to the task of getting my home in order. I walked outside to the awaiting carriage with my aunt and Natalino in tow. We returned to the city center with our moods and spirits greatly lifted.

We descended from the carriage and Natalino paid the driver. Someone called my name as the rickety vehicle rolled down the street.

"Valentina!"

Shading my eyes from the light of the late afternoon sun, I gazed up at my admirer. "Good day to you, Guido."

"I still love you no matter what people are saying about you," he assured me while leaning out the window, his dark eyes sincere.

"That boy," Aunt Gloria whispered while shaking her head.

I rewarded his loyalty with a smile.

Guido scrunched up his pudgy face. "Who was the fancy lady in the painted carriage?"

The three of us stared up at the boy.

Natalino demanded, "What fancy lady?"

"Her carriage stopped where you are now standing."

"What did she look like?" I asked.

"Funny, she didn't seem poor," the boy mused thoughtfully.

People appeared in various windows to eavesdrop on our conversation. To my irritation, they made no attempt to be discreet.

I inquired, "Why would you say that?"

Guido replied, "She was so skinny!"

"Was she wearing a black gown?"

"Yes, and pearls too. Do you suppose they're real?"

"It could only be Livia," I said to my companions.

Aunt Gloria demanded, "Guido, when did you see her? How long ago?"

He shrugged. "An hour, maybe two."

A wrinkled toothless crone with flashy gold hoop earrings interjected, “What are you saying, boy? That rich woman came by almost three hours ago.”

Another neighbor added, “She waited for a long time but none of you were home.”

The crone demanded, “Where were you, anyway? You were certainly gone a long time.”

Ignoring the nosy neighbors, I focused on Guido. “Did you speak to the woman?” He shook his head, so I asked, “Did she appear happy or sad?”

“Come away from the window this instant!”

Guido’s mother appeared at the window and frowned at me. Turning to her son, she added, “You shouldn’t be talking to women of ill repute.”

Aunt Gloria frowned in outrage. “How dare you say such a thing about my niece, Donna Margarita?”

The lanky woman put one hand on her hip while the other rested on the sill. Guido peeked over this mother’s elbow.

“I say it because it’s true. Valentina is pregnant with no husband. What does that make her?”

The middle-aged woman in the window above retorted, “Really Margarita? Given that Guido was born seven months after your marriage, it makes Valentina the same as you!”

More neighbors joined the conversation and a few of them laughed and jeered at Donna Margarita, causing her to shake her fist at them in anger.

Before being dragged away by his mother, Guido cried, “I’ll still marry you, Valentina. If no one will have you, don’t worry. You can count on me.”

I tried not to laugh. “Thank you, Guido.”

Two men clapped at the boy’s declaration of love whereas the women in the windows began talking about Margarita.

Natalino urged us inside. “Cackling hens, the lot of them.”

The fiasco didn’t dampen our mood in the slightest. Before long, we would be moving to Marechiaro.

CHAPTER 19

We were getting ready to close up shop on Monday when Natalino nudged me. I followed his gaze out the window to see Livia's carriage on the street. Together, we went outside.

"Signora Livia, hello," I said politely.

"Oh my dear girl," she said, her eyes filling with tears.

The last time I saw that look in her eyes, Ferrante had been stabbed. Panic squeezed my heart, making it difficult to breathe.

"Is he dead?" I demanded, my voice sounding far off.

"No, but I fear for him," Livia replied.

I turned to Natalino. "I'm going with her right now."

"As you should," he said before helping me into the carriage.

Livia tapped the side of the vehicle and the driver took off at a quick pace.

"He's been sick for over a week," Livia explained while drying her eyes with a lace handkerchief.

That's why he never came for you, Valentina!

Fighting back tears, I asked, "How bad is it?"

"The fever refuses to break."

"Why didn't you send word to me earlier?"

"Ferrante had already been abed for a day when Raimondo came to tell us the news. My nephew wanted to go to you directly but I forbade it. He believed he would be better in a day or two, but when that didn't happen he dispatched me to fetch you. I came here yesterday at his request but no one was home."

"We went to Marechiaro."

"Marechiaro, yes…I almost forgot that I am now addressing a countess. You are above me in the noble hierarchy now. Isn't life strange?"

"Signora Livia, do you think Ferrante will die?"

"I am preparing for the worst while praying fervently to God and hoping for the best. I suggest you do the same."

Reaching for her hand, I gave it a squeeze before pressing

her palm to my belly. She expressed confusion at first, then realization lit up her features. I nodded in response to the silent question in her eyes.

Livia smiled and whispered, "Thank you, God."

"Your nephew must live to help me raise his son."

The moment we arrived at the villa I went straight upstairs to Ferrante's room. I was unprepared for the sight of my beloved, thin and pale, against the pillows. His skin resembled white ash and his hair clung to his damp brow. The windows were shuttered and a cloying scent hung heavily in the air.

Lisa and Donna Florinda curtsied at the sight of me. Barely acknowledging them, I rushed to Ferrante's side.

Taking his hand into mine, I pressed my lips to his cheek. "My love, it's me."

He opened his eyes a little and a smile touched his colorless lips. "Don't leave me…"

He exhaled and closed his eyes again. My eyes scanned the table beside the bed and froze at the sight of a glass jar containing two fat bloody leeches. Pushing up the sleeve of his linen shirt, I cringed at the sight of various cuts.

"How many times was he bled?" I demanded.

Sandro, who lingered in the corner, replied, "More than I can count, my lady."

"Dear God," I whispered. "Donna Florinda, I need a hearty beef broth. If you have liver, crumble it up finely and add it to the liquid."

Donna Florinda nodded before vacating the room.

I looked to Lisa. "Open the windows to get rid of this stench. Add feverfew to the fire."

"Yes, my lady."

"Sandro, help me undress him," I said, grabbing one end of the linen shirt.

Livia appeared in the doorway. "Is that wise, Valentina?"

At the sound of my name, the servants stopped and stared at me in confusion. Ignoring them, I said, "I'm going to run a cool damp cloth over his body to temper the fever. He's burning to the touch."

"That's not what I meant," Livia said, eyeing me pointedly. "I was referring to the baby."

Again the servants paused to stare at me in surprise.

"I'm hearty and hale, Signora Livia. I'll be fine."

Sandro helped me wash Ferrante, then we put him in a fresh linen garment. The clean air from the open window had cleansed the room of its sickly miasma. I went over and closed the window since the chill of night would soon be upon us.

"I'm going to my studio to mix a curative for fever," I said, heading for the door. "I'll be back as soon as possible. Lisa, I could use your assistance. Bring candles, it will be dark soon."

I was glad to see my window garden flourishing when I arrived at the studio. I found the space untouched and exactly how I had left it. Lisa lit a few candles in the fading gloom of day as I searched through a few books for the best recipe.

While I selected various herbs and roots suspended from the rafters, Lisa stared at me. "Go on and ask," I prompted, giving her permission to voice her curiosity.

"Signora Livia called you Valentina."

"That's my real name. Valentina Gaetani…The title of Countess of Marechiaro has been recently bestowed upon me and I'm carrying his lordship's child. That pretty much covers everything. There's a story to go along with those facts but today's not the day for telling it."

"Felicitations, my lady," Lisa said.

"Thank you, now pass me the Peruvian bark since it's the best febrifuge I have on hand."

I boiled the bark along with several other herbs to induce stamina and improve health. After distilling the concoction, I raced upstairs to administer it to Ferrante. I found Livia spoon feeding her nephew the beef broth with liver.

"Is he eating?" I inquired.

"A little."

I looked into the pitcher by the table and poured the heavily diluted wine into a chalice before putting it to his lips. He drank a bit, then turned his face away.

Livia fed him some more broth and he swallowed it down

without complaint. At one point, he opened his eyes and looked at us briefly. We stayed with him until late.

Finally, I said, "You should get some rest, Signora Livia."

"What about you?"

"I'm staying here with him."

"You can't afford to get sick in your delicate state."

"I won't let anything happen to this baby, I swear."

She leaned over and kissed my cheek. "Thank you, Valentina. You are the heart and soul of this house."

Ferrante groaned. "Baby?"

Livia and I looked at each other before she leaned close to her nephew and said, "It seems I'm going to be a great aunt. Goodnight, my loves."

I watched her departure then turned my attention to Ferrante. Glistening green eyes stared at me from a pale face. Slowly, he reached out his hand and touched my belly. The love I saw reflected in his gaze melted me. No words were needed.

"Your son grows inside of me," I said, covering his hand with mine. "This is why you must get better."

"I love you…I'm sorry."

Covering his lips with my fingers, I shook my head to silence him. I touched his clammy forehead, then reached for the curative. "You seem to be keeping down the food, so I need you to drink a bit of this. It tastes terrible."

He sipped a bit of the potent liquid and made a face. I didn't give him too much for fear he would vomit. Later, I would administer more.

"Go…rest," he whispered.

"I'm not going anywhere, Ferrante."

He fell asleep and I dozed off for a bit too. I awoke to the sound of his moans.

"Shhh," I said, placing a hand on his shoulder. "It's only a nightmare. I'm right here, my love."

"I'm going to die."

I reached for the curative and placed it to his lips. "Here, drink a bit more. You won't die." *You can't die…I need you.*

He fell asleep again and I applied another cool damp cloth

to his forehead. Lifting a candle aloft, I noticed that a hint of color had returned to his cheeks.

The door opened and Sandro poked his head into the room. Seeing me, he ducked back out into the hallway. I went out there to speak with him.

"I wanted to check on his lordship," Sandro whispered. "I didn't realize you were still here, madam."

"When is the physician expected to return?"

"Tomorrow."

"I don't want him anywhere near Ferrante. My father was a chemist who dabbled in biology. He never believed in bloodletting and neither do I. He said it weakened the body by sapping it of its life source, which is blood."

"I'll send the physician away the moment he arrives."

"Thank you."

"Can I get you anything, my lady?" Glancing down at my waist, he added, "A fortifying tonic would be of benefit to you in your condition."

I smiled slightly, my hand resting over my navel in a protective gesture. "I'm fine. Go and get some sleep."

"With all due respect, madam, perhaps you should get some sleep. I can stay up and watch over his lordship."

"Thank you, but I prefer to stay."

"As you wish. I'm in the antechamber if you need me."

I watched Sandro go, then slipped into Ferrante's bedchamber. Carefully, I stretched out beside my husband and fell asleep.

I awoke to Ferrante's deep even breathing. A good sign. Relief washed over me as I touched his cool brow. The fever had finally broken. He appeared less pale too. Carefully, I rose from the bed and went down to the kitchen. Donna Florinda stood amid the servants, instructing them on what needed to be done for the day. At the sight of me, everyone inclined their heads in greeting.

"Good morning," I said, walking over to the hearth and peeking into the cauldron. "Donna Florinda, is there any of that beef broth left from last night?"

"A bit, my lady. Shall I heat it up?"

"I want you to make pottage with it."

Donna Florinda set her hand to the task.

Spotting a bowl of fruit on the table, I selected the ripest lemon. Turning to one of the scullery maids, I said, "You there. Squeeze the juice from this lemon, add a teaspoon of honey and a teaspoon of crushed oregano, stir it up well and take it upstairs for his lordship."

She took the lemon from my hand. "Yes, my lady."

I was about to return to Ferrante's bedchamber when Donna Florinda said, "What about you, my lady? You must not neglect your own health." Her eyes dropped to my belly.

"Eggs," I replied thoughtfully. "I'm craving boiled eggs."

Donna Florinda grinned and snapped her fingers at the nearest servant before pointing to the wire basket full of fresh eggs. "Get to it."

I entered Ferrante's room to find him wide awake. To my relief, his ashy pallor no longer appeared as startling as it did yesterday.

"I thought I had dreamed you," he whispered, reaching out a hand to me.

Rushing over to take it, I smiled. "I was in the kitchen."

Closing his eyes, he sighed. The fever had subsided but his weakened body needed time to recuperate. The servants came in with the food and I fed Ferrante spoonfuls of fortified pottage between sips of the curative. He fell asleep afterward and I took advantage of the opportunity to eat my eggs.

Lisa helped me bathe and dress before I returned to check on my husband. To my surprise, Ferrante stood by the open window with the sun on his face.

Turning around to face me, he inquired, "What was in that tonic? I feel rejuvenated."

"Peruvian bark, goldenseal root, liquorice, and some other herbs. I'm happy to see the color in your cheeks."

His eyes swept over me. "I'm happy to see you."

"Come to bed, my love."

A wicked grin stretched across his face at my words. "Oh I

plan to. You have no idea how much you've been missed."

I tried to appear stern. "There will be time for love play later. Right now, you need to regain your strength."

"I need a fresh shirt," he said, stripping of his linen garment.

My mouth went dry with desire as I took in his sculpted body devoid of clothing. Fever had stolen some of the fleshiness, but the hard muscles and elegant lines remained.

"You and the baby have given me the will to overcome illness," he said, coming toward me. "Shall I summon Sandro to help me wash or would you do me the honor?"

My fingers ached to touch him, so I went over to the pitcher and rinsed out the cloth I had used on his brow last night. After wringing out the fabric, I approached him.

Ferrante stood perfectly still, his eyes never leaving my face. I ran the cloth along his neck, collar bone, and chest before concentrating on his sinewy arms. Rinsing out the cloth again, I tried to control my racing heart. I cleaned his shoulders, back, and stomach. His erect manhood made me pause. Chuckling, he took the cloth from my hand to complete the task. I watched as he washed his thighs and shins, as well as his well-shaped feet.

Tossing the cloth aside, he said, "All clean. Now, I need a fresh shirt. There is a stack of them in the armoire."

I crossed the room to the mahogany armoire and selected one of the folded garments. He took it from my hand and shrugged into it. My eyes were continually drawn to his engorged member, which begged to be satisfied.

Following my gaze, he inquired, "Do you love me, Valentina?"

The sound of my name on his lips caused a flush of warmth to spread throughout my body. "More than you know."

"Do you want to continue being my wife?"

"More than anything."

"Now that I know what love is, I can't live without it. You are my reason of living."

I brought his hand to my lips and kissed it. "Now you have two reasons."

His eyes dropped to my midsection. "My son."

"Or daughter...but I have a feeling it's a boy."

Pulling me into his embrace, he nuzzled my neck. "I don't care. It's *ours*, and that's all that matters."

My arms slid around his neck of their own accord, which caused him to moan. We staggered toward the bed, our lips locked in a passionate kiss.

I pulled away. "We shouldn't...you're not fully recovered yet, Ferrante. Let's wait."

His hand reached under my skirt to stroke me intimately. "I don't want to wait."

Falling on top of me on the bed, he proceeded to lift my skirts. Our lovemaking left me breathless.

"I'm so sorry," he whispered into my hair before kissing my temple. "Casting you out was the worst mistake of my life. Never leave me, Valentina...promise me."

"I'm not going anywhere, my love."

***

Ferrante made a full recovery in a matter of a few short days. With the danger of contamination eliminated, we could visit with Nadia. To my delight, she hugged me tightly. We played with the child for the better part of the morning before retiring to the salon to discuss the future.

Settling on the settee, he studied me thoughtfully. "As the Countess of Marechiaro, you could possibly snatch a nobleman of higher rank. I'm only a mere lord. Are you certain you wish to remain here with me?"

I knew he was teasing but played along with the game. "I'll have to give it serious thought."

His eyes widened in feigned shock. "You little vixen."

"That's Countess Vixen to you, thank you very much."

At that he laughed, which made me giggle.

His expression sobered as he took my hand. "Raimondo has offered his private chapel if we wish to exchange vows again. Otherwise, he can simply authorize the changing of your name on our marriage certification."

"Drawing up a new document is more than enough as far as I'm concerned. No need to put anyone out. Besides, I never stopped being your wife in my heart."

"There will be talk, you know. Possibly a scandal."

"Gossip is inevitable. People use it to fill the voids in their lives much the same way as a mason uses cement."

"Have I ever mentioned how much I admire your practicality?"

I grinned. "All that matters is our health and happiness.

He kissed me. "May I offer you a suggestion?"

"By all means, my lord."

"Your aunt—Gloria, is it?"

"Yes."

"Aunt Livia mentioned that she's married."

"To Natalino, the finest butcher in the city."

"Why not allow them to live in your villa in Marechiaro? Unless, of course, the countess prefers to follow the current French trend and maintain a separate residence from that of her husband."

"The countess is a true Neapolitan and desires no such thing."

Joking aside, I immediately liked his idea. Natalino could fish in his old age and Aunt Gloria could be the lady of the finest house in the village—a role she would undoubtedly embrace with unabashed delight. "I'll speak to them, but I'm sure they'll agree."

"It's settled then."

"There are a few demands the countess wishes to make upon her husband," I said, snuggling close to his side.

Placing an arm around my shoulders, he smirked. "Oh? And what might those demands be, my lady?"

"Your time, my lord. Your daughter and I love you, and we both wish to see more of you. If you find such conditions agreeable, it would gladden my heart."

"I find them very agreeable, my love."

My love. The future stretched out before us and, for the first time, I felt no fear. Taking his hand, I stared out the window and admired the blue haze of the distant Naples Bay.

EPILOGUE
One Year Later

Sparrows frolicked in the garden's fountain, splashing water into the air. The droplets sparkled like diamonds in the brilliant morning sunshine. My son slept peacefully in my arms while Nadia tried to capture one of the small birds. Each time she got splashed, she giggled. The sound of her joy made Berta and I smile.

"Mamma, look!"

Nadia began calling me *Mamma* months ago when she had discovered that my big belly carried a baby. The child pointed to her father, who emerged from the woods on horseback. She squealed with glee when he blew her a kiss.

I chuckled and waved at Ferrante, so he blew me a kiss too.

Nadia clapped her hands. "Kiss-kiss."

"That's right, sweetheart," I said, glad that the child's speech was developing normally.

Ferrante and I named our son Raimondo, in honor of the prince. The healthy infant had instantly captured the heart of everyone. Livia couldn't be happier and visited her grand-nephew daily.

Lisa exited the villa and came over to me. "There's someone here to see you, my lady—a young woman and her baby. She said her name is Celeste Carducci."

I sobered instantly. "Bring her here to the garden, please."

A moment later, Celeste stood before me toting a plump baby in her arms. The child's bright eyes regarded me with clever curiosity.

"Thank you for seeing me," Celeste said in a quiet voice.

"Berta, take my son."

I carefully transferred the infant in my arms to my servant and stood. Folding my hands in front of me, I inquired, "Why are you here?"

"I've come to beg your forgiveness—your husband's too. I'm sorry for what I did to you and to Sister Assunta. I beg for God's forgiveness for my sins every day."

A moment of tense silence passed before I said, "I forgive you, Celeste."

"Thank you," she whispered, her eyes glistening.

My gaze slid to the baby in her arms. "You've been blessed with a healthy child."

"Yes, thank God. Patrizia is a good girl."

I smiled at the child and stroked her round cheek. "You seem well. Are you married now?"

She shook her head sadly. "Luigi married a woman of this mother's choosing. There was so much at stake, you see."

"Ah…"

"I've been staying with my uncle but he died a few weeks ago. The debtors, well…they took everything—" She broke off and sobbed loudly, her body convulsing.

I reached for Patrizia and carried her to the fountain where the birds played while Celeste composed herself. At length, I said, "Celeste, please sit down."

She sat down and wiped the tears from her eyes. "I'm sorry…I have no money, nowhere to go. The convent won't take me. I'm a ruined woman. I've come to offer my services. I'm a hard worker. I can scrub floors, do gardening work, I can cook too…I'll do anything. All I ask is that you give me shelter so that my daughter has a place to sleep at night."

Ferrante's footsteps caused our heads to turn. He stood beside me, his eyes on the child in my arms. "Who is this?"

"This is Patrizia, Celeste Carducci's daughter," I replied in a sweet voice for the benefit of the baby in my arms.

Ferrante smiled at the baby, then pinned Celeste with a hard stare.

"My lord, I have come here seeking your forgiveness and that of your wife," Celeste said quietly.

"She's more than my wife," he corrected, placing a hand on my shoulder. "You are addressing the Countess of Marechiaro."

Celeste's eyes bulged in surprise and I knew several questions burned on her tongue, but she wisely refrained from asking them. Instead, she curtsied before me.

"We don't require your services here, Celeste." When her face fell, I added, "My Aunt Gloria may need them, however. She and her husband, Natalino, are residing in Marechiaro, at my villa. I'll send her a note. You and your child will be given room, board, and I'll make sure she offers you a decent wage."

Celeste grasped my hand and kissed it. "Thank you."

"My maid will provide you with the address."

"God bless you both," she said, taking her baby.

"Good luck, Celeste," I said, dismissing her.

Ferrante watched Celeste's retreat with an unreadable expression. Turning to me, he said, "That was quite magnanimous of you, my love."

"You forgave me, didn't you? Folly and youth go hand in hand, and Celeste has already suffered the dire consequences of her bad decisions. Little Patrizia is innocent and I don't want her to suffer."

"Do you think your aunt will approve of your decision?"

"She has known Celeste since childhood, so I'm sure she will welcome the female company. I won't be surprised if she finds a husband for Celeste."

Ferrante touched my cheek and the love reflected in his eyes made my heart race. "Every day I love you more."

Did you enjoy this novel? The author would appreciate a review on Amazon. Thank you.

Turn the page for a sample of the bestselling novel, Ruthless: A Novel Set in Gothic Verona.

RUTHLESS

A NOVEL SET IN GOTHIC VERONA

C. DE MELO

www.cdemelo.com

ISBN-13: 978-0-9997878-4-7
ISBN-10: 0-9997878-4-5

Note from the Author

Italian medieval politics consisted of two factions: *Ghibellines*, who supported the Holy Roman Emperor, and *Guelphs*, who supported the Pope.

The power struggle between the Holy Roman Empire and the Papacy began in 1075 and ended with a mutual agreement in 1122. In Italy, Guelphs and Ghibellines continued fighting well into the fourteenth century.

Francesco I della Scala, commonly known as "Cangrande" or "Big Dog," was born in Verona on March 9, 1291. A fiercely loyal Ghibelline, he was a friend and patron of Dante Alighieri, and is mentioned with affection in Boccaccio's *Decameron*. His relentless military campaigns expanded his territories to include Vicenza and Padua.

After many failed attempts to conquer Treviso, the Veronese warlord finally succeeded in taking control of the city. On July 18, 1329 he rode into Treviso a victorious conqueror, only to die a few days later on July 22, 1329. The diarrhea and fever he suffered prior to his death was documented as the result of consuming water from a polluted spring. Rumors of poison began circulating shortly afterward.

In an attempt to solve the mystery of Cangrande's sudden death, his mummified body was exhumed from its tomb in Santa Maria Antiqua in 2004. Researchers from the University of Pisa studied the toxicology of his remains and found traces of chamomile, black mulberry, and pollen grains from the foxglove flower.

Cangrande's relationship with his wife, Giovanna di Svevia, is open to speculation. The couple failed to produce children, but the warlord sired eight bastards. The children's names were recorded, but little is known about them—or their mothers, for that matter. The following is a list of Cangrande's illegitimate children (in order of birth from oldest to youngest):

Gilberto
Bartolomeo
Francesco
Margherita
Franceschina
Lucia Cagnola
Giustina
Alboino

Most of the events and battles described in this novel are the result of historical research, but this is a work of *fiction*. Many artistic liberties were taken based on Italian medieval traditions, speculation, and a few rumors.

"The Devil is not as black as he is painted."

—Dante Alighieri

JULY 22, 1329
TREVISO

My beloved son,

I will be dead by the time you read this letter. There is so much I want to tell you, but I have little time left in this world. You will hear stories about me…Many will be true.

Forgive me.

Your devoted mother,
Agata, Countess Visconti

PROLOGUE
NOVEMBER 1311
VERONA

Cangrande sank to his knees before the magnificent gilded altarpiece. Staring at the intricate gold patterning on the Madonna's midnight cloak, the twenty-year-old warlord contemplated the burden that would soon be placed upon his shoulders.

A liveried page quietly crept into the Palazzo Scaligero's private chapel. "My lord, the physicians have done everything possible."

"Is my brother any better?"

"The barber-surgeon has been summoned."

Meeting Mary's benevolent gaze, Cangrande rose to his feet and crossed himself before exiting the small chapel with a heavy heart.

A cluster of nobles loitered outside the bedchamber where the current Lord of Verona, Alboino della Scala, lay dying. At the sight of Cangrande, the people fell silent and stepped aside to allow him access to the door.

Mastino detached himself from the crowd and intercepted his uncle. "Is Papa going to die?" the boy asked, his innocent brown eyes begging for a lie.

In that instant, the powerful warrior felt as helpless as a child. "I hope not, but we must accept God's will."

The boy sniffed and ran toward his mother, whose glistening eyes betrayed her fear of widowhood.

Cangrande felt the heat of several stares as he gripped the door latch. Taking a deep breath, he entered Alboino's bedchamber ready to face his destiny.

Chapter 1
January 1320
Verona

Cangrande's stomach growled as he got out of bed. Twice a week, he sacrificed daily sustenance in honor of the Virgin Mary. Having lost his own mother at a young age, he drew maternal comfort from the Queen of Heaven. Rubbing his lower back, he shuffled to the window. Icy air cooled his face as he threw open the shutters and peered down at the courtyard. A scullery maid was on her knees, her wet hands redder than the terracotta tiles she scrubbed. A nostalgic smile touched his lips as he recalled how Alboino used to love reading beneath the potted fruit trees.

Since his brother's death nearly a decade ago, he had done little else but fight for the Ghibelline cause. So far, his efforts had earned him the western region of Lombardy, an excommunication from the pope, and several failed attempts to conquer Treviso.

Ah, Treviso—the thorn in his side.

He closed the shutters and sat on the edge of the bed before massaging the upper part of his leg. His thigh had been pierced by an arrow last summer during the battle against Padua. To prevent stiffness, the physician had instructed him to rub the damaged muscles every day. Such a wound would have barely made an impact during his youth. Now, with his thirtieth birthday fast approaching, the aches and pains were daily reminders of the inevitability of old age.

His valet entered the bedchamber with a bowl of scented water and a cotton cloth. "Good day, my lord."

"What news, Ercolano?"

"Signore Ottavio awaits downstairs."

The warlord ran the dampened cloth on his face and chest,

both of which bore battle scars. "Ah, yes. This morning's discourse should be interesting."

"I'm certain it will be." Ercolano helped his master don a wool tunic dyed the color of blood. "Shall I have the servants prepare fruit and bread, or would you prefer pottage?"

Scooping a handful of dried figs from a silver bowl, Cangrande replied, "I'll break my fast along the way."

The Lord of Verona exited the imposing Palazzo Scaligero and crossed the busy Piazza dei Signori with his most trusted advisor at his heels. "Make haste, Ottavio. I don't want to be late."

Eager vendors and dignified magistrates buzzed around the stalls that were set up along the edge of the piazza. Veronese silk merchants tried to entice potential customers by holding up bolts of fine cloth. One even approached Cangrande with a length of ermine.

The Lord of Verona shook his head. "Not now."

The vendor bowed and retreated.

Shivering with cold, Ottavio did his best to keep up with his overlord's brisk pace. The damp winter fog seeped through his wool cloak, settling into the marrow of his bones. "I'm looking forward to hearing the discourse."

"As am I."

"My lord, you *are* aware that Artemisio has already been promised the position of chair."

"So I've been told."

"Signore Dante will be disappointed."

"Of that, I am sure."

Teaching at the Studio di Verona would no doubt have pleased the aging poet. A man of his intellect and literary fame deserved a position of prestige and comfort in his final years.

Ottavio frowned. "So why allow him to—"

"Dante Alighieri is dear to the Scaligeri. He is always welcome in Verona. We will listen to his words today, and treat him with the utmost of respect."

"Of course, my lord, but—"

"*Basta*, Ottavio." Enough.

The arcaded façade of Santa Elena loomed into view as they rounded a corner. Cangrande acknowledged the noblemen and scholars loitering outside the humble church with a polite nod, then entered to take his seat.

Dante Alighieri struck an imposing figure in a long black robe with his silver hair neatly combed beneath a leather cap. The Tuscan studied his audience with an appraising eye before addressing the congregated men. "Good day, my lords. Today I will be discussing the *quaestio de aqua et terra* in the hope of securing your consideration."

Having already read the treatise, Cangrande allowed his mind to wander while the divine poet articulated his cosmic theories. Veronese scholars engaged the guest speaker in a lively debate afterward. Artemisio, famous for his teachings on logic, challenged the Tuscan on many issues. Dante never raised his voice and maintained the stoic demeanor for which he was known.

Cangrande eventually approached his old friend. "An excellent talk, Signore Dante."

"Thank you, my lord, but your stubborn scholars are not convinced by my arguments. It would have been pleasant to stay here for a while."

"And create another literary work in my honor?"

Everyone knew that *Paradiso* was dedicated to the Scaligeri—specifically, Cangrande.

Dante smiled. "Perhaps."

"My cooks are preparing a special meal in your honor."

"Then I shall summon my appetite in their honor." Casting a glance at Artemisio, Dante added, "After that debate, I would relish a walk along the river to clear my head."

"A fine suggestion."

Ottavio remained with the scholars as the poet and the warlord discreetly exited the church. A dirty sky dominated the landscape, transforming the Adige into liquid lead. A few vessels floated down the river, and a spattering of peasants huddled by a fire on the bank.

"Your nephews are doing well, I hope," Dante said while

maintaining the relaxed pace of his companion.

"Mastino never ceases to amaze me. Two years younger than his brother, Alberto, and he's already a fierce warrior. The lad if fearless."

"Scaligero blood courses through his veins, so I'm not surprised. They are lucky to have you as a mentor."

"Although I'm a warrior at heart, I do strive to be like my older brothers when it comes to matters of diplomacy."

"You display prudence, my lord, for Bartolomeo and Alboino were fine rulers. They would both be proud of your accomplishments."

"Would they?"

Startled by the Lord of Verona's self-doubt, Dante replied, "Yes, my lord. You are continuing their legacy."

"You flatter me, Signore Dante."

"I may be many things, but a false flatterer is not one of them. Your military conquests are known throughout most of the European continent, thus making you a legend within your own lifetime. That alone must bring you a measure of satisfaction."

Cangrande nodded. "I've been victorious in many battles, it's true, but Treviso is always there to remind me of my failure. You cannot imagine how this troubles me."

"It is only *one* city, after all."

"One city that *challenges* me, *mocks* me."

Aware of the warlord's obsession, Dante concluded, "I dare say to the point of consuming you."

"I am indeed a man consumed."

"There are other cities worth conquering, my lord."

"You are correct, but *heat cannot be separated from fire.* Those are your words, my friend, and they are an apt description of my relationship with Treviso. Our destinies are intertwined, and I will not stop until I have succeeded in my goal."

"One cannot help but admire your determination."

"I appreciate that."

They continued along the river in thoughtful silence. Sooty clouds gathered in anticipation of rain, prompting Cangrande to head toward home. Palazzo Scaligero's impressive Ghibelline crenellations could be seen in the distance.

Dante cleared his throat. "My lord, as far as Treviso is concerned…"

"Yes?"

"Have you ever considered that, *perhaps*, Fate is urging you to focus your efforts elsewhere?"

Cangrande smiled without mirth. "Fate be damned."

CHAPTER 2
MARCH 1320
VERONA

A lone swallow glided across the milky expanse above Verona's rooftops, its forked tail quivering in the wind. My favorite bird signaled the coming of spring; a time of sunshine, blue sky, and flowers. I watched the bird's frenzied flight with a grin.

"Come away from the window," Mother said, placing a meager bunch of kale on the scarred wooden table. "Throw these into the pot. Hurry."

The pathetically thin baby in her arms regarded me with dull eyes as I chopped the coarse leaves. My younger sister recently died, and we were amazed that he didn't follow her to the grave. Despite my sadness over her death, I didn't dare question God's will. I loved Him above all things—even more than I loved Verona or Aunt Serafina. My aunt once told me that God had a plan for everyone, including me. I hoped His plan included wings so that I could fly with the happy swallows. The silly thought almost made me laugh aloud as I tossed a handful of chopped kale into the simmering lentil stew. Unfortunately, some of the pieces missed the target.

Sighing, Mother bent to retrieve them. "Daydreaming again, Agata? Stir the embers lest the fire goes out."

I grasped the poker by the hearth and coaxed the embers to life. Our drafty cottage was in a sad state of disrepair—the thatched roof sported holes, and wood rot had consumed the window shutters.

Mother placed the baby on the straw pallet in the corner. "I'm going to the market. Mind your brother while I'm gone."

"Did Father give you enough money for a new frock?"

Eying my threadbare garment, she shook her head. "You can

easily patch that tear in your sleeve and let down the hem."

"Pina hasn't outgrown anything in years. This dress is getting too tight for me."

"Nonsense, it fits you fine."

Father sauntered into the room. "You'll be married soon enough, Agata. Your husband can buy new clothes for you."

Mother glared at him. "You promised me that she would remain here until she turned fourteen. I need help with this one and, in case you've forgotten, there's another one on the way."

Father glanced at her protruding belly. "Stop whining, woman. Ernestina can help you once the baby is born."

Father often referred to the mute spinster living across the road as an "idiot" but I liked Ernestina. She taught me how to weave dandelion crowns so that I could wear them on my head like a princess.

Mother pursed her lips. "How will Ernestina be paid?"

He waved away her question with a flick of his wrist before helping himself to more ale.

She continued, "So, who is it?" Father's blank look made her frown. "You said Agata would be married soon."

"Don't be meddling in the affairs of menfolk."

"I have a right to know."

"The blacksmith's son—"

Horrified, I whipped around. "Father, please—"

"Shut your mouth, girl. Alvino and his son are respectable men. What's more, they've got coin."

I knew better than to defy my father, whose temper easily ignited at the slightest provocation. My feisty mother, on the other hand, often sported a blackened eye or a bruised lip.

"The boy has a clubfoot," she pointed out, regardless of the risk to her face. "He's practically lame."

Father slammed his fist on the table. "He won't be fucking our daughter with his foot, will he?"

She scowled at his vulgarity. "You're drunk."

Mumbling incoherently, he strayed into the tiny garden behind our cottage to finish his drink in peace.

Mother hastily hid the pitcher in a cupboard, then plucked a basket from the shelf. "I won't be long, Agata."

No sooner had she left than I felt Father's eyes burning into my back from the open doorway. I reluctantly turned around and met his insistent stare.

"Start showing some gratitude. A decent husband, a roof over your head, and food in your belly—that's more than anyone can ask for, don't you agree?"

I nodded and kept my mouth shut. I had no desire to marry, but the thought of staying at home with my parents held even less appeal. Pina, my older sister, wedded the butcher's son last summer. The city's prettiest girls had competed for his affection, but Pina had outshone them all. She reminded us of her "God-given beauty and charm" whenever she gifted us a greasy lump of bacon or a meaty bone. Father enjoyed claiming the latter from the soup and sucking the marrow—when he did this, I hated the sight and sound of it.

"Well, I'm off to find some work," he said before swigging the last of his ale and practically stumbling out the door.

I glanced at my drooling brother. Poor runt. It was only a matter of time before the Angel of Death swooped down upon our household—*again*. The misery trapped within these moldy walls seeped into our words, our food, our clothes...

Obviously, God was testing our faith. Like Job, we would someday be rewarded for our loyalty and devotion to Him.

God has a plan for me.

I wandered to the window and spotted the carefree swallow circling high in the sky. Overcome by envy, I turned away and returned to my chores.

CHAPTER 3
EASTER 1320
VERONA

The Lord of Verona frowned while studying his reflection. Ercolano's head poked out from behind the polished looking glass, which he held upright in his hands.

Cangrande sighed. "Well?"

"You are the epitome of elegance, my lord. The violet silk suits you."

"I feel more comfortable in a hauberk."

The valet hid his amusement.

A mouthwatering aroma from the kitchen prompted Cangrande to sniff the air with satisfaction. "Smell that, Ercolano? We shall feast today."

"You host the finest banquets in Verona."

The valet spoke the truth. His nobles expected good food, fine wine, and decent entertainment during Easter, and he had no intention of disappointing them.

The Veronese nobility and their overlord attended Holy Mass at the Duomo of Santa Maria Matricolare. At the service's conclusion, Cangrande slipped into a brightly frescoed chapel. A magnificent altarpiece depicting the Coronation of Christ dominated the space. He lit a candle while uttering a brief prayer of forgiveness for the sin of gluttony he intended to commit later that day.

Exiting the chapel, he veered toward the rear of the cathedral where an old Norman vestibule still stood. Consecrated in 1187, Santa Maria Matricolare had been built on the site of two much older churches, both of which were devastated seventy years ago during a great earthquake. Cangrande looked forward to visiting the sacred space after the Sunday service, and people knew better than to follow him. His breathing slowed as he entered the cool, dim interior.

The sound of a light footstep drew his gaze. To his surprise, a pretty girl stood amid the columns studying the carved capitals. She wore a tight-fitting frock of homespun wool that accentuated her budding breasts and shapely hips. Obviously, she had outgrown the garment and her family couldn't afford a new one. No father in his right mind would deliberately allow his blossoming daughter to exit the house in such provocative attire. Approaching the girl with silent steps, he took in the flowers strewn into her haphazard braid. A surprised gasp escaped her sensuous lips when she turned her head and noticed him.

Cangrande frowned. "What are you doing here?"

"The same as you, my lord. Enjoying a bit of solitude."

Such impertinence! "Do you know who I am?"

She nodded, her eyes lingering on the sword at his side. "You are the Lord of Verona, the most loyal Ghibelline on Earth, sanctioned by God and favored by the Madonna."

Silver-tongued, too. To his surprise, she didn't flinch when he closed the gap between them. In fact, she pinned him with a steady stare, her eyes glittering in the dimness like gemstones.

He pointed to one of the columns. "You were admiring the capitals when I walked in."

"I like them and so does God."

"We must not presume to know God's thoughts."

"Well, these columns *are* survivors."

"Survivors?"

"God preserved them during the great quake, so..."

"Who told you all of this?"

"My Aunt Serafina. She is a nun at the Convento di Santa Agnes."

"I see…"

"She taught me to read. Father believes it's useless to teach a girl to read. Do you agree with him, my lord?"

Cangrande stared at the precocious girl, baffled. Not even his trusted advisors spoke to him so candidly!

"Well, do you?" she pressed.

"Learning is a privilege afforded to very few," he replied, his tone stern.

"That's exactly what my aunt said, too! She says I'm clever, and that a fertile mind should not be wasted."

"What's your name, clever girl?"

"Agata."

"Your parents must be wondering where you are, Agata. It's not prudent for unchaperoned girls to linger in deserted places." He deliberately eyed her as a wolf would a lamb, then added, "I urge you to be more careful in the future."

This time, he'd succeeded in frightening the girl. She offered him a clumsy curtsey and ran off.

Stopping at the vestibule's exit, she turned around and said, "A blessed Easter to you and yours, my lord."

Resisting the urge to smile, Cangrande inclined his head at the girl. He waited until she was gone before running his hand along the cool, hard surface of a "survivor." Closing his eyes, he inhaled deeply and exhaled until there was no air left in his lungs. He repeated this exercise a few more times, savoring the stillness and silence. After a long moment, he rejoined his entourage.

The Veronese nobles followed their overlord to the Palazzo Scaligero. Everyone congregated in the main hall for the midday meal, and their host raised his chalice to the numerous guests in a toast of good health. Fresh spring greens adorned trestle tables groaning beneath the weight of platters piled with roasted lamb. Dancing and games followed the bountiful feast, but the guests tempered their revelry with moderation for Easter was one of the holiest days of the year. The merriment lasted well into the evening, long after the sun had set.

Somnolent and satiated, Cangrande watched the dancers with detached interest as a pair of oversized mastiffs foraged for scraps at his feet. It was late, and he desired the comfort of his bed—preferably with a partner. He winked at a pretty servant and caught his wife glaring at him over the rim of her chalice.

Arrayed in a gown of samite trimmed with mink, what

Giovanna lacked in charm she made up for with elegant clothing. Once an attractive woman with a shy smile and a pleasant demeanor, the passing of years had transformed his wife into a corpulent shrew. Childless and resentful, she went out of her way to make his life—and the life of his mistresses—as unpleasant as possible.

Fortunately, his sons and nephews held the power to lift his mood whenever Giovanna irritated him, which was often these days. His eldest son, Gilberto, had been entrusted to the care of his best knight and currently served as a young squire. Mastino, the younger of his two nephews, got on well with Gilberto. Both boys were warriors in the making, which pleased Cangrande, who had been knighted by his own father at the age of ten due to his love of the sword.

His second son, Bartolomeo, was like his oldest nephew, Alberto. Pensive and quiet, the studious boys preferred to stay indoors. Someday, they would become political strategists trained in the art of diplomacy.

At one point in the evening, Gilberto approached his father with a falcon on his forearm. "Look, my lord! Do you see how she obeys me?"

"You handle her well, my son. Remember—only offer her a reward *after* she has done your bidding, never beforehand."

"Once she catches the prey."

"Correct." The warlord's eyes shifted to Bartolomeo, who sat beside his mother, Grazia. The sensuous young woman accompanied her aunt and uncle to the Palazzo Scaligero on a regular basis. "What of your brother? Does he enjoy the sport?"

Gilberto shook his head. "He's afraid of the birds."

"Which is why *you* are my favorite. Don't tell your brother I said that." Cangrande ruffled the boy's dark hair while noticing Grazia's low-cut gown. The sight of her ample bosom caused a stirring in his loins. "It's late. You and your brother should be in bed. Go, tell your mother I'll be along shortly."

A servant came forth to take the falcon back to the aviary where the rest of the carnivorous birds were housed.

"Is it true that Bartolomeo is afraid of the birds?" Cangrande demanded once Gilberto was out of earshot.

"Yes, my lord—to the point of fainting if I force him to handle them."

"Let the boy faint. I'll beat the fear out of him, if needed."

The servant nodded, then backed away.

Cangrande saw Gilberto whisper in his mother's ear. Grazia met her lover's hungry eyes and, taking both of her sons by the hand, exited the main hall. The chilly wind outside compelled her to hurry across the piazza to her uncle's palazzo.

Once she had put her sons to bed in the cozy antechamber adjacent to her room, Grazia prepared for her lover's visit. She wiped the perspiration from her brow, chest, and armpits with a dampened cloth before dipping a point of the fabric into a small container of crushed sage and salt crystals. Running the cloth along her teeth, she carefully removed traces of food, then rinsed her mouth with a combination of vinegar, water, and ground mint. Hearing footsteps in the hallway, she hastily let down her long black hair and doused herself with rosewater.

The knock served only as a perfunctory courtesy, for Cangrande possessed the keys to the palazzo's side entrance. He entered quietly and locked the door behind him. Poking his head into the antechamber, he smiled at the sight of his sleeping sons.

Grazia stood beside the bed with open arms. "My love."

The Lord of Verona kissed her lips before burying his face in her big breasts.

Chapter 4
Verona

Many women were forced into godly service out of poverty or after a marriage annulment. Such was not the case with Aunt Serafina. In fact, she had spurned two suitors before joining the convent. My mother's older sister was my favorite person in the world—a true blessing from God.

Serafina visited me often, usually after dispensing bread and comfort to the sick at a hospital near our home. She came over shortly after Easter, so I greeted her at the door and ushered her inside.

Extracting a tiny prayer book from the inner pocket of her gray nun's habit, she said, "I have something for you."

I accepted the book with reverence.

She continued, "You must be careful, for it's worth a tidy sum. If you return it to me unharmed, I'll let you borrow another one."

"Thank you, Aunt Serafina."

"Go on, read the title."

I stumbled over the words written on the cover, sounding them out slowly. Father entered the room and scowled at me.

Narrowing his eyes at Serafina, he demanded, "Why do you teach my daughter such nonsense?"

She regarded him coolly. "I would hardly call reading the word of God *nonsense*."

"Agata will be married soon. She needs to know how to cook, clean, and rear children—nothing more."

Disappointment was clearly etched on Serafina's face as she stared at me in shock. "Is this true, Agata?"

Father took it upon himself to reply on my behalf. "Yes, and it's a good match, too!"

I added sheepishly, "Father has arranged for me to marry Nunzio, the son of Alvino the blacksmith."

Before my aunt could utter any protest, my father pointed his finger at her. "Don't try to talk her out of it, Serafina. Your job is to pray and be an example to Christian women. Marriage is a sacrament, not that *you* would know."

Serafina bristled. "True, but not every woman is suited for matrimony. Mother Anastasia has been praised by the bishop many times for her piety and chaste conduct. She encourages all of us to read and study, so that we may contemplate spiritual matters."

"Oh, I'm sure the bishop doesn't know *everything* about that abbess of yours, does he?"

That my father would refer to a holy woman in such a disrespectful manner shocked me, but I was even more disturbed by Serafina's reaction. Rather than defend her superior, she hung her head in defeat.

"Regardless of what you think of me or the abbess, the sisters at Santa Agnes adhere to the philosophy of the Cluniac monks. Prayer is important, but so is wisdom and understanding of the Holy Scriptures."

Father crossed his arms. "I still don't see the point."

Indicating an empty chair at the table, she said, "You're more than welcome to sit with us and learn. That way, you might see the point."

He grunted and made a comment about women not knowing their place, then stormed out the front door.

Mother, who had witnessed the entire exchange, shook her head in disdain. "He's right, Serafina. There is no need for Agata to be as educated as you are."

"That's where you're wrong," she countered.

"It's not your place to decide what is best for my daughter."

"Women should know more than only dull domestic things."

"You say this because you've never been married."

Serafina crossed herself. "Praise God for *that*!"

"You've always been rebellious. Even now, as you hide behind that nun's habit, you try to corrupt your own niece."

"How can you say such a thing to me? I'm your sister! I want the best for Agata."

"Maybe you don't remember how much you made our parents suffer, but the memories are quite vivid in my head."

"Our parents were fools."

"Serafina!"

There was a moment of tense silence before my aunt said, "How I wish you had chosen the same path as me. Right now, we could be serving God together instead of you being…"

Mother lowered her eyes when her sister trailed off. "You knew my situation...I had no choice but to marry."

Serafina shook her head sadly. "You traded a moment of pleasure for a lifetime of pain. You could have married that well to do—"

"*But I didn't!* What's done is done! Leave it be."

"Forgive me," Serafina offered contritely.

Mother's eyes glistened with unshed tears. Pressing her lips tightly together, she returned to her chores.

I looked from one woman to the other, intrigued. Was my older sister conceived out of wedlock? I didn't dare ask. In that moment, I felt a surge of pity for my mother. She must have had hopes and dreams when she was my age. Had she also fostered the desire to fly away like the carefree swallow? Gracefully swoop into a better life with better prospects?

Serafina leaned close to me and whispered, "Marriage can be a prison sentence if you wed the wrong man. Being a common wife is a terrible waste of a fertile mind. Is this what you want in life—to be miserable like your mother?"

"No, but what can I do?"

Serafina's brow creased in thought as she folded her hands on the table top. "You can claim sanctuary at the convent and declare your desire to marry Christ instead of an ordinary blacksmith."

"Is that what you did when your parents tried to force you into wedlock?"

She smiled wryly. "I scared the first suitor away with my sharp tongue, but the second one had managed to strike an advantageous bargain with my parents. My father beat me when I refused to marry the man, so I ran away."

I pondered her words, then asked, "Why do you hate marriage?"

"I don't hate marriage....Let me explain. The majority of people in this world are poor, dull-witted fools destined for mediocrity. You are neither male nor noble, which lessens your options in life. Becoming a nun is by far the best solution for an intelligent girl like you—trust me."

Mother returned to the room and we both fell silent.

"I need to get some things at the market," she announced, refusing to meet our eyes. "Agata, watch your brother."

I waited until my mother was gone, then said, "I don't want to marry Nunzio, but the Bible commands children to obey their parents."

"You would be disobeying them in favor of serving the Lord—a forgivable sin. Imagine if Hildegard of Bingen chose marriage over God. What a loss to the world!"

The famous German nun had achieved greatness and fame within her lifetime. An artist, a scholar, a musician, and a poet, she had even garnered the respect of famed holy men like Bernard of Clairvaux.

I stood and announced, "I want to claim sanctuary at the convent. Neither of my parents are home, so let us make haste."

"You wish to go there *now*? Are you certain?"

"Yes."

"What about your brother?"

I glanced at the silent child watching us with wide eyes. "I'll leave him in the neighbor's care. Mother won't be long."

I convinced Ernestina to stay with my brother, then left with my aunt. My steps were light as we crossed the city. We arrived at the Convento di Santa Agnes and Serafina produced a key to unlock the gate. Once inside, I marveled at the cleanliness and orderliness of my future home. I offered a silent prayer of thanksgiving to God as my aunt led me to the abbess. I was surprised by Mother Anastasia's youthful appearance.

She offered me a warm greeting, then took Serafina's hand into her own. "I've heard so much about you, Agata. I'm happy that your aunt has managed to convince you."

Serafina tossed me an indulgent smile. "My niece will make a fine addition to our convent."

The abbess stroked my aunt's hand in a manner that was oddly intimate. "I have no doubt of that, Sister Serafina. Tell me, Agata, did your parents offer you their blessing?"

I cast a nervous glance at Serafina. "Actually, no."

My aunt added, "My brother-in-law may try to claim his daughter now that he's negotiated a marriage."

The abbess eyed me steadily. "I see."

"Please don't send me home, Mother Anastasia."

"Rest assured, child," she said soothingly. "You are free to live among us as a novice. Later, when the time is right, you will have the opportunity to take the vows. It's a shame you didn't come to this decision before your father promised you to a man. Hopefully, we'll convince him to accept your choice."

My body sagged with relief. *Thank you, God.*

Serafina placed an arm around my shoulder. "Come on, let's get you settled in."

My aunt and the abbess exchanged a lingering look before I was offered a tour of the convent. I was delighted by the pretty cloister garden and the extensive library. I imagined myself researching interesting topics and reading about the lives of various saints. There was also a room dedicated to the mixing of medicines and curatives. Mortars and pestles dominated the surface of a long table laden with various herbs. I liked the art of flower lore and already knew a little bit about it.

"Well? What do you think?" Serafina inquired at the tour's conclusion.

"I am so happy."

She embraced me. "So am I."

I spent my first few hours at Santa Agnes in the library trying to read the titles of books and scrolls. At one point, I smiled and sighed contentedly. Aunt Serafina, seated beside me, offered me a heartfelt smile.

My happiness was cut short when my father showed up at the convent later that day. Banging on the gate, he demanded to see me. Mother Anastasia went outside to deal with him while

Serafina and I lingered in the background.

Father pointed at me through the iron bars. "Insolent girl! I am going to beat you senseless! Do you think you can run away and make me look like a fool?"

The abbess remained silent as my father ranted and raved like a lunatic. He was drunk, of course. People with nothing better to do began to gather around to watch the scandalous scene unfolding outside the convent gate.

When he calmed down a bit, I said, "Father, please, I want to serve Christ and devote myself to God's work."

"Marriage is a sacrament, created by God."

"Yes, Father, but I don't want to marry Nunzio."

"I've already given Alvino my word! You've been promised to his son and you'll do as you're told." Turning his attention to Serafina, he added, "And *you*! Putting her up to this—"

Mother Anastasia raised her hand to silence him. "No one is forced into service. Agata came here of her own accord."

Giving her a dark look, he said through clenched teeth, "Open this gate and give me my daughter."

The abbess peered down her nose at him. "I cannot do that. Santa Agnes is an extension of the church, which is God's house. Anyone can claim sanctuary here, including Agata."

Father leered at her, shocking the three of us. "Is that what you call it in this place? *Sanctuary?* I know all about you..."

His implication prompted the abbess to cast a wary glance at my aunt. "I don't know what you mean."

Lowering his voice so that only she could hear, he said, "I know all about Serafina. My wife told me the stories…Caught her in the act, too. You would know all about those acts, wouldn't you, *Mother* Anastasia?"

The abbess blanched. "How dare you—"

Lowering his voice, he said, "As God is my witness, I will make your relationship public if you don't hand over my daughter. Do you understand?"

To my astonishment, she nodded. I could see from her shocked expression that she didn't anticipate his ruthlessness.

Father glared angrily at me as my aunt and the abbess retreated into the corner. Both were visibly shaken as they spoke in hushed tones. I tried to eavesdrop, but I couldn't make out the words.

Serafina broke away from the abbess and walked toward me, her face a mask of pity and regret. "I'm so sorry, Agata."

"Aunt Serafina, what's happening?"

"It's complicated..."

"What was my father talking about?"

Mother Anastasia rushed over to us, grabbed my wrist, and pushed me toward the gate.

"No," I begged.

"You can't stay here."

I struggled to release myself from her grip, but she was too strong. "Why? Please, don't!"

She unlocked the gate and thrust me toward my father.

***

The twenty-first of May drew many people to Verona from the neighboring villages. The Festival of San Zeno inspired the finest noble households to display colorful tapestries outside their windows. Most of these costly and elaborate fabrics boasted the family's coat of arms or holy images. A solemn procession, which wound its way through sunlit streets, was headed by six priests carrying a statue of the city's patron saint. The Lord of Verona followed the bishop, then came the nobility, wealthy merchants, and, finally, the Veronese citizens.

Serafina accompanied me and my family as we followed the great multitude of people. My parents had accepted her sincere apology—and mine, for that matter—but we were no longer allowed to be alone together. True to his word, my father had administered a sound beating for my disobedience. The entire incident came to be seen as a folly of my inexperienced youth.

I was disappointed with my aunt for not standing up to my father, but I accepted my fate with as much dignity as possible. God's plan for me obviously included the blacksmith's son, and who was I to question His will?

We entered the Basilica of San Zeno and I tilted my head

back to admire the large whale bone suspended from the vaulted ceiling. To my left, a chapel boasted a crocodile bone. Aunt Serafina once told me that it was from the Holy Land. A brave crusader had slain the ferocious crocodile beast—a creature she described as a giant reptile. I imagined it being similar in appearance to St. George's fearsome dragon. Whale and elephant bones hung in other basilicas throughout the city, each one brought to Verona by Christian men. It was widely believed that these exotic bones served as talismans against evil and protected the congregation from the machinations of Satan.

The procession concluded in the crypt. Forty five columns supported the ceiling, each boasting a different design. My favorite capitals depicted expressive faces. The bishop stopped before the wrought iron gate protecting the relic containing Saint Zeno's sacred remains. Mass was sung, communion was offered to all, and confessions were heard after the service.

From where I stood, I could clearly see the Lord of Verona and his entourage. The fur adorning the cuffs of his brocaded tunic appeared enticingly soft and I longed to touch it. He stood beside his fat wife, who wore an expression of disapproval on her doughy face. Perhaps her annoyance had to do with the fact that her husband's gaze kept wandering toward a voluptuous woman standing in attendance with the other nobles.

If the Veronese warlord's eyes looked my way, would he even remember my face after our recent encounter in the vestibule? I doubted it. After all, he was the most powerful man in the Veneto. I was nothing.

After the service, I wandered toward the old marble statue of Saint Zeno. Depicted smiling with a silver fish in his hand, the talented sculptor had rendered the saint's face in such a pleasing manner that worshippers often found themselves grinning back at the effigy. I was no exception.

My aunt paused beside me to study the statue. "You must be terribly angry with me, Agata."

"I'm not angry, Aunt Serafina. Only disappointed."

"Your father's threat frightened Mother Anastasia."

"You as well," I gently reminded her.

She blushed, nodding. "I'm so sorry...How can I correct the wrong I've committed?"

"Continue to teach me and be my steadfast companion."

Tears welled up in her eyes. "Always."

I caught a glimpse of a large, robust young man in a dark wool tunic exiting the church. One hand held a walking stick, the other was placed on his father's shoulder.

My aunt inquired, "Isn't that Nunzio?"

"Yes," I replied, relieved that he didn't hobble like a beggar.

"I hear he's a hard worker and a good son to his widowed father. Hopefully, he'll treat you well."

"Hopefully," I repeated.

Alvino and his son visited our household the following day. Under the watchful eyes of our fathers and my mother, Nunzio and I exchanged pleasantries for the first time.

He carried an iron pot, which he set upon the kitchen table with great pride. "I made this for you myself. A new pot for you to cook in once we are wed."

Most men offered their betrothed a sweetmeat or a posy. Instead, I got a pot—heavy, plain, and practical like my future husband.

Mother declared, "A fine pot, indeed."

I forced myself to appear grateful. "Thank you."

Father suggested we retreat to the garden to get acquainted with each other while he and Alvino discussed the details of our marriage. Mother gave me a warning look as I led Nunzio to the tiny patch of land outside the kitchen door. Three sets of eyes watched our every awkward move from the open doorway.

Nunzio stood with his back to our parents, his eyes glued to the swell of my breasts. "Father says we can marry before the harvest. You're nearly fourteen, yes?"

"I'll be fourteen in August."

"I turn eighteen in December." He studied me with an appraising eye. "You're very pretty, Agata. I would marry you tomorrow. I'm honored to have been chosen by your father."

Lowering my head for the sake of modesty, I saw that his left foot was misshapen and clumsy, turning inward. His clubfoot required a bigger shoe than the one on his right foot.

Out of the corner of my eye, I caught Mother exiting the doorway with two ceramic cups. She handed one to Nunzio and offered me one as well. Father rarely shared his ale with us.

I waited for her to retreat into the house. "Where will we live after we are wed?"

"In my father's house. He's a widower, as you know."

Would I be required to cook and clean for two men? "Do you have a servant?"

"My father pays the baker's widow to cook. Sometimes she tidies up the house and does our laundry."

Relief washed over me. "Donna Giulia?"

"Yes. We won't need her once you become my wife."

He smiled so guilelessly that I didn't know whether to laugh or to be angry. *Oh, how I wish I could join the convent!*

As the silence stretched, his smile faded. "Have I said something to upset you?"

"No..."

My face must have revealed my dishonesty because Nunzio balled his meaty hands into fists and cursed under his breath. "I wanted to bring the ring, but my father said it was best to meet you first. Now, I regret heeding his advice."

"What ring?"

"A wedding band fashioned from gold."

Gold? No one I knew could afford gold—even the parish priest only sported silver. Gold was for high-ranking clergy and members of the nobility.

Nuns didn't wear gold.

He continued, "It was my grandmother's ring and she passed it to my mother. Because I'm an only child, I must pass it on to my wife."

"Where did your grandmother obtain such a treasure?"

"She was a capable midwife who saved the wife and child of a wealthy goldsmith."

A gold ring! I preened at the thought of owning something so fine. Perhaps being married wouldn't be so bad after all.

Noticing my smile, he ventured, "You are pleased, then?"

I nodded. Glancing downward, I smoothed the skirt of my threadbare frock. "I hope to marry you in something better than *this*. It wouldn't do to wear rags on my wedding day with a gold ring on my finger, would it? I say this only to please you, of course, and bring honor to your household."

"I'll see if I can arrange something." His eyes were glued to my breasts again. "I do wish we could marry sooner."

The sound of chair legs scraping across the floor startled us.

Mother appeared in the doorway. "Agata, come inside."

Nunzio followed, his hungry eyes no doubt glued to my backside. Alvino, who hadn't addressed me once, inclined his head in my direction before ushering his son out the door.

Father said, "The wedding will take place in two weeks."

Mother crossed her arms. "I still think it would be better to wait until after the harvest."

"You heard Alvino. Nunzio is eager to marry, and rightly so! He's a healthy young man despite his defective foot." Looking at me, he added, "Alvino's smithy provides most of the weapons for the Lord of Verona's knights. Did you know that, Agata? You'll be living in a house that's bigger and better than Pina's."

While my father's words might be true, my brother-in-law wasn't lame, and my older sister didn't have to care for two men. Naturally, I kept these observations to myself.

"Your father has done well by you," Mother chimed.

"Indeed I have," he agreed. "Smile, and show some gratitude for your good fortune."

CPSIA information can be obtained
at www.ICGtesting.com
Printed in the USA
BVHW030808300520
580605BV00001B/228